EMANCIPATED

EMANC

I P A T E D

M. G. REYES

KATHERINE TEGEN BOOKS
An Imprint of HarperCollins Publishers

Katherine Tegen Books is an imprint of HarperCollins Publishers.

Emancipated

Library of Congress Control Number: 2014949409
ISBN 978-0-06-228896-7

Typography by Carla Weise
16 17 18 19 20 PC/RRDC 10 9 8 7 6 5 4 3 2
❖
First paperback edition, 2016

For Hoku,
with fond memories of a wonderful drive through
Malibu Canyon and lunch at the beach cantina
—all in the name of research, of course!

CALIFORNIA FAMILY CODE SECTION 7120-7123
EMANCIPATION:

7120.

(A) A MINOR MAY PETITION THE SUPERIOR COURT OF THE COUNTY IN WHICH THE MINOR RESIDES OR IS TEMPORARILY DOMICILED FOR A DECLARATION OF EMANCIPATION.

(B) THE PETITION SHALL SET FORTH WITH SPECIFICITY ALL OF THE FOLLOWING FACTS:

(1) THE MINOR IS AT LEAST 14 YEARS OF AGE.

(2) THE MINOR WILLINGLY LIVES SEPARATE AND APART FROM THE MINOR'S PARENTS OR GUARDIAN WITH THE CONSENT OR ACQUIESCENCE OF THE MINOR'S PARENTS OR GUARDIAN.

(3) THE MINOR IS MANAGING HIS OR HER OWN FINANCIAL AFFAIRS.

GRACE

It happened like this: Candace needed to leave home and Grace found the solution.

The two stepsisters had taken as much as they could of Grace's mother's behavior—the screaming fights, the threats to get a divorce. Since her seventeenth birthday, Candace had been sharing confidences with Grace, anxious that she herself might be the cause of their parents' unhappiness.

The girls lay on the lawn, long fair hair trailing in the grass, bare legs tan against the bright green. Grace peered through her fingers at her stepsister. At sixteen, she was the younger of the two, but often she felt like the older one. Candace had spent so much of her life in various forms of coaching: voice, drama, dance, horseback riding, fencing; she'd had a lot less time to read, think, listen, and reflect.

Or maybe Grace was simply more mature because of something that had happened much earlier in her life?

"It's probably not you, Candace. But isn't that totally classic?" Grace rolled over onto her side. "It's the first place therapists go when they counsel kids from 'broken homes.'"

"Oh. Right," Candace muttered. "I'm a cliché?"

"You are, but how is that relevant?"

Grace grinned as Candace kicked at her shins with bare feet.

The problem was, Grace suspected deep down that her stepsister's fears were real. That she was the cause, 100 percent. Without a single moment of bad behavior, Candace had managed to put their folks' marriage on the line. The girls could both hear the argument raging inside the house.

Grace's mother said, "I won't stand by to see our daughter throw her career away just because you won't move."

"Tina, sweetheart, what am I going to do in Los Angeles?" Candace's father asked.

"Fine, stay here then. But let me take Candy to Hollywood."

Grace heard Candace's father pause, try to get past the nickname again, and fail. "Don't call her that."

"Candace, fine," said Tina, straining audibly to keep her voice under control. "I've already lined up her first TV audition. It's in a month. She needs to be living there, goddamnit. That's what all the experts say. *Move to LA*."

"Look, Tina, you—*we*—have four other kids to worry about."

Grace knew that the "we" was euphemistic. All four were, biologically speaking, her mom's kids and not his. Tina's obsession with the sole child he'd brought to their blended family was something that none of them could openly address. But now Tina wanted to leave him, Grace, and her three younger brothers in San Antonio and head for the madness of a Hollywood dream.

Grace watched the frustration grow in Candace's face. Her eyes strayed to Candace's long legs stretched in front of her from under denim shorts, lithe and slender. She watched as Candace turned her head slightly, reaching over her right shoulder, just enough to get a quick look into the house. Their parents had moved from the living room, with its French windows, and into the kitchen. The girls couldn't hear them clearly now.

Grace concentrated on the sensation of hundreds of blunt prickles under her thighs, the coarse blades that she'd mown that afternoon. When Candace finally glanced up at her once more, there was a rueful grin on her face. Grace smiled back. The fights were becoming a bore for everyone in the house. A repetitive, predictable bore.

Candace scowled. "Man, it's like Tina thinks that if she keeps whining he'll eventually crack."

"She's doing it for you," Grace reminded her carefully.

"You know I love your mom, Grace. But we both know she's not just 'doing it for me.' You saw how she was about the jeans commercial. Me, this—it's all part of Tina's vicarious Hollywood life."

Grace nodded. "I saw." It was a strange thing about stage moms. Their motives seemed so altruistic, but they rarely escaped the scrutiny of intense examination.

Grace hesitated. "There's another way."

"I know," Candace said. "I already said I'm cool with waiting until after high school."

"That's not what I meant." Gently, Grace added, "And we both know you can't. This is your time, Candace. Now."

They were silent for a moment. It was the inescapable truth at the heart of the family's dilemma. Candace was a fruit on the cusp of ripening. Her hair was long and fell as straight as honey being poured, golden brown with hints of strawberry. Her skin was, without any recourse to a strenuous routine of diet and cleansing, clear and smooth with a peachy tone. Her eyes were light brown, her lips full and soft; a perfect shade of raspberry. She had a way of moving that looked like a ballet dancer unfolding from a tight hold.

It even surprised Candace herself. Grace had seen it on occasion—noticed the way Candace would catch sight of herself in the mirror and pause. Not admiringly, but as if startled by a stranger. Sometimes Grace wondered who was sharing her room. It wasn't the lanky girl she'd spent the past few years with, years over which they'd forged their firm, sisterly bond. Candace had become someone else, a young woman of understated sensuality and grace. If she slouched a little, curled her lip just a tad, a smoldering teenager returned her gaze. Total transformation. As though all it took was a small shift inside her brain, a subtle tweak of an attitude, and she could be whatever anyone wanted to see.

Of all the people on the planet to receive the undeserved gift of the face and body of a chameleon-goddess, it had to be the first person Grace saw when she woke up every day.

It wasn't fair, but there it was.

"Stay in San Antonio," Grace said, "and your best years are going to waste away."

"I'd be getting an education."

"I hear they even have schools in LA these days."

"It's about time."

Grace smirked. "Yeah, those airheads. No fair they all get to make a living from being pretty, like, forever."

"Whiny brats," Candace retorted.

"Get yourselves to school already, 90210."

The two girls laughed. Candace gazed into her stepsister's eyes for a second. "I can't leave. And you of all people should know why."

"I know, you'd die without me," Grace returned, deadpan. "But what if I could come, too?"

"Never. Gonna. Happen. Tina's going to give in to Dad. Any day now he'll make me apply to UT. And that'll be the end of it."

"You could always move back in with your mother."

Candace frowned. "The Wicked Witch of Malibu? She can barely stand to stay in the country long enough to get through a week of visitation."

"But she's loaded, right?"

"Strictly speaking, the cash belongs to the Dope Fiend."

"Pretty disrespectful term to apply to your stepfather."

"Don't even remind me," Candace said. "It's too bad I don't want to break into the art world. At least then the

Dope Fiend might be of some use."

"If you could switch your official residency back to your mom's, we might have another option."

"Grace, I'm serious. I don't want to live with them."

"What if–technically–you didn't have to?"

"Okay," Candace admitted, "you totally lost me. How can I live with my mom if I don't live with my mom?"

Grace pulled a slow, revelatory grin. "I have one word for you, my defeatist friend. *Emancipation.*"

"Huh?"

"If you're a California resident, you can petition the courts to be legally freed from parental control at fourteen. Keep all the money you earn, rent your own place. And your mom lives in California, which makes *you* a California resident."

"So Tina wouldn't get my cash?" Candace said with a sudden, wicked grin. "Hey, cool. Or is this about getting your room back for yourself?"

Grace's smile widened. "Not so fast, sis. In Texas, you have to be sixteen. Which, of course, I am."

"So this would be both of us?" Candace asked. "You and me, emancipated minors?"

Grace nodded. "Heck yeah."

PAOLO
MALIBU LAWN TENNIS CLUB,
WEDNESDAY, NOVEMBER 5

Things had gotten to the stage where Paolo wasn't even sure why he bothered. No one at the tennis club could beat him. He still coached a couple of people, rich girls who insisted on Paolo and only Paolo. But the money was, relatively speaking, a pittance. The last competition he'd entered had netted him more than he'd earned in all his time as a part-time coach.

Then he remembered the bottomless pit of tuition. Unless he could swing some major scholarship to Stanford or the Ivy League—which wasn't all that likely—an undergrad degree and law school was going to add up. So, even though he was exhausted from his training session, Paolo headed for the shower. He scrubbed away the sweat, washed his hair with a shampoo that smelled of green apples, and then dried off. From his locker he took a fresh set of tennis whites, neatly laundered and pressed by his mother. He dressed. He checked his watch. His student would be here any minute. He checked his hair. Slicked back wasn't the best look for him. With this girl, that was all good. He was running out of ways to turn her down.

Livia Judge was waiting for him on the court. She called out to him: "Hey, sweetie." She drawled on the "hey." She probably thought it sounded seductive. A couple of months ago, Paolo might have agreed. Since then, he'd slept with a couple of "slow-hey" types at the club. They hadn't been all that. There was more to seducing him properly. Paolo knew that much now. He didn't know what, but these pampered princesses didn't do whatever it was. He was looking to have his mind blown and his heart shredded. People told him that love was painful, yet all he'd found was an endless stream of pleasant but insipid smiles. Beautiful smiles, prizewinning orthodontic work. Empty, nonetheless.

But sex was sex. He grinned at himself in the mirror. The cute little boy he'd always seen grinned right back at him. To Paolo, he looked about twelve. He couldn't imagine what these twentysomething women saw in a boy like him. But hey, why fight it?

After the lesson, Livia invited him back to her place. For "cocktails."

"I don't drink," he reminded her politely. "I'm in training."

"A cup of chamomile tea then." She smiled a slow grin. Her face and chest were glowing a healthy pink, moist as if from stepping into a mist. He could smell the faint aroma of clean sweat. He tried to imagine her naked and reaching for him. But, nothing.

"I need to get going," he said. "My mom's making a special dinner for me tonight."

"Ooh, aren't you the special son."

He nodded. "I guess I am."

"Lucky Caroline. I'd love to have a son like you."

Paolo bit his lip. *I bet you would.*

Livia patted his arm affectionately. "Until next week?"

"Uh-huh."

"And maybe next time you'll keep the rest of the afternoon free?"

He swallowed. "Maybe," he managed to say.

What was wrong with these women? Livia Judge was the daughter of a Hollywood studio executive. She mixed with movie and TV stars. Why didn't she leave him alone? He just wanted to do his job and move on. But no. Not a single lesson could go by without some comment about the power in his thighs, his washboard abs, or the glimpse she'd caught of his waist when he'd reached for a high ball.

He drove his Chevrolet Malibu home and parked on the road. Both his parents' cars were in the driveway beside his older sister's. He sniffed the air—the unmistakable aroma of charred fish. He strolled into the backyard to find his mother, father, and sister, Diana, sipping from glasses of white wine. When she saw him, his mother, Caroline, gave him a welcoming smile. She poured him a tall glass of freshly made iced tea. He noticed her glance sideways at his dad. Paolo's father looked away from his conversation with Diana and met his mother's eye. They were nervous, Paolo was sure of it.

"I hope you're hungry," his mother said.

"Always."

"Then I suggest we get to it!" His father laughed a hollow sort of laugh and clapped a hand to Paolo's back. "Are you okay, son?"

"I'm great."

"Everything okay at the club?" continued his father.

"Everything's cool."

His father stuck a fork in his own food, which was piled high. "Get some of that good salmon your mom made, go ahead. And take some of the coleslaw. I made it myself. Special recipe!"

"Yeah, I know, the secret ingredient is Tabasco sauce."

It usually was.

Paolo relaxed into a chair and ate rapidly, watching his parents. He really was hungry, but something about his parents' behavior this evening was unnerving. He ran through all the possibilities that might be linked to him. There was no report card due from school. As far as he knew, his parents weren't undergoing any medical examinations. His sister was visiting from UCSF, where she was a biochemistry major, so it wasn't likely to be anything to do with her. He found himself stealing a peek at his mother's belly. She couldn't be pregnant again, could she? She was forty-seven years old; it wasn't possible. Was it?

But they were obviously waiting to tell him something. With every second that went by, the air grew thicker with tension. Strained smiles met him when he caught their eye. Paolo put his plate down carefully on the grass. He stood up and joined the other three where they were clustered around the grill, slicing up a large, smoking hunk of salmon.

His mother spoke first. "So, Paolo, darling, we kind of have something to tell you."

He nodded.

"Your father's been offered a great new job. It's an incredible opportunity."

"Cool, what's the hitch?"

His mother's face fell. "What makes you say that?"

Paolo's dad shook his head. Reluctantly, he grinned. "Caroline, you didn't raise any fools here." He turned to Paolo. "You're right, there's a hitch. The job's in Sonora. In Mexico."

"Sonora?" Paolo said. "That copper mine you're always visiting?"

"Yup. They need me on-site full-time. It's just for two years."

"But it's, like, in the middle of nowhere!"

His father nodded. "That it is."

"Can't you just . . ." Paolo stopped. He didn't understand his dad's business even close enough to follow any argument. A few years back he'd have argued anyway. Now he knew there was little point. He gazed imploringly into his father's eyes. "Dad. Please. Can't you turn it down?"

"I can't. They're my main client. If they pull out that's like eighty thousand I gotta find from someone else. And they're gonna pay me twice that if I move there for a couple of years. Plus relocation costs."

"But, school. And my tennis."

Paolo's mother squeezed his arm, reassuring. "It'll be okay, Paolo. There's a way."

In disgust, Paolo said, "Some Mexican international school and an occasional tennis coach? I don't think so."

She shook her head. "No. You can stay here in California."

"With Aunt Janet? Tell me you're kidding."

His dad coughed. "I think we can all agree that Aunt Janet isn't the answer."

Paolo's mouth was half open. "So what *is*? You gonna leave me here alone? I'd totally manage."

His father shook his head. "Legally, we'd be responsible for your actions. Frankly, son, we're not comfortable with that unless we're in the same state at the very least. We know what teenagers can be like—we survived your sister. Plus, this way you legally get to keep all your earnings from coaching and tennis competitions. Although we'd prefer it if you still put them straight into a high-interest savings account. There's college to save for, after all."

"What a crock," Paolo said. "You're just dying to get your long-awaited freedom."

"Well, son, I didn't like to say." His father gave Paolo an affectionate grin.

Finally, Paolo's sister, Diana, spoke. From behind her glass of sauvignon blanc, she'd watched the whole conversation with a secretive grin, as if awaiting her moment.

"Don't worry, it's better than being left here alone, kiddo. Way better."

Paolo turned to her. "What then?"

Diana's grin grew wicked. "You just won the jackpot, little brother. They're gonna *emancipate* your ass."

ARIANA CALLS CHARLIE
WEDNESDAY, NOVEMBER 5

"He didn't act scared. I remember that. He didn't scream. There was no noise."

The voice on the other end of the phone was hesitant, scared. A teenager on the brink of some terrifying revelation. It wasn't easy to tease out the secret. But failure wasn't an option. Ariana Debret knew she'd have to draw it out slowly, like prizing an oyster from its shell, alive and intact.

She was right; eventually the words began to flow, and Ariana encouraged them along.

"Sounds like a pretty awful memory," Ariana said sympathetically.

On the other end of the line the voice sounded thoughtful. "It's more like a dream."

"My therapist says that recurring dreams can begin to feel like a memory," Ariana admitted. There'd been a time when all they talked about was the therapy they shared. Ariana had grown to relish her friend's acerbic jokes at the expense of the therapists. The younger of the two, Ariana's friend had barely started high school when they'd met. Ariana reflected on how much her friend had grown up in the past two years.

"You still have a therapist?" Charlie sniffed. "Huh. I ditched mine after I left the group."

For a moment Ariana said nothing. Why had she mentioned therapy? Stupid. The last thing she wanted was for this kid to hire some no-account child psychologist and start spilling the beans. She made her voice all soothing. Confidential. "Tell me how the dream goes."

There was a long sigh on the other end of the line. "Well, okay," began Charlie. "It's nighttime. I'm at the party, but everyone else must have gone home. I hear voices from around the pool. I'm looking through a window. That's when I see him. He's lit up from below. His face is glowing, watery highlights from underneath the pool. He's wearing a real nice suit. You know, expensive. When he falls he throws his arms up to protect his face. He doesn't look afraid. No yelling, no nothing; just the slap of his body hitting the water. Behind him there are dark shadows, palm trees. And there's someone back there, in the shadows. Then the person from the shadows is kneeling down. Yeah, I remember white knees. There's a hand on his head. Holding him down.

"I don't want to think about that hand." The voice paused. "I'm not supposed to think about it.

"He doesn't struggle much, the guy in the water. I want to move but I can't. I'm on the stairs, looking through the open window on the first floor. All anyone has to do is look up and they'll see me. It would be smart to move away. I wish I could. But my feet are, like, planted."

"I get that, too," Ariana interrupted. "In dreams. Everybody does. That feeling of being rooted to the spot."

The voice continued. "Then someone's calling me. A whisper, really, but it reaches me across the water: 'Charlie . . . hey, Charlie.'

"I can't speak so I do this tiny wave. And real, but real slow, the feeling returns to my feet. I'm turning around, I'm all shaky . . ."

Ariana nodded. "You don't know what you've just seen."

"I don't know what I've just seen. Then a hand is taking my hand, all gentle-like. Telling me: *You're sleepwalking, honey. Dreams grabbing you by the throat.* Those exact words. And: *Time to get back to bed, Charlie.*"

"You're 'Charlie'?" Ariana said. "Like the character you played in that TV show?"

"It's what everyone called me back then. I didn't mind. Back then, I liked being Charlie. I was sad when I had to stop."

"What about now?" Ariana asked. "Do you wish you were still Charlie?"

"I think . . . I think I wish I'd never been Charlie. 'Charlie' saw a man drowned."

"Huh? From what you're saying, we're talking about a dream," Ariana said. "A dream that got all caught up with what you must have heard afterward. About Tyson Drew."

"If it was just a dream . . . why am I still dreaming it all these years later?"

"I don't know, honey. Could be many reasons."

The voice on the other end of the line was barely audible now. "You think it's got anything to do with why I'm . . . you know . . ."

"What?"

"Why I'm acting out?"

Ariana frowned. "You think you're acting out?"

Charlie's response sounded fragile. "Someone does. Why else would they want me to leave my own house?"

"You're leaving home?"

"It looks that way."

Ariana didn't have to fake her disapproval. "But you're still a kid! Where are you going to live?"

"I'm moving to Los Angeles. Getting emancipated."

"LA? Damn. But why?"

There was a sour laugh. "Must be 'cause I'm 'acting out.' 'We're not going to be the ones who have to pay for your adolescent misdemeanors.' That's a direct quote from my mom."

Ariana rolled her eyes. "You saying your folks are actually going to *emancipate* you? Where they let you live on your own, sign legal agreements, have a job—that kind of emancipation?"

"That's it. No parents. No safety net."

Ariana said, "Heck, I live on my own. My folks haven't given me any cash since I turned seventeen."

"But Ariana, you're eighteen. You're done with high school. You have a job. Emancipation is different. There's a court order. Makes me responsible for my own business."

"Sure, baby, I know that; I work in a legal practice. We've handled the paperwork on some emancipation cases. Your folks have to prove to the court that you've got enough cash to live on."

"That's right. They're gonna set me up with a monthly allowance, enough to pay for me to rent a room somewhere, buy some food, take the bus a few times."

Ariana found herself nodding. Now that she thought about it, emancipation made a kind of sense for her friend. "On the other hand, you do get to choose what school you go to."

There was a sigh. "Oh, that part my parents still want to control. Here or LA—guess when it comes to school, I'm going wherever they send me."

JOHN-MICHAEL
CARLSBAD, MONDAY, DECEMBER 1

"Everything will be okay now, Dad," John-Michael murmured.

The sight of his father's clenched fist resting on top of the quilt made it hard for John-Michael to concentrate on the task at hand. His dad was rolled over, facing the window. Apart from that single fist, all angry blue veins and tension, he looked peaceful.

John-Michael's eyes closed as he reached for his father's hand, gently relaxed the fingers, and tucked the hand under the covers.

He breathed, "You don't have to worry about me anymore."

The clock on his father's nightstand had the time at 10:35 p.m. Chunky digits an inch high, white on black; the choice of a man with failing eyesight. John-Michael had always hated that clock. He'd resented any sign of his father's growing age and mortality. It sucked to be the son of an angry widower, even before age had begun to take its toll. He moved to the other side of the bed. His father kept his most treasured mementoes of John-Michael's mother there. When he was a little boy, his father would lay the objects on the bed for him to touch and hold. Sometimes he'd even tell him a story about his mom. It hadn't happened for a very long time.

John-Michael emptied the nightstand drawer onto the bed. For a moment he stared at the collection of handwritten envelopes, the necklace of Chinese pearls, the black-velvet box containing diamond and gold rings from an engagement and a wedding, the metal box of photographs. *I never knew what to keep*, he remembered his father saying.

At first, John-Michael had been pathetically grateful for anything. Resentment only came later. His father should have kept much, much more. There wasn't even one voice recording. No video. It was the twenty-first century, but John-Michael didn't have any digital record of his mother's existence. And his only memories were dim now, faded. He wasn't even sure if they were real, or the memories of dreams.

His eyes went once again to the bulk of his father's body in the bed. Reluctantly, his thoughts returned to the events of the past hour. He couldn't stand to think about them for more than a second or two. The things his father had said—worse than anything he'd heard before from the man. Things that couldn't—that never would—be taken back.

He rummaged beneath the bed for a shoe box and removed a pair of his father's Italian loafers. He gathered his mother's possessions into the box, covered it with the lid, and placed the box at the bottom of the empty backpack he'd brought along.

It took another few minutes to collect the papers he'd come for. His father had told him where to find the cash. Not exactly under the mattress, but not far from it. He kept everything he'd saved in Krugerrands and hundred-dollar bills, never less than five thousand at home; the gold and most of the cash was in a safe-deposit box.

There was no point taking anything else. It would only look suspicious. As much as possible, things had to look normal. "Better leave by the back door," his father had advised with a nasty cackle. "These days, anyone who sees your sorry ass on my porch is gonna get to wondering what the ungrateful little faggot is doing visiting his pa."

John-Michael felt a stab of pain at the memory of those words. Even now, it still hurt to hear his father call him names. He wanted to tell his dad he was sorry. But the truth was, he wasn't. Not for any of it. He'd done his crying a long time ago. Most of it alone, on rainy nights, trying to find shelter in a phone booth, a doorway, anyplace where he might avoid waking up to feel greedy hands around his throat.

He'd finally freed himself from the misery of Chuck Weller's eternal bile and disappointment. Not tonight, but sometime in the last year. Tonight had merely been the outward expression of a sentiment he'd long ago internalized.

Yet John-Michael's hands still trembled slightly at the memory of his father's words.

You're more like me than you know. Your mother could never have done anything like this.

He placed a gloved hand on the handle of the back door. As instructed, he turned the key in its lock and then replaced it in the hanging basket of geraniums. He crossed the backyard, vaulted the wooden fence, and strolled across the brown field of undeveloped land at the back of his father's house. He'd used exactly the same escape route a thousand times at least, ever since he was twelve.

There was something cold and ominous in the idea that this time would be his very last.

John-Michael turned to gaze one last time at his father's house silhouetted in the neon streetlights from the front. The two-story building cast a long shadow, intensely black. For a moment that darkness seemed to stretch toward him. A little closer and it might swallow him up. He took a step backward. His heart was pounding, hammering so hard that it rattled the bones in his chest.

"Good-bye, Dad," he whispered.

It was scary to be out in the city, alone, carrying several thousand dollars in cash. John-Michael wished he could just take his dad's car right away. But his Dad's instructions had been clear. *Hold your horses. Be cool; wait it out.*

He'd be safe soon enough. The money would buy him a night in a comfortable bed and a big breakfast; the first time in weeks he'd manage to find that without having to get some guy off first. Not that he always minded—some of the guys who'd picked him up over the past year had been pretty hot. Some of them had wanted to see him again. But the idea of being anyone's boy toy didn't appeal to John-Michael. He wanted a guy his own age, someone who was still in high school. Maybe even someone a little younger. If he couldn't have a relationship on equal footing, then he wanted to be the one with the upper hand.

So far, life kept handing him the fuzzy end of the lollipop. Tonight had been John-Michael's chance to change that. His father's exact words had been, "You're a screwup, son. For once, I want to see something different. Prove to me that you inherited some balls."

Now John-Michael would finally have the opportunity, maybe even for the upper hand. Freedom had come at last. The price had been high.

But then, wasn't it always?

CANDACE
CULVER STUDIOS, FRIDAY, DECEMBER 5

"Didn't they say they wanted blondes?"

Finally, the moment had arrived, the part of any casting call that Candace most dreaded: walking into the waiting area to be surrounded by a gaggle of identical girls. Same age, same slender bodies, same loose blond hair. Any idea of your own uniqueness went right out the window.

To her surprise, this time was totally different. There were at least a dozen or so blondes, brunettes, black girls, white girls, Latinas, and Asian girls.

Candace chose a seat and then Grace sat beside her, giving her an encouraging smile. She and Grace had arrived in California just four days ago after a month of packing and paperwork. Two days before, they'd taken a trip to court to pick up the permission for Candace to live as a legally emancipated individual. Grace's emancipation had been arranged in Texas before they'd left. Now they were able to enter into legal contracts, to choose their own school, and most important to Candace—to keep all the money they earned.

Candace turned to a stunning Filipino girl who was flicking through pages of the script. "Is this the right place for auditions for 'Gina' in *Downtowners*?"

The girl nodded and smiled. "My agent told me: 'Age seventeen to twenty-three, fresh-faced, athletic build, stage combat training essential, previous screen experience preferred. Wear clothing suitable for physical training.'"

"So you don't have to be blond?"

"I think the character's head is shaved, so it doesn't really matter."

"Her head is shaved . . . ?" broke in Grace, but Candace silenced her, eyes flashing a warning.

Candace's mother, Katelyn, strode into the room, trailing an oriental-floral scent that had been personally blended for her by one of the noses at Guerlain. Katelyn swept an appraising glace across the dozen or so other girls before sitting down next to her daughter.

Doubtfully, she glanced around, then placed her Chanel handbag on her lap. "Darling, this looks like a crapshoot."

Candace didn't reply. She rolled her eyes at Grace, who suppressed a grin.

The two stepsisters had been lucky enough to get along from the day they'd first been introduced to each other about six years prior. The girls immediately discovered that they shared a sardonic sense of the ridiculous. There was something surreal about seeing your parent dating someone else's parent. One pointed this out to the other and the chemistry was instant.

Candace was nervous, staring at the script. There were only two lines—the pages were just somewhere to focus her attention, somewhere she might escape for a few minutes from her mother's incessant, unsolicited advice.

Candace had wanted only Grace at the audition, but Katelyn was going to drive the two girls to the Venice Beach house right after. Then they were going to pick up the car Candace's mom had leased on her behalf—a Prius. Katelyn had insisted. "It's that or you can use a bicycle. Bad enough we have to increase the family's overall carbon footprint by having you live apart from me, but you know how it is with Jarvis. His work demands such intense privacy."

Grace was counting the minutes until she and Candace moved out of Jarvis and Katelyn's Malibu house and into a place of their own. They'd been staying with Candace's mother and the Dope Fiend since their whirlwind move from San Antonio. Katelyn had insisted on doing everything by the book: "In my Venice house, you're my tenant, not my daughter. Legally responsible for keeping the place in order. You'd better remember that."

There was definitely a weird atmosphere at the Malibu house. Candace could see that it wasn't easy on Grace. Katelyn hated Grace's mother, Tina. She blamed her for the failure of her own marriage to Candace's father, even though it had actually been Candace's mother who'd done the dumping. But mainly, Katelyn resented Tina's obsession with Candace's career. It made her own relative disinterest seem distinctly unmotherly.

Luckily, all the bad vibes would soon be a thing of the past. Katelyn's recent generosity more than made up for her helplessly supercilious manner. She'd decided, without any prompting from Candace, to let them live in her own house on Venice Beach. She'd even lined up the first of four other people that she'd insisted had to share the house. He was a guy named Paolo King, a sophomore who coached tennis at Katelyn's country club.

Candace and Grace had already checked him out online. They'd agreed that he was a total hottie. Katelyn had mentioned that she'd heard Paolo was going out with some rich girl that he coached, a college student.

"No hookup potential for you then," Grace had told Candace.

"Eww, I don't do younger guys, thanks," had been Candace's response. "I don't care if he goes out with college girls. Even if he *is* cute."

A couple of girls were practicing a combat sequence a little way down from the waiting area where the corridor opened into a break room with watercooler, candy machine, and beanbag chairs. Both girls were tanned, lithe, and dressed almost identically to Candace in cargo pants, sneakers, and snug-fitting sleeveless tops. For a few minutes, Candace watched.

"I should have made you practice a fight with me," she muttered to Grace.

Grace raised an eyebrow. "I'm game if you are. Let it never be said I wasn't willing to look a fool for my girl."

"Don't be ridiculous." Katelyn scowled. She adjusted her flowing linen trousers so that the hems fell evenly, then crossed one leg daintily across the other, dangling an elegant black-and-white Jimmy Choo slingback. "Look how sweaty they're getting."

"This Gina is some riotous badass," Candace said fiercely. "She kills a guy with her own hands in the first episode. 'Sweaty' is a good look for her."

"Is this really the kind of part you want, darling? You're such a gorgeous girl. More of a graceful type. Dancers, singers; that's what you should play."

"They get actual dancers and singers to do that, Mom. I'm an actor. I can play any part. It's on TV and it calls for a degree of pretending to be someone else. So yeah, this will do just fine."

"But it's such a teeny role," Katelyn said. "It's going to tie you up and keep you from auditioning for other things while you're under contract."

Candace rolled her eyes at Grace, who merely raised an eyebrow in response. "Mom, that's bull."

"Even if it doesn't," Katelyn continued, now defensive, "I'm not going to support you taking more parts. Not while you're still in high school."

"Seriously?! God, I wish Tina were here instead of you! She'd never say anything like that. She'd put me up for any TV part going."

"Well, that's a difference—one of many—between that woman and me," Katelyn said loftily. "She wants you to be famous so that she can come along for the ride. Whereas I'm your mother, I love you, and I want you to have some kind of balance in your life. If anyone knows what the life of an artist can be, what it can do to those who love you, it's me."

Grace didn't say a word, but Candace could see the rigid control in her face as she tried, yet again, not to rise to Katelyn's daily criticism of Grace's mom.

Through tight lips Candace said, "Could you leave the martyred-wife-of-an-artist speech for some other day, Mom, please?" A note of desperation entered her voice. "I need your support. Do you have any idea how much Tina did to encourage me? It's not easy to lose that. Honestly, any kind of break into TV would be amazing. So I don't care if I have to play a boxer with a shaved head—anything that gets me screen time is good."

From down the hallway a voice called, "Candace Deering?"

Grace stood up with Candace. She hugged her tight for two seconds. After a moment, Candace released her and turned, following the woman with the clipboard through clear plastic swinging doors. The churn of butterflies in her stomach began to calm. It was always like this just before she auditioned. The nerves left her, just seconds before the moment of truth, leaving her slightly sleepy and numb.

PAOLO
VAN BUREN HIGH SCHOOL,
MONDAY, DECEMBER 15

"You're looking for a *gay* roommate? Why don't you ask the weird new kid? From what I hear, he sleeps in his dad's car."

The court permission for Paolo's emancipation had come through about a week ago and he'd already found a great place to live. One of his tennis students at the country club in Malibu had recommended him to a woman who was looking for young tenants to live with her daughter.

She wanted to set up a "family" type of atmosphere in the house. In the interview, Paolo had gone all out on the charm offensive. It seemed to have worked, because not only did she want Paolo to move in but she'd asked him to find another guy, too.

"Maybe you know a nice gay boy?" she'd suggested hopefully. "Someone who likes to keep a place all neat and clean."

Paolo didn't dare admit that he didn't actually have any

close gay friends. Anyway, how ridiculous. *He* was neat and clean. Gay men didn't have a monopoly on that. Just the same, he'd asked the only gay student he knew at school, who just laughed. But then the guy had mentioned John-Michael.

Paolo wasn't sure. John-Michael Weller had only been in his school a week, in the same homeroom, and they'd barely exchanged a word. Paolo couldn't tell if it was the classic jock-nerd divide, although he prided himself on being able to play in either camp, if he felt so inclined.

Or maybe John-Michael just didn't like him. Paolo was perfectly aware that despite his alleged popularity, there were those who avoided, even despised him, because of his perfect teeth, skin, and hair. Add the tennis on top, and he was just about toxic—to a certain type.

John-Michael, Paolo suspected, was secretly cool. For the first few days he'd been silent, just this ghost at the back of the classroom, taking everything in, sizing everyone up. Not a word about himself, why he'd transferred to Van Buren High weeks before Christmas break. Then suddenly, in response to a teacher's question about the significance of rap as modern-day, urban poetry and its spread through all forms of popular music, John-Michael had recited the entirety of some obscure, rap-influenced lyrics from a British indie rock band.

The class had turned as one to watch, at first embarrassed, not knowing where to put their eyes, then finally, grudgingly, impressed. John-Michael had said his piece, then stopped and disappeared into the background just as swiftly as he'd emerged.

With that pale skin, angular features, jet-black straight hair, and the guyliner he wore, it wasn't surprising to hear girls slyly refer to him as "that vampire wannabe." Except that Paolo noticed John-Michael never returned their curiosity, never even looked at the girls. He wasn't "out," but Paolo was fairly certain John-Michael was gay.

And stupidly, that made Paolo nervous. You couldn't easily ask some guy to live with you and it not sound a bit strange. Hugely more complicated when there was a frisson—which there definitely was. Paolo sensed John-Michael's eyes on him. Not that he minded—Paolo was used to that kind of attention, too. But how to go about making the proposition without it sounding like, well . . . a proposition?

Paolo waited for John-Michael outside the lunchroom and followed him as he carried his tray to one of the empty benches near the peace garden. He watched John-Michael unwrap a grilled-cheese panini and take a sip from his juice box before sitting down opposite him.

"Hey." Paolo suppressed his usual winning smile.

John-Michael hey-ed back. He took a bite of the panini, which dripped melted cheese from its edges.

"That looks good."

John-Michael nodded. "It is. You should get one."

Paolo shrugged. "I'm on this diet, for my tennis. I'm supposed to avoid stuff like that."

"Sounds like a hoot," John-Michael said carefully. Clearly, he was interested to know what Paolo wanted.

"We've never really spoken before," Paolo began awkwardly. John-Michael looked disconcerted. He seemed to be controlling the urge to say something. Probably a snarky response, Paolo decided.

Better get it over with. Paolo was acting like a doofus.

"So I'm, like, looking for a housemate. And I heard, well, I heard that you might be . . ."

"Homeless?" John-Michael said it like it wasn't a thing to be embarrassed about, as if it were a challenge.

Paolo blushed. "Yeah. To be honest, that's what I heard."

"That's not a strictly accurate description of my current situation," John-Michael said, "because this week I'm staying with a friend of a friend of a *friend*. . . ."

"But it will be?"

"Yeah." For a second there was a catch in his voice, a hint of vulnerability. "This weekend. I gotta move out."

"How d'you manage?"

John-Michael put down his half-finished panini. "You mean, like, money-wise? There's no problem there. I got cash. What I don't have is a place that will take me. Most people want a college-age student. Not a high school kid."

"So how about it?"

"Your folks looking to take in a boarder?"

Paolo let himself grin, finally. "Not exactly."

John-Michael looked confused. "You and me?"

"You and me and some girls . . . ideally. Although if it's

a deal breaker we could always look for a third guy. But between you and me, I'd feel better with girls."

"I get it. You don't need the competition. And I'm not exactly what you'd call competition, am I?"

Paolo stared into John-Michael's eyes. Okay. So he *knew* he knew.

"It's not that at all. It's just that this setup I'm looking at—we already have two girls locked in. You and me makes four, so far, out of six. Sharing three rooms. The girls want clean guys. Nice, housebroken types."

"Housebroken. Right." John-Michael nodded. "Because I'm gay?"

Paolo didn't know how to respond.

"You think all gay men are clean freaks with a penchant for interior decor?"

"Whatever, man, you seem . . . trustworthy." Paolo sighed. "Okay . . . but could you pretend to be neat and clean? Just until the girls say yes?"

"What kind of setup are we talking about? Three bedrooms? An apartment? A house?"

"It's a sweet deal. Wait until I tell you the location—right on Venice Beach."

John-Michael laughed. "You barely know me."

"You and me," Paolo said firmly. "Assuming your references check out, that is. These two sisters, it's their mom's second house, or something like that. If we get our deposits in by the end of the week, we can move in over the weekend."

John-Michael swallowed some juice and nodded, giving Paolo a half smile of semicommitment that Paolo knew only too well. Every girl he'd ever hooked up with had worn the same expression—a look that screamed *hell yeah* while trying to appear smooth.

ARIANA CALLS CHARLIE
SATURDAY, DECEMBER 20

"You remember that dream I told you about?"

Ariana Debret nodded. "I remember." It had been almost two months since Ariana and Charlie had last spoken of the dream. She'd been wondering when the topic would raise its ugly head again.

"What if I told you that I'm pretty sure it wasn't always a dream?" Charlie said.

"Did you ever tell anyone else that idea?"

"Like who?"

"Like anyone," Ariana said, frowning. "Another friend. Your parents. The police?"

The reply came in considered bursts of speech, with frequent pauses. "I *thought* it was a dream. For years. But it can't be. Can it? It's his face I see: Tyson Drew, the guy who was murdered. I try to see the person who pushed him in, who held him down—"

"And?" Ariana said expectantly.

"I can't. It's like a block." The voice on the other end of

the line sounded resigned. "Like my eyes won't open."

"Because in real life you saw nothing," Ariana stated.

"I guess. But what if it's because I'm afraid to look?"

"Honey, I'm going to have to call you back," Ariana broke in. "My momma's on call-waiting. She goes nuts if I don't pick up."

Ariana waited until she heard the line go dead before she switched to the other call. When she spoke to the older woman her own voice was noticeably lower, as though the warmth had been sucked right out of her. "I just got off the phone with our old pal, 'Charlie.'"

The woman replied in her usual smooth, confident voice. "Excellent. All good?"

"The bad news? Still mightily preoccupied with Mr. Tyson Drew. Good news is we're still talking in terms of a dream."

The line went silent for a long time. Then, "All right. What's next?"

"Well, you and me, we have ourselves a problem," Ariana said. "I can't keep doing this."

The reply was full of derision. "What—suddenly you've developed a conscience?"

"I did what we agreed, I made friends with her. But it's about to be over."

The woman gave a hollow laugh. "I think *I'll* tell *you* when it's over."

Ariana sighed. "The kid is leaving home. Moving—a long way from me."

"So what? You can just keep calling her."

"I don't think so. I always call with the usual excuse—checking in on each other, the way people who've shared therapy do. But we finished therapy awhile ago. It's getting harder to call so often. You don't have any kids of your own or you'd know—people under twenty don't talk on the phone. They text, or use some kind of instant message."

There was a hostile silence. Tentatively, Ariana continued. "You need to find someone local. What am I gonna do—call her up out of the blue and demand to talk about all this historical nonsense?"

"I see. Can't you move, too? I helped you find one crummy job; I can get you another."

"You know how I feel about LA. I hate the big city. And as for my 'crummy job,' I happen to like it. I'm finally settling down, saving some money. Not that I don't appreciate the offer." Ariana was hesitant. "This living arrangement thing—it may be an issue. I know what I'm talking about—I remember how I was when I moved out of my folks' house. I shared an apartment with my cousin and her friends. A lot of fun. Late nights, unsupervised teenagers. All kinds of shenanigans."

The woman didn't seem perturbed. "I appreciate your concern, but I'm not exactly without other options. One way or another, Ariana, I've had my eye on this girl for the past eight years. And I'm not about to let her out of my sights now."

"Maybe so, but things just got a whole lot more

complicated. You need someone on the ground. I'm talking on-site, in Los Angeles."

"LA? Not a problem. I know just who to send–"

Ariana cut her off. "Don't say any more! The less I know about what you got planned the better."

GRACE

"There'll be other parts. My agent's already lining up more auditions. Yeah. This is why I had to come live here, Tina. I'm here in the middle of the action."

Candace was quiet then, listening to the flood of sympathy that ensued from Tina's end of the cell phone. Grace, sitting next to her in the car, glared at her stepsister in irritation. She mouthed, *Tell her you're driving!*

Paolo was already in Venice Beach when Candace and Grace drove up in Candace's gleaming blue Prius. With a wave, he ushered them into the parking spot next to his Chevy Malibu.

"Nice car," he said, offering a hand as Candace stepped out of the car.

"Likewise," said Grace. The guy was as pretty as his picture. And it was obvious that he knew it.

The other male housemate, John-Michael, was the last to arrive. Grace's eyes widened when she saw his car—a pearly-silver Mercedes-Benz convertible. Beside her, Paolo perked up. By the time John-Michael opened the door Paolo was already running one hand over the hood.

"This your old man's?"

John-Michael nodded. One hand, clad in a fingerless purple glove, pushed dyed-black bangs away from his face. From behind gorgeously applied black-and-purple eyeliner, his eyes were a clear blue-gray. "It was."

"You kill him for this or what?" Paolo asked.

John-Michael shook his head and said very softly, "No. But he *is* dead."

Grace watched Paolo's smile vanish. "Dude! I'm sorry, but, damn, this car—"

John-Michael blinked. Grace noticed his mouth open and close for a second like a fish. The mention of his father had rattled the boy. She made a mental note to tread carefully.

"Okay, so we're all here," Candace said in a business-like voice that Grace rarely heard her use. "Let's go see the house!"

As they walked down the path that ran behind the houses on the beachfront, Grace said to John-Michael, "So— your dad died?"

"He did," John-Michael said.

Grace guessed that his short, clipped tone was meant to discourage further questions, so she stopped talking. But Candace wasn't put off, not a bit.

"Was he sick?"

He nodded. "You could say that."

"What was it? Heart attack? Not cancer?"

Grace nudged her. "Candace!"

"It's okay," John-Michael said. "I'll tell you. He committed suicide."

There was a blunt silence. Paolo was the first to break it. "And you two didn't get along?"

"No. The bastard threw me out last year."

"What for?" Candace asked.

John-Michael seemed to ignore Candace's question. "At least he left me his loot. Silver linings and all."

Grace commented, "I guess you don't need to be emancipated then."

John-Michael looked confused. "Who's emancipated?"

"Me," Grace said, then nodded at Candace and Paolo. "Her, him. My parents live in Texas. Candace's mom isn't interested in supervising a couple of teenage girls. And Paolo's folks moved to Mexico."

John-Michael asked Paolo, "They couldn't just leave you alone?"

"They want me to be responsible. For my own mistakes." Paolo smirked. "Guess they assume I'll be a good boy now."

"And will you?"

Paolo blinked. "Dude. Please." He turned his attention back to the car with a wistful air. "You sure you didn't kill your old man? Car like that, I dunno. Some people would do some extreme stuff to get a ride like that."

John-Michael turned a glacial stare on him. "I'm pretty sure."

"I never knew anyone who killed himself," Paolo said.

"Me either," John-Michael said. "Until now."

"Were you shocked?" Candace asked.

John-Michael shook his head and shrugged, noncommittal. Grace watched him for a second. He was trying to seem flippant, yet not far beneath the surface, there was a kind of trauma in his manner. She wondered how much further they might be able to take this. Maybe what John-Michael needed was to talk?

But Candace changed the subject. "So anyway, my mom said we can't move in until she has everyone's first check."

Paolo handed Candace an envelope. "Got mine. John-Michael, you got yours, too?"

"I got cash," he said. "I don't have a bank account yet."

Grace turned to him. "How do you get money?"

"My dad's attorney. He's the executor of his will. When I need money, he gives it to me."

"Are you loaded?" Candace asked.

"Not really. My father made sure I can't get too much at any one time. There's a basic annuity, and I mean basic. I'll get to keep some of the rent from my dad's house, if his attorney ever manages to find some tenants. Above that, every dime I spend needs to be accounted for. Until I turn twenty-five."

"Twenty-five!" said Paolo. "That's a long wait."

Grace asked quietly, "Are you sad?"

John-Michael seemed to consider this. "He was the only parent I had left. I don't have anyone else. No brothers or sisters."

She placed a hand on his. "I'm sorry."

Candace chimed in, "Yeah, John-Michael, me too. Not everyone gets along with their parents, but it's got to be hard to lose one."

"Then I must be pretty careless," he replied with a bitter chuckle. "Because I've lost *two*."

They'd perfectly timed their arrival on the waterfront. The sun was setting, the whole sky over the ocean was lit up: layers of fiery gold, pink, and blue interrupted by the stark silhouettes of tall palms. A neat strip of pavement in front of the row of houses opened directly onto trimmed patches of scrub grass and then smooth white sand, all the way to the water's edge, which foamed, about six hundred feet away.

For a moment they all stood, practically paused mid-stride. Grace turned with a half smile. She watched the boys react, recognizing in their response herself from just two days ago.

In a low voice Paolo said, "Dude!"

"You gotta be kiddin' me," John-Michael mumbled.

Candace dangled a set of keys. "And you haven't even seen the house."

They followed her along the boardwalk, gazing at each

house they passed. Every house was different, an exercise in cool architectural self-expression. One house had made a life-sized stone statue of the Buddha into a frontispiece, with a fountain and glowing lights. Some houses had vast windows through which the new housemates could see pristine living rooms with minimal furnishings, all watched over by huge plasma-screen TVs. Artwork—almost certainly original—occupied the walls, which were either plain white or brick.

The people inside looked rich, as though they'd never known a day's uncertainty or discomfort in their lives.

Candace stopped in front of a house.

It was a blocky modernist building with three floors, narrow, like the other "beach shacks" in the nearby strip of beach. The first two floors were covered with white stucco, all horizontal lines of gray and steel. The outside walls of the third floor alone were brightly colored—a deep, sunset yellow.

There was a single eccentric feature—a yellow spiral staircase that stood beside the main front door. It ran from the first floor to the third and opened onto a large balcony that looked out onto the beach. The balcony was bordered by a low, white stuccoed wall.

A pale gray, ultrasmooth concrete wall ran around the perimeter of the house. A white metal gate stood at one side.

"Paolo said it's three bedrooms?" John-Michael asked.

Grace answered, "Yup, three. Two bathrooms. We'll

have to share. Candace and I took a quick look the other day. After her last audition."

Paolo said, "You're auditioning?"

Candace nodded. "I've done a few now."

"Exciting!"

"Maybe one day," she answered flatly. "But not this time. I didn't get the part. Again."

"Tough business," Paolo said with sympathy.

John-Michael turned to Paolo. "So, guess I'm sharing with you."

"Nope," Paolo replied. "I've already talked it over with the girls. Two of the rooms are huge. One is teeny. Well, it's me-sized. I'm coughing up a bigger share of the rent so I get to have privacy."

John-Michael said, "You mean you're the only one who gets to bring someone home?"

Candace interrupted. "I think we should have a rule— no sex in the house. It's too small."

"Why would we be having sex?" Grace said with a straight face. "None of us are married."

It took the boys a few seconds to realize that she was joking, or at least hope that she was.

"If that's an issue," Paolo said gallantly, "I could always propose."

They all laughed. Paolo smiled, enjoying the attention. "I only offered to take the small room because I thought it would save the rest of you from having to deal with me in your own space. Predatory male beast that I am."

His second quip got a bigger reaction than the first. When they'd calmed down Grace said, "I think it's best if we get two other girls. Or else the room sharing gets weird."

"You don't mind sharing with me?" John-Michael asked.

"You'd be welcome in either room," Grace said. "The other bedroom has the same layout, only two beds. One's a double but Candace already called dibs on that."

"And you're not sharing with your sister?" Paolo asked.

Grace found herself blushing. "It's kind of embarrassing. My folks only agreed to this if I pay the lowest rent possible. They've got a bunch of other kids to support, yada yada."

"And my super-mean mom won't let her stay for free," Candace added carelessly.

"Maybe my friend Lucy Long could share with both of us," John-Michael said.

Grace turned to him slowly. She could hardly believe what she was hearing. *It couldn't be.*

In the calmest voice she could manage she said, "Tell us about this Lucy Long."

LUCY

"You cannot be serious."

Lucy checked the GPS on her cell phone. "Totally serious."

Her brother, Lloyd, frowned. "Right on Venice Beach?!"

"Uh-huh."

"Sis, you are one lucky girl, you know that?"

Lucy gave him a piercing look. "If it gets me off your student-ass floor, that's good enough for me. I'm tired of waking up smelling like beer."

"Girl, do not make fun of my hobbies."

"Hobbies, nothing," Lucy shot back. "Apart from drinking beer and watching TV, I haven't seen you do anything where your head wasn't in a book since the day I arrived."

"When it's Dr. Lloyd Long, MD, PhD, you'll be eating your words," her brother said. "Need any help with your bags?"

"I'll take the acoustic guitar; can you grab my Telecaster?" Lucy said. "Thanks, Lloyd."

He reached into the trunk of the car. "Got it."

They strolled along the beachfront, stepping aside at times to avoid two small clusters of cyclists and kids on scooters. After a few minutes they arrived at the house. The white front gate was open. Lucy stepped into the front yard and took in the house. The front door was all but obscured by an exterior yellow spiral staircase that led to the two upper levels. As she approached, Lucy could see that the door was a solid, cherry wood carved in the Spanish style and varnished to a high polish.

Through the two front windows she could see the kitchen. There were no blinds. A French press had been left on the counter but otherwise the place looked spotlessly clean. Gleaming, modern kitchen appliances were visible inside. A dining table dominated the kitchen, and a large bowl of green apples had been thoughtfully placed as the centerpiece.

It looked like a show home. Not the "beach shack" she'd been led to expect at all. She wasn't sure how she felt about living here. It looked like the kind of place a bunch of hipsters would rent. Just the atmosphere she was trying to escape.

From above, a voice called out. Lucy looked up to find herself staring at a good-looking white boy with short dark hair. Leaning over the balcony, he grinned—clean-cut, wholesome smile. "Hey! You must be Lucy! I'm Paolo. We all moved in yesterday—we've been waiting for you!"

Paolo bounded down the spiral staircase and bumped

fists first with Lloyd and then Lucy. He picked up the rectangular case that held Lucy's second guitar, a Fender Telecaster. "Let me help you get this stuff upstairs. You're on the middle floor, with Grace and John-Michael. They're both totally cool."

"Finally, I get to meet the famous John-Michael Weller," Lloyd commented.

"I guess you and he are pretty good friends?" Paolo asked Lucy.

Lucy smiled. "We played in a band together a couple of years ago at camp."

"John-Michael plays guitar? He didn't mention that."

They arrived at the threshold of the middle floor. John-Michael was standing in the doorway. He held his arms out to Lucy, who carefully put down her suitcase and walked right into them. In silence, they hugged tightly.

"I'm so sorry about your dad," Lucy murmured against his neck.

"S'okay. The old coot was a bastard anyhow."

But she heard the catch in his voice when he mentioned his father and hugged him harder. After a few more seconds, Lucy gently pulled away. She realized that Lloyd and Paolo were watching them uncomfortably.

Lucy sat on the edge of the single bed nearest to the door and glanced around the room. The size wasn't bad. It was newly painted, the buttery, maple wood floor polished to a matte sheen. All the furniture looked IKEA-fresh. But with three beds crammed in as well as two desks and a closet, not to mention a couple of nightstands, there wasn't a lot of extra space.

She looked back at her friend. "So now we've *both* been kicked out."

John-Michael nodded. "Pretty weak, huh?"

"I gotta tell you, John-Michael, I did not enjoy it very much."

"What exactly did you do?" asked Paolo.

Lucy turned to him. The boy looked like he belonged on a Disney Channel show, a dazzling white smile and clear green eyes. "Well—Paolo, is it? Seems that my folks did not appreciate my turning our basement into a creative space for the expansion of minds in the general direction of the arts."

Paolo laughed. He came in and sat in the swivel chair next to one of the two desks. It looked as though he planned to hang around to watch her move in.

"What my sister is saying," Lloyd said, placing one suitcase carefully on the bed next to Lucy, "is that she had some of her stoner buddies over for a late-night jam session. Our parents walked in on two of her friends having sex, and Lucy and her friends tripped out on crystal meth, while trying to play something by Green Day."

Lucy leaned back against the wall. "That's so not true. They weren't having sex. She just had her hand in his pants. And they were behind the amps, it's not like we could see anything. It wasn't crystal, it was weed. Seriously, Lloyd, what's with you? Like I'd mess with methamphetamine!

And hey, also, it wasn't Green Day–it was Rancid."

Lloyd sat in the other desk chair, nearest to Lucy's bed. Lucy wondered fleetingly if she should claim the desk. It didn't look as though anyone had yet, but there were only two desks between the three of them. How was that going to work out?

"What difference does it make?" Lloyd said languidly. "Point is, my sister blotted her copybook somethin' awful and Mr. and Mrs. Long did *not* take it well."

There were footsteps on the landing. A petite, slim girl with wavy blond hair and piercing blue eyes stepped into the triple room. "I'm Grace," she said, smiling. "It's so good to meet you."

Lucy stood up for a quick hug. "Hey, Grace. I was just telling the others how my folks threw me out."

"Did it have anything to do with your dad being in the government?" Grace asked.

Lucy's eyes narrowed for a second. "Someone's been doing their research."

"My stepsister's mother owns the house," Grace explained. "She had everyone checked out. Even me!"

Lucy sat back on her bed. "The other girl–Candace Deering. That's your *stepsister*?"

Grace nodded. "But yeah, we both take her dad's name now. My mom remarried, changed her name and every-thing."

Lucy frowned. "And is it awkward? With Candace's mom, I mean. Was your mom, like, the 'other woman'?"

Grace crossed the room to sit on her bed, the larger of the two against the far wall. Unlike the other beds in the room, which were spread with plain blue-and-white bed linens, Grace's was already decorated with a tasteful floral design and piled with lime-green pillows.

"Kind of the opposite," she said. "Candace's mom left my stepdad for a dude in Malibu. Jarvis Adler. He's a sculptor, or something, or maybe he does installations. If I had a clue about art, I might be able to tell you more."

"What happened, did Candace argue with your mom or something?"

"Nothing like that. My mom is crazy about her. Too crazy, I sometimes think. . . ." Grace paused.

Lucy caught her eye. "Must be kind of annoying for you." She smiled gently.

Grace shook her head, resolute. "I'm real happy for my mom. She'd been super-depressed. Things improved a lot when Candace and her dad came along. It was like a miracle really."

"Candace seems pretty cool," John-Michael admitted. "Kind of . . . acerbic, though."

"Don't let that bother you," Grace said. "That's just Candace. Wait until you hear her Shakespearean insults. She doesn't mean any of it. You'll know she loves you when she calls you something bad."

Paolo frowned. "How will we know if she hates us?"

Grace looked at him darkly. "You'll know."

Lucy looked around the room again. The walls were

pure white, with some type of adobe finish. The beds didn't match, nor the furniture, and yet there was a pleasingly eclectic feel to the decor. It was like someone had carefully chosen each piece because of some particular moment of delight or nostalgia it had caused.

At best, there was enough floor space for two extra people to sleep. There were no rugs, pictures, or any other kind of decoration on the walls so far.

Lucy decided it had to be mentioned. "There are only two desks."

"Yeah, the rent per person is lowest for this room," Grace said. "We'll have to share."

"But there's Wi-Fi in the whole house," Paolo offered. "Come on, I'll show you around."

Lucy followed Paolo out of the room to the open landing that led outside to the spiral staircase and two other doors. "Bathroom," he said, tapping the door nearest to the triple room. "One of two. The other one is directly above, on the third floor. And—my room," he finished with a push at the far door. As he held it open, Lucy saw a compact arrangement—a single bed, desk, and chest of drawers fitted closely with barely room left over for a desk chair.

Lucy poked her head around the door. A glossy poster of a movie star dressed as Superman hung over the head of the bed and a full-length mirror was mounted on the opposite wall.

"You like to check yourself out?" she teased.

"Hey—all the bedrooms have one behind the doors."

She smirked. "Superman?"

His eyes grew wide, innocent. "He's the Man of Steel. What could be more inspiring?" When she didn't say anything, he continued. "If it's a problem that you don't have a desk, you can work in my room sometimes. I almost always study sitting on my bed." He grinned invitingly. "Or you could have the bed. I'm willing to share."

Paolo really was very cute, but he looked about as sexy as a cuddly little puppy dog. Discreetly, Lucy checked his arms and neck for tattoos. Nothing. Athletic, wholesome. He probably liked to study, too. The popular girls at the Catholic girls' high school where she'd just started would probably throw parties in the hope of getting a guy like this to show up. He was exactly the kind of boy Mom and Dad had been dying for Lucy to bring home.

But a younger, cutie-pie athlete? Even if he turned out to be smarter than she thought, Paolo was definitely not her type.

"So Lucy," Grace asked, stepping into the room. "Candace told me you might have found us a sixth person for the house?"

"Oh yeah. I told Candace I'd post something on my school's Facebook page. I got a reply the next day. This girl Maya is a little young, just fifteen. Her parents are from Mexico. They had to leave, problems with immigration or something, but Maya stayed. She's been living with her aunt but she seems pretty eager to move in with us."

"She's Mexican, and she's at your private school?"

Paolo asked. "So she's not poor?"

"Not all immigrants are poor," Lucy said, eyeing Paolo flatly. "Maya's dad ran into trouble with his papers. Her mom left with him while the problem gets cleared up. Could take eighteen months, could take longer. Maya's a citizen, so she can stay. So yeah, from what Maya told me, I guess they emancipated her."

"It's just that the rent here . . ." Grace said. "Okay, we're sharing the rooms so it's not too bad. But we gotta know she has the money."

Lucy arched an eyebrow. "I see that white Cadillac her aunt drives her in to school. I don't think we need to worry about that."

"Candace sent all Maya's references to her mom. If everything checks out, then we're all set." Grace beamed. "On Monday, we'll be going to school from our own house!"

Lucy flashed a dazzling smile in Paolo's direction. "Well, all right. Let the good times roll!"

PAOLO

Maya Soto, the new girl, was hot, although not as hot as Lucy Long. She had very dark brown hair but her skin was fair, almost white. It looked as though Maya didn't spend much time in the sun.

Paolo turned to John-Michael to share this assessment. Then he stopped. He'd never had a gay friend before. Did you share this kind of stuff with a gay dude? Would it make Paolo seem sexist? He wasn't being sexist; he simply appreciated a beautiful woman. Especially when they looked as though they could wrestle him to the ground, like Lucy. But if he started up with the comments about hot girls, John-Michael might start pointing out hot guys that he was into. Then Paolo would have to either pretend to go along or make a big deal about not being interested.

There was no way for it not to backfire.

"She's not bad, hey?" John-Michael whispered. "Maya's pretty hot. I wonder if she has a brother? He'd be just my type."

Paolo smiled. "She's only fifteen, though. So we're gonna have to take things easy around her."

"True. We should look out for Maya."

They both leaned forward, resting on the cedarwood bar of the balcony.

Paolo said, "So Lucy and Maya go to the same school?"

"That's pretty much how come Maya's in the house. Lucy posted an ad on her school's Facebook."

"The girls in this house are all pretty hot." Paolo sighed.

John-Michael chuckled. "What's *that* mean?"

"What does what mean?"

"That sigh. You sighing 'cause you can't have them all? Or because you can?"

Paolo grinned. "I'm sighing because there is no way of knowing."

"You're kidding? A guy like you? I bet you could have every girl in this house."

"Maybe. Such is the mystery of women, John-Michael."

"What's the mystery?"

"They choose, dude. I've never had to make the first move with a girl, not once."

"You've never had sex?"

"I didn't say that."

John-Michael's jaw dropped slightly. "They all asked you?"

Paolo shrugged. "They made it pretty clear what they wanted." He regarded John-Michael quizzically. "It must be so easy being gay."

"Why?"

"Because dudes are such a safe bet. We're always going to say yes to sex. All you have to do is figure out if a guy is gay or straight."

"I've said no to sex."

"To a guy? Was he gross?"

"Nope," John-Michael said with a lazy smile. "He was prettier than you."

Paolo nodded his appreciation. "Interesting."

"But not as interesting as Lucy," John-Michael ventured. "Am I right?"

Paolo dipped his head with a rueful grin. John-Michael had noticed his interest in Lucy, which began the moment John-Michael first mentioned her.

Lucy was from Claremont, a college town, east of Los Angeles. She'd recently moved to LA because her parents had agreed to emancipate her, but only on the condition that she live in the same city as her older brother.

"Lucy is this, like, amazing guitarist," John-Michael had told the group the first time they'd visited the house. "Seriously talented. Her dad is some government type, he commutes over to Washington, DC. Her mom is the dean, or president, or whatever, at one of those Claremont colleges. Bottom line—Lucy defected to the school of rock. Well, that, they did not like so very much."

Paolo had been taken aback. "I can't believe they threw her out for that!"

He remembered that Grace had become suddenly

rather silent. "Is Lucy black?"

"She's a person of color, yes," John-Michael had said.

Grace had become thoughtful. "I was just wondering if I'd heard of her dad. You said he works in the government—which department?"

"Her dad is Robert Long," John-Michael said. "He's assistant secretary of defense."

"Robert Long. Yeah, I thought the name 'Long' rang a bell."

Paolo had been impressed with Grace's knowledge of politics. His ambition to go into law made politics a natural fit with his future. It might be good to have someone to discuss legislation and policy with—it would help him to learn. Lucy, as the daughter of a government guy, might prove to have useful contacts for him one day.

Already his housemates were looking like the type of people Paolo's parents liked to refer to as "a great network."

The boys' attention returned to Maya, whose aunt was helping her carry suitcases and zippered laundry bags up to the top floor.

"We should help them," Paolo said.

They helped install Maya's luggage into the top floor room, which she would share with Candace. But when Paolo answered her question about the rent, she balked.

"The ad said 'from four hundred dollars.'"

"Yeah, that's what everyone in the triple is paying. The double is more."

Maya seemed anxious. She glanced at her aunt for a

second, then wrung her hands. "I only have four hundred a month."

Paolo watched, observing her unease. "Maybe someone can switch with you. Candace doesn't want to room with a guy. But Lucy might be able to move in with her."

"Where are Candace and Grace?" John-Michael asked.

"They went to IKEA to get pretty stuff for the rooms."

"Wish I'd known. I need things for the kitchen."

Maya looked at him. "You cook?"

John-Michael smiled slightly. "I've been known to bake."

Paolo placed a hand on Maya's shoulder. She was tense. "Relax. There'll be a way to sort this out. I'm gonna talk to Lucy." Maya's aunt also looked uneasy. Paolo wondered if he'd been right to guess that money would be an issue with Maya. He'd been around people with money—they didn't get this upset when the price went up by a hundred and fifty dollars. Maya might be enrolled in some fancy prep school and her aunt might drive a Cadillac, but something told Paolo that her family wasn't well off, after all.

"Come and see the kitchen," John-Michael told Maya and her aunt. They followed him down the hallway.

Paolo knocked softly on the door to Lucy's room. He could hear the strumming of a guitar, playing five chords in succession. It didn't sound as though she was practicing particularly hard. Paolo poked his head around the door.

"Hey. Whatcha playing?"

Lucy glanced up. "I'm practicing a song."

"Can I hear it?"

"Sure, why not."

Paolo closed the door behind him and looked for a place to sit. Lucy was sitting cross-legged on her own bed, an acoustic guitar across her lap. He decided to take the red swivel chair from under the nearest desk.

"You ready?" Lucy began to play, singing along in a slightly crunchy voice. The song sounded great. Raw and uncompromising.

"You didn't write that," he interrupted with a shy smile.

"Of course I didn't. It's 'Holiday in Cambodia' by the Dead Kennedys."

"Who?"

She cocked her head to one side. "Not your style?"

"What's not my style?"

"Punk rock."

"That's what you're into?"

Lucy merely raised an eyebrow in confirmation. Paolo glanced along the sleek line of her arms, perfectly toned shoulders, and triceps. The swirled ink of a tattoo coiled around her right arm, all the way down to her long fingers. The fingernails on her left hand were painted black and filed down, neatly, whereas on the right hand each fingernail was individually decorated with a miniature image. It was impossible not to imagine what those slender, dark fingers might look like wrapped around him. She watched him calmly, her stare surprisingly penetrating. With a dry throat, he tried to swallow.

"You have a nice voice."

"I can sing a little. But I play lead guitar. Sometimes it's hard to carry the tune as well as play."

Paolo picked up a copy of *Rolling Stone* magazine that had slipped from the bed and onto the floor. "I like Green Day."

"Well, they're pretty vanilla."

"Oh, like me?"

A smile touched the corner of Lucy's mouth. Gently, she told him, "Your word."

He shrugged, but her comment struck him with surprising force. "You play any songs by them?"

"Sure I do."

"Can I take a video of you?"

"Go ahead."

Without taking her eyes from his, she propped up the guitar and began to play. Paolo recognized the tune immediately—"Good Riddance" by Green Day.

When she was done, Paolo could only gaze in astonishment. "Marry me."

Lucy smiled a little awkwardly. "Glad you liked it."

"I freakin' loved it. You're better than that Billie Joe dude."

"And yet he's the one with the stadium tours."

"You'll get there."

"My dad didn't think so."

"Your dad, the assistant secretary of defense? Does he know *anything* about music?"

"He thinks he does."

"Well, he can't. It's obvious you've got amazing talent."

Lucy lowered her eyes. "He never really doubted that."

Paolo looked at his phone and hit play on the video he'd just made. "I should put this on YouTube."

Lucy wrinkled her nose. "I don't know. . . ."

"Gotta have a channel. Put vids of you online. Get discovered. It happens."

"I know, but . . . we need better equipment to record decent sound."

"You'd be surprised. The sound on this thing is pretty good."

Lucy frowned and then broke into an unexpectedly bashful grin. "Is this what you came in here for, Paolo? I thought you came in here to hit on me."

"I came in here to ask if you'd like to switch rooms with Maya. She's gonna have a hard time finding five-fifty a month for the room upstairs."

"That how much it is?" Lucy whistled. "Not gonna lie, it's a lot. But then again, I could use my own desk. Yeah. My savings will cover that. I can make an academic case for it."

Paolo raised his phone to his right eye. "But also, I *did* come in here to hit on you, by the way."

Lucy didn't react.

"Just to get it out of the way, you understand?"

"Sure, sure," she said, indulging him.

Paolo stared at her through the phone's camera lens.

She hadn't so much as flinched. A totally cool customer. He'd flirted like this once before, both him and the girl so calm in the approach they were practically flatlining. Right up until the electric first touch. That time he'd been the one in Lucy's position, calmly waiting for the other person to make the first move.

He decided to push things straight to the next level: the joke that wasn't a joke. It had worked on him after all. "So we'll record this song, and then we'll . . ."

And he stopped.

With this girl, Paolo didn't know how to take things to the next level. It was like his neurons were temporarily blocked. Lucy was already smiling, a little resigned if anything, and shaking her head. Rather lamely, he finished, "And then I guess . . . I'll leave . . . ?"

"See now, we've gotten it out of the way."

For a second, Paolo was confused. They hadn't gotten anything out of the way as far as he was concerned.

Lucy fixed him with a gaze of devastating cool. "You hit on me. It's done. Now we can move on."

Paolo felt as though his chest had been chilled by a sudden, frozen blast of air. It took a few seconds for sensation to return. But when it did, it was like a rush of wildfire to his extremities. Unsteadily, he rose to his feet and backed out of the room. He babbled something nonchalant. He closed the door behind him and leaned against the wall.

She'd blown him off. It wasn't possible. And yet what

he felt wasn't embarrassment, but desire. There had to be something very wrong with the way he was wired. Because before, he'd only liked her. Now he wanted her. The image of her shoulders, arms, and fingernails, the swell of her breast were already seared on his brain, tattooed onto the backs of his eyelids.

MAYA

Finally, her aunt left and Maya was alone in her room. Behind the closed door, she could hear John-Michael talking quietly to Paolo. Lucy's name was mentioned. After a few moments, she heard them go back downstairs.

She thought about unpacking but decided to wait; it would be a hassle to do it twice. Better to wait for Candace to return and confirm the switch.

A pity, because this room was *way* nice. Two beds, one of them a double, spread with a metallic, anthracite-colored quilt, bloodred pillows, and a crimson chenille blanket tossed in a stripe across the end of the bed. Two desks, both against a wall, not facing a bed as she'd spotted in the triple room. There was even a generous white closet with an attractive, abstract pattern in pink, green, and blue across the middle. And still tons of floor space.

Maya left the room and went outside along the cedar decking of the outdoor corridor, past the spiral staircase and to the third-floor balcony. Three woven rattan easy

chairs faced outward, a round, glass table with a matching rattan base in between them. She eased into the chair farthest from the staircase and gazed over the low wall of the balcony toward the beach.

It was the best view in the whole house, looking out over the ocean. The sun's reflection glittered off the water, bright silvery white, almost too dazzling to bear. A wide strip of sand separated the house from the sea. A paved path wove through sand dunes and tall palms. Every now and then a group of Rollerbladers or skateboarders would stream past.

It was incredible that she had the opportunity to live in a house this amazing, considering Maya's situation. There was no point getting antsy about the specific room she'd have to share—she couldn't really afford any of them.

If it had been up to Maya, she'd have taken the single room. She doubted that her housemates were going to be too happy when they figured out what it was she liked to do until the early hours of the morning. Solitude had always suited her.

But it wasn't up to Maya.

Who'd have thought that a person Maya loved so much could want her out of the house so bad?

She opened up her pink Kipling messenger bag, slid out her MacBook Air, fired it up, and checked her in-box. Her eyes went straight to the latest email: *Cheetr—Bug Report*. Tensely, she opened the message, started to read.

There were footsteps on the spiral staircase. She glanced

around–John-Michael, asking whether she'd like to go to the grocery store with him and Lucy. Or maybe she'd prefer to go to the hardware store with Paolo? He wanted to get some tools to fix up the garden.

She felt the familiar tug. She wanted to go, definitely. Bonding with the housemates. A chance to get some of her favorite foods. Not being able to drive was going to be a real pain now that she didn't have anyone to drive her around. She was dreading having to get to school every day. It was a ten-minute walk to the school bus stop. Maya really should take any opportunity to get a ride to the market.

If only she hadn't opened the stupid computer. Once open, it was impossible not to work. It always started with a little tweak to her project. Five minutes' worth, nothing more. Yet five minutes so easily turned to fifteen, one hour, three.

John-Michael poked his head around the edge of the stairs.

"Knock, knock. You coming?"

"I kind of have a thing I need to do."

"Will it take long? We can wait."

Maya wanted to tell him sure, it would take five minutes, and then she'd be flying down those zany yellow stairs with her two new roomies. But it wasn't worth it. She'd grown used to the hostile glares of a disappointed friend who'd been forced to wait an hour while Maya tweaked a line of computer code. She couldn't risk that with these people.

Not yet, anyway.

"Ehhhh. Oh man. I want to." She gritted her teeth.

"No problem," John-Michael said. "Do what you gotta do. You've got my number? If you think of anything you need, text me."

Maya smiled in relief. "Thanks, John-Michael."

"No problem, *señorita*."

She gave a gracious nod. *"Muy amable."*

"Means 'you're very kind,' right?"

"Close enough."

"It's so cool that you're Mexican," John-Michael said. "We should have, like, Spanish conversations. I could seriously use an A in Spanish this year. That's my best chance to get my grades up so I graduate. Last year was kind of a washout for me. I'm working on catching up."

"I'm not exactly fluent, but sure, anytime."

"Bueno." He grinned and backed toward the staircase.

Barely two minutes went by before Paolo made his way up the staircase. He poked his head above the decking and gave a whistle to get her attention.

"Hey. How'd you like to come buy a shovel with me? I'm going to fix up the yard."

"I can't right now."

"Homework?"

"I'm—ah—well, I'm actually writing an app."

Paolo looked stunned. "Wow!"

Maya had seen that look before, especially from jocks. They made a judgment about the types of people who did techy, digital stuff. She was guessing that they didn't expect a girl like Maya to be one of them.

"It's not that impressive. But I started and now I want to see it work properly. After a while it's like an itch you just gotta scratch."

He said nothing but his eyes spoke volumes. "Okay."

"Is there a lot to do?"

"In the yard? A little. It's just dirt now, and a bit of lawn. I'm going to put in some flowers. Something with color."

Maya beamed. "Good for you! Listen, by the time you get back, I'll be finished. I'll help you plant."

About fifteen minutes later, on the ground floor, the front door to the house opened. Maya heard two female voices. It had to be Candace and Grace. Maya put her Mac-Book down. She should really introduce herself.

But instead, she remained on the balcony, trying to listen to their conversation through the open kitchen window. She could just catch the occasional snippet. They were talking about Lucy, too, like the boys. That girl had obviously made some major impression on everyone. Maya hadn't missed the fact that Lucy hadn't even opened her door to say hello to her when she'd arrived. It was impossible not to feel that Lucy might be rather aloof. She wondered if the other housemates were saying something similar.

She heard footsteps on the spiral staircase. Maya stepped back inside and ducked into the double bedroom so she wouldn't be spotted. One of the girls was coming upstairs. Probably Grace, because she stopped at the second-floor room, the triple. Maya waited until she'd gone into the room, and then quietly descended.

She stood on the open threshold of the triple room for a few seconds without knocking. Grace hadn't noticed her—she was watching something on a laptop, with an earbud in one ear. Maya looked at the screen. It was a video of Lucy, playing the guitar and presumably singing.

Maya knocked on the door. Grace looked up swiftly. Her instant guilty expression gave way to confusion. After a second or two, she managed a veneer of welcome. Grace pulled away from the laptop and yanked the earbud out of her ear.

"You must be Maya. I didn't know you'd already arrived."

Maya smiled, apologetic. "I was upstairs. Sorry, I only just heard you guys get home."

Grace gave her a welcoming hug. Over her shoulder, Maya glanced down at the laptop on the bed. The video of Lucy continued to play. The image of Lucy strumming her guitar, smiling gently through her lyrics at the unseen witness.

There was no obvious reason to be suspicious exactly, but Maya couldn't help being struck by the image of Grace watching Lucy on the screen. There was a connection there that wouldn't have been obvious to everyone, perhaps.

But then, Maya had inside information.

CHARLIE CALLS ARIANA
SUNDAY, JANUARY 4

"Hey," Ariana exclaimed. "Good to hear from you! You all settled in?"

She put down her grilled cheese and sat in the brand-new reclining chair in her living room. The chair was a gift—more compensation for keeping up the "friendship" with the child actor she'd first known as "Charlie."

"Getting there." It was a cheerful response.

Ariana decided to push it a little. "Good to be back in LA? Been checking out your old haunts?"

"Old haunts?"

Ariana dropped her voice. "You know what I'm talking about, hon."

"Oh." The tone changed. There was a long pause. "You mean the place where it *happened*."

"Yeah. You ever think about it?"

A halting reply, slow. "I remember the house. It was up in the hills somewhere. A twisty, long drive. Big clumps of bright pink bougainvillea on the walls. When it got dark you could see the city lights down below spreading out like a sparkly picnic blanket."

Ariana interrupted. "Mulholland Drive."

"Excuse me?"

"That's probably where the party was," Ariana said with easy confidence. "It's a long road in Los Angeles. Plenty of movie and TV people live there. Goes up, all twisty, just like you said. And down into Beverly Hills."

The response was doubtful. "I don't know. I was just a little kid, I got used to jumping into a limo with a driver and one of our chaperones. Most times, I didn't know where I was going."

"Who was your chaperone?"

"Different people. They looked after all the kids on the network's shows."

Ariana changed tack. "Did you go to a lot of those parties?"

"With the Hollywood folk? A few. If it was someone from our TV show, they usually invited us, but we'd leave at around nine."

"The other kids from the TV show?"

The voice grew colder at the memory. "Yeah. They'd set up some special table for us, you know, real party food that kids actually eat. Not the fancy-schmancy bits of seafood crap they'd feed to the adults to impress them. They'd hire some kids' entertainer to keep us happy. And then come nine o'clock—*vámonos!*"

"They'd kick you out?"

"They'd escort us to our limos."

"But not that night?"

"No." A pensive silence. "No. That night the chaperone got sick. She didn't want to get in the car for that twisty ride. She begged the hosts to let us kids stay over. They found us a room, put a cot in there for me, next to the couch where the chaperone slept. They sent me to bed around nine."

"The chaperone didn't wake up?"

"Someone gave her some medicine. I guess it made her sleepy. She was snoring after an hour. I slept for a bit. Sometime in the middle of the night, I got up to pee."

"You should have woken the chaperone."

The girl released a deep sigh. "Yeah. You don't know how much I wish I had."

PAOLO

"We should totally have a party."

John-Michael had been the first to say it, but Paolo knew it was on everyone's minds. When they'd first discussed the idea, they'd been living in the Venice Beach house for almost a month, but hadn't had a chance to truly celebrate their freedom.

Paolo dropped a cushion onto the checkerboard-patterned rug between the green futon and red easy chair. He rested his feet on the cushion and put his Diet Dr Pepper on the round coffee table that occupied the space between the sofa and the French windows.

"I'm in," he said.

Maya had been the only one who didn't look excited about the idea. But then again, since she'd settled into the routine in the house, Maya hadn't done much except eat, go to school, and disappear behind her computer screen, forever working on the code for her app.

Paolo could understand. He'd become seriously addicted

to World of Warcraft when he was twelve years old, and ended up heading a guild and sitting on a pile of WoW gold. He'd done it by playing day and night, often without his parents' knowledge. He was soft and flabby in those days, still waiting for the final push into puberty. WoW had given him another life, one in which he was powerful and gave orders—probably to adults. That thought he'd enjoyed even more. When his parents found out, they'd forced him to quit cold turkey and increased his tennis lessons from one hour a week to five. The weight had dropped off him; he'd thrown all that frustration into his tennis game. Since then, Paolo hadn't let himself near any kind of computer game. It was just too risky.

He understood the kick that came from creating something on a screen. It wasn't real and yet it *was*.

They'd delayed the party awhile. The first three weeks, Candace's mom had made a habit of dropping by unannounced to check up on the house. Lucy and Maya were particularly wary—probably worried that they were one phone call away from being dragged back home.

The housemates had agreed to let things settle down, prove themselves capable of getting to school every day, not starving to death, and not letting the house get too untidy.

The not starving to death bit had been easy enough—everyone in the house seemed to know how to make a sandwich or a salad. Paolo and Maya were pretty good with eggs. Maya made *huevos rancheros* and Mexican omelets that had the others begging for a taste. John-Michael, however, turned out to be an amazing cook. He never ate the same sandwich twice and would create combinations that made the others go *ewwww*—until they tried them.

Keeping the house tidy was harder. If Paolo hadn't been a neat freak, it might have been impossible. He'd persuaded the girls and John-Michael to operate a rotating system for chores. Only Lucy had been reluctant to take part.

"You're my mom now?"

"He's nicer than my mom," Candace had warned. "She threatened me with pop-ins."

They'd had less than fourteen minutes' notice of the first spot check—a breezy text from Katelyn about a casual swing-by.

Everyone in the house had launched into action with orange-scented kitchen spray, pine toilet cleaner, and lemon-scented wooden-floor wax. Ninety seconds before she'd walked through the door they'd ditched the cloths and mops in the kitchen cabinet and thrown themselves onto the sofas in the living room, glued to the TV as if nothing would ever shift them.

They set a date for the party—the end of their eighth week in the house—and assigned all the party jobs.

The night of the party, Paolo was sent to fetch tacos from a taco van. He'd phoned in the order and was going to pick up a trayful of chicken, fish, and char-grilled steak tacos. Lucy decided, last minute, that they didn't have enough booze. Half an hour before Paolo was planning to leave, he heard her telling John-Michael that she was going to try to get a couple of bottles of vodka. So he decided to leave a little sooner.

Ever since that awkward first encounter in her room, Paolo had found it increasingly difficult to stop thinking about Lucy. Within a few days he was waking up from dreams of her. He hadn't obsessed like this over a girl since he was thirteen. Soon he realized that six weeks had gone by since he'd last had sex. The beautiful twentysomethings at the country club were getting used to seeing Paolo leave the minute their lesson was done, not even bothering to shower.

Paolo caught up to Lucy outside the house. "Hey! So, do you have a contact? At the liquor store?"

Lucy turned to him with her customary amused smile. "No. But I usually find a way."

"We should just get some fake IDs."

She gave him a look that said *Who me?*

Paolo was silent for a moment. He idled slightly as Lucy walked ahead so that he could watch the backs of her toned legs.

"You checking me out?"

"Totally." There was no point lying. She was onto him at every level. Yet it would be all the sweeter when he finally won her over.

"Paolo."

"Yes?"

Lucy stopped walking, closed her eyes for a second as if weighing up a multitude of thoughts. She turned to him slowly. "It's never going to happen."

Paolo forced himself to grin. He raised the tip of a finger to her nose and touched it lightly.

"Life is long . . . Lucy."

"Sugar, it ain't that long."

When Paolo arrived home with the tacos, there were already about forty people at the party. At least fifteen were outside on the balcony, smoking cigarettes. The smoke trailed in the air as far out as the paved path.

He glanced around, hoping that it wouldn't cause a problem. They had some pretty precious neighbors who liked to walk, jog, and cycle along the boardwalk—the kind who liked to shop at Whole Foods. Lucy had once slyly referred to them as the "SoCal offenserati" on account of how easily they took offense. The nickname had stuck.

John-Michael had been waiting anxiously for him in the front yard. He snatched the tray of tacos out of Paolo's hands and took them straight to the kitchen. Through the window, Paolo could see Lucy emptying a bottle of vodka into a large glass punch bowl full of ice cubes and pinkish-red liquid.

He was about to go inside for round two of their bout, when Maya appeared beside him, clutching her MacBook. She looked a little frustrated.

"Candace and Grace are saying I can't have more than two drinks. They won't let me into Lucy's room, on account of the sketchy stuff goin' on in there. And obviously the hookup room is out-of-bounds."

"Good for them! They're looking out for the baby of the house." Paolo paused. "We have a hookup room?"

But Maya just scowled. "Okay, so I need you to let me use your room. I might as well work on my coding."

Paolo stared, disappointed. "Oh, come on, Maya, don't be that way."

She looked a little red-faced, almost teary. "Just let me, okay? If I'm too young to join in the fun then at least don't make me waste my time."

Reluctantly, Paolo let her into his room and then stuck a sign that said *Private* on the outside of the door. As he left, he spotted Candace behind the yellow spiral staircase, unsteady on her feet and blinking. She looked as though she'd had a flashlight shone into her eyes and was leaning on the staircase for support. In one hand she held a cell phone.

"You okay?" he asked.

Candace suddenly focused on Paolo. "Omigod. I don't believe it."

"What?"

Her eyes lit up. Slowly but surely an expression of pure wonder spread across her face. She raised both hands to her mouth and gasped.

"I got the show. I'm gonna be on TV. Paolo!"

"Really? How? Did you go for another audition?"

"No . . . it's . . . I can't take it in . . . I was one of the alternates. For the part of Gina, in *Downtowners*."

"You were an alternate? I didn't know that."

"I didn't know it, either! My agent decided not to get my hopes up. But the girl who got the part was in some kind of accident. She broke her leg. The other girl they called isn't available."

"So—you're in?"

"Yeah. I mean, kind of a bummer for the girl who first got it. Obviously. But she's on crutches for eight weeks. And filming starts tomorrow morning. So, *hell yeah*, I'm in!"

"Jeez, Candace. That's amazing!"

Candace did a little jump for joy. She threw her arms around Paolo's neck and squeezed.

"I got it! I mean, I know it isn't a big part or anything. But that's good, right? Too much and I'd have problems with school."

"It's awesome!"

She held her breath, smiling at him. "It really is, isn't it? And the beauty of it is that the other girl's agent had already convinced them to let her have hair."

"Excuse me?"

"Yeah, originally Gina was going to rock the shaved-head look."

Paolo made a face. "Not a good look for a girl."

"Obviously."

"We should go inside and tell everyone. Yeah, Candace! Yeah, TV!"

A few minutes later everyone was raising a glass to Candace's news. She herself, however, was apparently finding the news increasingly hard to absorb. She grew noticeably quieter. After a while, she disappeared into her room.

The energy level inside the house soared as the alcohol began to flow even faster. Paolo wandered through the house, picking up discarded plastic cups and plates, cleaning occasional stains from the walls with a kitchen wipe. In his other hand he carried a glass of the cocktail that Lucy had mixed.

It was the first party he'd ever hosted. Hosting really wasn't as much fun as attending. He couldn't relax. He remembered getting totally wasted at parties when he was fourteen. But lately, tennis had dominated his existence. He wasn't supposed to drink too much. Calories. He glanced at the trickle of people going into Lucy's room. She'd promised to get hold of some weed. There was a bong party going on in there. Maybe he could risk just a few tokes without getting too bad a case of the munchies. Uncomfortably, Paolo watched the kids waiting to get their chance to go inside. It wasn't difficult to see the difference between him and them. Everything about their clothes, hair, tattoos, and attitude screamed rebellion.

Maybe that was why Lucy wasn't into him?

JOHN-MICHAEL

John-Michael made his way downstairs, pausing to admire the decorations that hung in the main hall and living room. He'd insisted that the housemates make the house fancy for the party. The building itself had a certain shabby, bohemian-Bauhaus chic. But inside, the walls were pretty bland. He'd bought a pile of *papel picado* paper decorations from a Mexican supermarket that Maya recommended and strung them along the ceiling, together with whatever colorful, slightly random decorations he'd been able to find. Silver foil paper chains, leftover Day of the Dead *papel picado*, Chinese lanterns in red tissue paper. It was kind of an eclectic mix, he realized, now that he was able to enjoy it without the stress of getting everything done on time. Somehow, it worked.

He moved through the throng of teenagers. To judge from the raised, excited voices, the buzz and general energy levels, this was going down as something a little bit special. Not every day you got invited to a party with no sign of parents, not even in the furnishings or bedrooms. This place was every inch theirs.

He'd recognize someone from school, watch their faces crease with momentary puzzlement to find him at such a hip party, and then give them a tiny wave as he sauntered over. Then he'd very casually slip in a reminder that yeah, he lived here and yeah, he'd made the snacks, well not all of them, not the tacos, obviously, but the teeny little cheese-cakes, the jam tarts, and chocolate chip cookies, he'd done all those. Then he'd watch the expressions of sheer respect form on their faces.

And: "Dude. This is the sweetest setup ever. Seriously. Who do I have to kill to live here?"

John-Michael merely smiled a Sphinxlike smile and floated along to the kitchen, borne on a cloud of praise.

A girl was by the fridge, petite and with long, very straight chestnut-brown hair. She had large, light brown eyes lined with dark kohl. She was smoking a skinny, hand-rolled cigarette, or at least trying.

"Hey, got a light?" she asked John-Michael.

"There's no smoking in the house. Sorry. Our landlady would kill us."

"Landlady?" She laughed. "Good one. I should call my mom that, too."

"You know Candace's mom?"

"No, seriously, Candace's mom is actually your land-lady?"

He looked at her sideways. The girl didn't look stoned. But she seemed to have difficulty following what he was telling her. "Candace's mom is our actual landlady, yes."

"Oh. Gosh! I only know Candace vaguely. She's a friend of my girlfriend's ex."

"Who invited you?"

The girl's expression fell immediately. "Wasn't this, like, an open thing? I just heard there was gonna be this killer party at Venice Beach. Jeez. How embarrassing."

"No, it's fine—you're welcome. I'm glad you came," he said as gallantly as he could. "You want a drink? Lucy just made a pitcher of Sea Breeze."

The girl followed him to the punch bowl in the living room. He poured her a glass, enjoying what was rare for him—some unalloyed female attention.

Girls could usually tell he was gay and didn't look at him the way she was looking at him. It wasn't that he wanted to string her along, but just that it was nice not to be dismissed. Any minute now she'd catch sight of Paolo, or one of the other tennis players who'd come to the party. Then she'd be gone and he'd be alone. The only gay guy in the house to judge by the total lack of interesting-looking boys.

"I'm gay," he said, lifting a glass to hers. "Just thought I'd get that out there. You're very cute and I like talking to you, though. So please don't go away."

She grinned, mischievous. "I knew you were gay. And I'm not going anywhere."

"Seriously, you knew? Huh. I thought I'd at least have a shot with you."

"Are you bi?"

"Bi? I wish."

"Why?"

"More options. You, for example. Or the four other hot girls I live with."

"You live with four girls?"

He laughed. "Do you know anything about this house?"

"I know that Candace lives here. And she's having a party. I thought that'd be enough."

John-Michael grabbed a plate of cookies from a passing boy, who barely noticed.

"Try one."

She took a bite and gave a blissful smile.

He said, "I made it."

"Really?" A pout. "Now I wish you were bi, too."

He shrugged. "What are you gonna do?"

"Candace is emancipated," the girl said. "I knew that. I didn't realize you all were."

"Free as birds."

"Oh. I'm sorry. That must suck."

He glanced at her for a second, but the girl didn't seem to be joking. She licked chocolate off a finger and gave him an expectant, sympathetic look.

"Are you kidding? Most people are, like, seriously envious."

"Really?" She shrugged. "Not me. I love living at home."

He just stared.

"My folks are, like, these amazing people. I'm very lucky. They're cool. My mom teaches music and my dad runs an ice-cream factory. Well, actually, he owns it. And a parlor, too. They're really interesting and fun and they cook so well, I mean, both of them. I have my room and my own bathroom, my bike, my electric scooter, my car. They take me to concerts at the LA Phil and the ballet. . . . Why would I want to live apart from them? Doing all my own housework, laundry, no one to help with homework?"

"Who *are* you?"

She laughed. "Honestly, doesn't it sound good? Breakfast in bed on the weekends. Mom's blueberry waffles and bacon. I mean, I guess something must have gone wrong in your lives for you to want to be emancipated. Am I right?"

He paused, wondering if what he was feeling was jealousy or skepticism. "I guess."

The girl continued to stare at him, then let out a huge laugh. "All right, I'm messin' with you."

"What?"

"My life isn't like that, not at all!"

"So your folks don't do any of that cool stuff?"

"Not really. Just the work bits. My brother and I hardly see them. But maybe if we didn't actually live in the house, they'd make time to see us. Like, real time."

John-Michael stared straight into his Sea Breeze. The mention of parents was having its predictably gloomy effect on him. "And you want that?" he said, aware that he sounded mournful.

"Yes," she concluded. "Definitely. They're not a bad set of 'rents."

"Then you're right," he admitted wistfully. "You *are* lucky."

GRACE
BALCONY, FRIDAY, FEBRUARY 27

"Thinking of joining the stoners?" Grace stared down at Paolo, an ironic smile on her face. "You know, you don't have to do it their way." A couple of seconds later she was joined on the second-floor landing by Candace.

"I don't want to . . . I mean . . ." He frowned. "I don't?"

Grace grinned the mischievous grin she knew caught people off guard. "I mean, you don't have to wait for the bong. I got Lucy to give us enough for a joint." The smile and comment had the desired effect. Paolo couldn't hide his surprise.

"You guys smoke?"

Candace replied, "Hardly ever. Tina—Grace's mom—is real strict. A total health nut. And Grace doesn't drink. Now, on account of having to get up at stupid o'clock tomorrow morning, neither do I. Still . . . some form of intoxication seems appropriate given my news. I mean, TV! Kind of life-changing, you have to admit. So, you wanna join us on the *ver-ahn-dah*, my dear?"

"You gonna smoke that in the open air? Hey, maybe you want to invite some cops, too?"

Candace laughed. "Relax. We're not big smokers. Two tokes and then we turn into pumpkins."

They headed upstairs. There was only one area of the balcony that wasn't occupied by couples already well on the way to hooking up. Turning their backs on the ocean, the three housemates tucked themselves into a corner. Grace lit up the misshapen cigarette and took a drag. Candace relaxed in anticipation as Grace exhaled slowly through smiling teeth. Candace took the joint from her fingers, inhaled, and passed it to Paolo. "Oooff. I'd forgotten."

Paolo drew in the smoke and held it there for a couple of seconds. "Been a long time?"

Grace gave a beatific grin. "We don't get out much."

"Well, Tina's not here to stop you," he reminded them.

Candace pulled a lopsided grin. "True. She's far away in San Antonio, getting bugged by Grace's bratty little brothers."

"But you," stressed Paolo, "you can get out all you want. Who's to stop you?"

Grace nodded. The edges of her senses were already fuzzy, tingling. "I know. Suddenly, it isn't as much fun."

Paolo sniggered. "I'm glad you said it."

"I didn't pick you for a giggler," Candace remarked. She batted her eyes at Paolo, sophisticated disdain. For a second, Grace thought, she looked just like her mother.

Candace continued. "You never can tell who's going to be the type to giggle when they smoke," she said. She paused lengthily, for obvious dramatic effect. "Personally, I prefer men who can still keep their cool."

"That's a great impression of your mom, Candace. I can just see her saying that to the Dope Fiend. *I liked you so much better before you giggled, dahhhhling.*"

Paolo burst into laughter, joined after a second by Grace.

If Candace was annoyed, she hid it with consummate skill, and ignored the comment entirely. "Don't get me wrong. The whole emancipation thing. It rules."

"Yeah," Grace said. "It totally does."

"But I hate laundry. And having to whine at people to clean up after themselves."

Paolo laughed harder. "Oh, I get it. This is all part of your cunning scheme to get me to do the dishes."

Candace said, "Yeah, lazy brat, could you do the frickin' dishes, already? 'Cause you're something of a disappointment, Mr. King."

"And there I was thinking I was all about the eye candy for you babes."

"You and Lucy. You could do your dishes. Like, *ever.*"

"Okay, okay!" Tears came to his eyes. "Can we be serious for a second?"

"What makes you think we're not being serious?"

"No, but really." He managed to bring his chuckles

under control. "Look, you guys must have an opinion: Does Lucy like me?"

A little too quickly, Grace answered, "No."

He sighed. "I was afraid of that."

Candace said, "Did she ever act like she likes you?"

"No. Kind of the opposite."

Grace rolled her eyes. "There's your clue."

"I guess."

She continued. "I hope you don't want to be a detective when you graduate."

"It wouldn't be my first choice."

"Okay, good," Grace said. "I'm just saying. I mean, I assumed you'd be sticking with the tennis."

He shook his head firmly. "I'm gonna be a lawyer."

Grace peered at him, surprised, amused. "Really? What kind?"

"Human rights."

Grace knew her amazement was showing on her face. For a moment, she couldn't speak. Paolo went on. "Yeah. I'm real interested in all the abuses that go on in our own country. You know, we're so worried about, like, Afghanistan and Iraq and Syria and all, but we don't think so much about the shitty stuff that happens right here."

Candace interrupted. "You mean Gitmo?"

"That's not here, but yeah, that, too."

"Gitmo's not here? Then where?"

"Are you kidding me? It's in Cuba."

Candace stared in disbelief and then snorted with hilarity. "For a minute, you had me."

"No, seriously! Google it. Anyway, I'm talking about stuff that happens to poor people, immigrants, people on death row."

Grace could hardly believe her ears. Wordlessly, she took the joint from Candace. "You'd do that? Work your butt off to qualify as a lawyer and then work with people like that?"

Paolo turned to her. "I think so."

Grace decided to keep playing devil's advocate. "Why?"

He seemed taken aback by the challenging note in her voice. "Because . . . because it matters. There are too many lawyers, that's what my dad always says. Clogging up the system, making work for themselves so they can get more clients. We don't need that, for sure. But I'm interested in how the law can be used to protect people. The innocent. The vulnerable." He gave her an intent look. "Don't you think?"

"I guess." Grace blew the smoke softly into his face. If he was faking it about the law stuff, he was managing to come across as remarkably sincere.

With an air of finality, Candace said, "I'm gonna leave you two to put the world to rights, and go check up on the triple room."

Paolo said, "The *hookup* room? I thought we agreed it was private."

Candace interjected, "No, Grace and I decided. One

of us has to check in every so often to make sure no one's getting, you know, forced to do anything they don't want to do."

"Jeez. You girls. You think of everything."

"Yeah, well, we like living here," Grace told him. "Don't you? But there are people who think we shouldn't be allowed to. Like Miss Olivera, the counselor at school. If anything horrible were to happen in this house, everything would change. Candace's mom would throw the rest of you guys out. She'd make us live with, like, med students; someone she thinks sounds respectable."

Candace pouted. "True."

"That's good thinking," Paolo said.

Candace pulled a tight smile as she disappeared downstairs, saying, "Glad you agree." She reappeared on the staircase after a couple of minutes. Grace thought she could detect a slight blush. Candace lowered her eyes and headed for the balcony. Paolo and Grace watched her approach, leaning on the stair rail.

Paolo turned to Grace. "Is it just me or did you get a little weird with me just now?"

Grace inhaled slowly, rolled her back along the concrete wall until she was facing the front of the balcony. She gazed out past the tall palms and to the ocean beyond. "Define 'weird.'"

"It's like you don't approve of my plans to be a lawyer."

Grace snorted. "More like I think you're bullshitting us."

"What?! Why would I?"

"To get us to say something good about you to, oh, I don't know, maybe Lucy?"

Paolo looked genuinely stunned. "Is that what you think?"

Grace shrugged.

"It's not a lie," he said, a little indignant.

"Not saying it is. Just that I know something about death row prisoners. Maybe it's given me an oversensitive BS detector."

"What do you know?"

"I write letters to them," she said.

"No shit."

"I've been doing it for years."

"Seriously?"

She nodded. "Yep."

"Why?"

"Because. Someone needs to."

"Why you?"

"I . . . I guess I don't like to talk about it much," Grace said. "It can get stressy."

"I'll bet. Like, when it gets right up to the date and you think one of them is gonna . . . you know."

"What?"

"You know," he said, making quotations marks with his fingers. "Get 'iced'?"

Grace felt the familiar cold steel in her chest at his question. She wanted to brush it off but the weed had swept away the controls she'd constructed around the idea. He asked and all she could see in her mind for a few seconds was the one place in the world she never wanted to see—the viewing gallery of the execution chamber.

Paolo seemed momentarily stunned. "Grace," he was saying, "are you okay?"

Grace watched his eyes travel from her face to the joint in her hand, which she was carefully extinguishing against the concrete wall. A cool wind blew in from the ocean. It rustled the palm fronds. It felt chilly against her bare legs.

She handed him the joint and tried to smile. "You take it. I think I've had enough."

JOHN-MICHAEL

Candace was the first to wake, but only because of her alarm. It set the cell phone under her pillow buzzing like a mosquito. Next to her, on the floor and arranged over three pillows, John-Michael gave a soft grunt and stirred.

"Goddamnit, Candace."

"Shhhh—go back to sleep! Grace and the others still are."

Impossible. Once awake, there was no going back to sleep. The room was already fairly light, even with the shutters closed. Those shutters weren't much of a barrier to the rising sun. He guessed that they were there mainly to stop people looking in than to keep the morning light out.

John-Michael squinted around at the general dishevelment. Behind Candace, Grace lay peacefully dozing on her side, having spent the night on her stepsister's bed. Lucy was nowhere to be seen. Instead, a fully dressed boy-girl couple lay back-to-back on her bed, with the comforter twisted around their legs.

He couldn't even remember how he'd ended up in Candace and Lucy's room.

Now he remembered. He'd spent the last hour of the party evading a guy who he'd looked at for about a microsecond too long. Okay, maybe he'd been staring at him. But in truth, John-Michael had merely zoned out. Then he'd come to, pupils suddenly focusing on a guy with sandy hair and blue eyes, with a stubbly beard. The music had changed and the dude had begun to dance. Hideous, horrible dancing. Bad shoulder-shimmying, uncoordinated little kicks, and a huge cheesy grin on his face as he began to snake over to John-Michael. His heart had plummeted.

The next couple of hours hadn't been much fun. John-Michael was terrible at rejecting sweet guys who just didn't do it for him. He always talked to them for too long, to compensate for the fact that he wasn't into them. Then they ended up wondering why he wouldn't get with them. He knew the score, yet he didn't learn.

Eventually, John-Michael had sneaked out on a trip to the bathroom and snuggled down alongside a couple of stoners who'd fallen asleep on Lucy's bed. He'd heard his stalker opening the door to the bedroom and whisper his name very softly, breathily, *John-Mi-hi-chael*, like that.

And John-Michael had held his breath.

He cracked open an eye and looked at Grace. She shifted slowly, waking up. He didn't budge, playing dead. He heard Grace mutter, "Already?"

Candace took her earrings out and whispered back,

"Weekend shoots, baby. The perks of being a schoolgirl TV star." She disappeared through the bedroom door into the adjoining bathroom. He heard her turn on the shower.

The instant Candace was gone, Grace moved, not slowly and sleepily as she'd been doing up until that moment, but swiftly, with purpose. She slid across the double bed, neatly avoiding the need to land on the floor and disturb John-Michael. Within a second she was sitting at Lucy's desk. He peeked upward but the angle was all wrong—he couldn't see what Grace was doing, only that she was using Lucy's laptop. Whatever she was doing, it went on for a few minutes. Click, tap, click.

John-Michael closed his eyes until only a narrow slit remained. An electric sense told him that Grace didn't want to be observed. He was about to say something when Candace stepped back into the bedroom. Seeing her, Grace froze for a second. John-Michael took the opportunity to stir noisily. He opened his eyes in time to see how hastily Grace clutched at two sheets of notepaper that were beside Lucy's open laptop.

Candace stared. "What the—? Are you looking through Lucy's letters?"

John-Michael sat up, pretending to be sleep-slow.

"What? Don't be an idiot," Grace hissed. But her right hand continued to guard the notepaper.

Candace took one last look. Then, resolutely, she strode over to the desk. She glanced at the handwritten scrawl that covered much of the top sheet of paper. There was an awkward pause. "Oh," she said flatly. "Right. I'm sorry."

Grace snatched back the notepaper.

"Anyway," Candace said in a more friendly tone. "Why are you writing to those prison losers in my room?"

John-Michael caught his breath. The sound of his slight gasp turned both girls' heads.

"'Prison losers'?" He looked from Candace to Grace.

Grace frowned. "It's kind of a private conversation."

"But it sounds so interesting."

"Where did you come from anyway?" Candace asked. "Don't you have your own room?"

"I was hiding from someone."

"Oh, that blond dancer I saw you with? Aww." Candace pouted. "I had such hopes for the two of you." She turned to Grace. "You shouldn't snoop on people."

Irritated, Grace replied, "I was just using Lucy's computer to look up something, not that it's any of your business."

Candace hesitated. "Is one of your guys up again for—you know?"

Grace shook her head. John-Michael stared in silent appreciation at the cold fury that blazed in her eyes. "No. Just that I'm awake now, I could write a letter before I head out. If you had the first clue what it means to him—what it means to *any* of these guys to get a letter from someone who actually gives a damn—you'd understand why I do it."

Candace gave her a long, hard look. "Grace. Tell me the truth. Do you have the hots for one of your death row guys?"

John-Michael's mouth fell open. "Did you say 'death row'?"

Grace ignored him completely, screwed up her face in disgust. "God, is that what you think? That's messed up and you know it."

"You wouldn't be the first girl to fall for one of them. They're lonely, misunderstood, and doomed. I'm just looking out for you. I don't want to see you get hurt. It's not worth it, just for a hobby."

John-Michael blinked. "Could we get a time-out and you tell me what the hell you're talking about?"

"If it had anything to do with you, I might," Grace said, flashing him an angry glare. Then she addressed Candace. "This isn't a *hobby*!"

"Okay, *college application* material, whatever."

Grace stared at Candace with an expression of sheer disbelief. After a moment she rose to her feet, shaking her head. "Think what you like. I'm outta here."

Candace watched her leave. "Hey, aren't you going to tell me to break a leg?"

"Yeah. Why don't you break *two*?"

With a final, furious glare, Grace left the room.

Candace put the palm of her hand to her chest.

John-Michael stared. "No way!"

"Such a dweeb. But I feel . . . amazing!"

"Seriously?"

"Yeah. Put your hand here." Candace lifted John-Michael's right hand and placed his fingers close to her heart. "Feel that!" She sounded delighted. "Grace did that."

He pulled his hand away. "What do you mean?"

"The way she looked at me. Did you see?"

"Not really. I was pretty caught up in the whole 'prison losers' and 'death row' thing. Candace, is Grace writing to guys on death row?"

"You shoulda seen it. Like real, passionate rage!"

"She was kinda bummed out," he agreed.

"I gotta remember this feeling."

"Why?"

"'Cause this is exactly how I need to be in a scene I'm doing today."

"Angry?"

"No—shaken. I need to be all rapid heartbeat and breathless."

"Oh, that. Well, yeah. Get someone to yell at you first."

Candace wasn't listening to him, though. She'd begun to focus on Lucy's laptop, which Grace had left open on the desk. He watched as she perched on the chair and clicked through the open windows on Lucy's desktop.

"Hey . . ."

"What?"

"Isn't this kinda what you told Grace not to do?"

"I didn't touch anything."

"Well, yeah, you did."

"I didn't touch anything that wasn't already open."

"Kind of nosy," he commented. But Candace was already lost in what she'd found on the screen. Reluctantly,

John-Michael looked, too.

There were two open windows—Lucy's internet accounts, a Word document in which Lucy had been writing a term paper on Voltaire's *Candide*, and a second browser open to a YouTube channel belonging to LucyLong. Only one video had been uploaded. In the frame-captured still, Lucy was caught in a rather sweet grin, sitting on her bed holding an acoustic guitar. A rare moment of vulnerability for a girl who was mostly pretty chill. The song was a cover of one of Green Day's.

"Lucy's YouTube. Big deal—we've all seen it. Are you going to tell me about Grace and her prison losers?"

"Huh. Insensitive," Candace murmured.

He gasped. "They're your words!"

"It's different. I'm her stepsister. I've seen what this has been doing to her."

"Writing the letters?"

"She gets upset sometimes," Candace pointed out. "I've seen her cry."

"Sure, it's got to be upsetting. But also, a pretty cool thing to do. Good for Grace."

"I guess." Candace seemed distracted again.

"Shouldn't you be heading to the TV studio?"

"Uh-huh."

"What's your problem? Are you seriously worried that Grace is spying on Lucy?"

"I guess not."

"Then what?"

John-Michael leaned back as Candace stepped over him on her way back to the bathroom.

"I like to look out for my sis," she said, speaking loud enough for him to hear her in the bathroom. "She doesn't tell me much about the guys she writes to. Sometimes I think she's going to leave clues on the computer. Browsing history, what she might have searched for. That kind of thing."

John-Michael rose to his feet, dropping the fleece blanket he'd had wrapped around himself. He glanced at the couple in the bed. Incredibly, they were still sound asleep.

"These two would sleep through the sinking of a ship," he said. Then louder he added, "You never found anything about who she's writing to?"

"No. She once said that she wouldn't search for them because the more searches, you know, the more their names would get a high ranking for stories about them in the papers. And that's not good. It could influence appeals, give the impression that there was 'negative public interest.'"

"Oh. Good point. So you don't know what they did?"

"They're on death row, so I'm gonna take a wild guess that it's murder."

John-Michael didn't say any more. Even hearing the word "murder" made him feel faintly queasy. It was odd, how he was reacting. Not what he'd expected—not by now.

PAOLO
SECOND FLOOR, SATURDAY, FEBRUARY 28

He'd woken up when he heard the creak of the spiral stair-case as Candace made her way out for her audition. But then he dozed for another hour. By then it was too bright to sleep. Blearily, he checked his watch. Eight o'clock and his room was already hazy with morning.

People had hooked up at the party last night—Paolo was sure of it. But not him. A couple of girls had approached, one very sweet and unassuming, the other aggressive and raunchy. Months ago he'd have hooked up with one if not both. Yet he'd made excuses with both these girls. What was wrong with him?

Paolo's thoughts strayed to Lucy. For a few blissful moments, he imagined her lying in bed alone. Almost cer-tainly, that wasn't the reality of what lay behind the door to Lucy's room. It had filled with weirdoes of all types as the night went on. They'd probably all passed out in their clothes.

Paolo slid out of bed. Okay, so he seemed to be

developing something of an obsession with Lucy. But it would wear off. Eventually. How long could he be expected to feel this bad?

The house was entirely still. Dressed only in shorts Paolo padded down to the kitchen, where he opened the fridge to get milk. When he closed the door, John-Michael was standing next to the sink wearing a white terry-cloth robe, grinning. It looked like he was still a little drunk, or high.

Paolo muttered a quick "good morning" and then returned to his room. He was fully awake now, and slightly wary of falling asleep again for fear of what he might dream. Instead, he pulled on a T-shirt, some tennis shorts, socks, and his sneakers. From his closet he picked out his second-best racket. He filled an empty water bottle from the cold water tap, grabbed two bananas from the fruit bowl on the kitchen table and left the house, heading for the tennis courts farther down the beach. Once summer vacation started he was booked to hit the tennis tournaments. It was time to begin some extra training, more than the hour or two he was able to snatch at the country club.

The beach was almost deserted, aside from joggers and people walking their dogs. It was surprisingly chilly out on the sand. Last night's cool air had persisted, whipped into a steady onshore breeze. Paolo finished eating the second banana, tossed the peels into a nearby garbage can, and broke into a gentle jog.

The courts were about a mile down the beach. When he arrived, he was slightly surprised to find someone already there. A jet-black-haired guy in his early twenties, tanned, and with a slim, wiry frame; a body you more often saw on a cyclist than a tennis player. Paolo watched the guy hit a few serves. He was obviously working on some kind of killer ace, throwing all his weight and energy into noisy serves, at least 30 percent of which weren't landing inside the box. Paolo did a few stretches and then returned to watching the guy serve. After a few minutes, the tennis player stopped, turned to him, and said, "You waiting for someone? Or looking for a game?"

Paolo doubted very much that this guy was going to provide much competition. Last time he'd been ranked, Paolo was twenty-fourth in the United States and tenth in the state. He was a little surprised that the guy didn't recognize him. But Paolo reminded himself that outside the precious enclaves of the country club and tennis circuit most people just played. They didn't watch.

Yet, once in a while, this guy landed a serve that impressed Paolo. There were a few that Paolo wasn't even sure he'd be able to return. The serve, however, was no more the whole game than putting was in golf. A game would be more fun than just working on his serve, as he'd also intended.

"Sure," Paolo answered. "I'll play." They played a set. For a while, Paolo hardly dropped a point. The fifth and sixth games, however, proved to be more of a challenge. Out of the blue, the guy broke his serve. In the end though, Paolo still won the set 6–1.

They shook hands and each sipped from their water bottles.

"My name's Darius," the guy said. "Play again? I bet you fifty dollars that next set I can take a game off you."

"Make it two games," Paolo said, "and you got a deal."

"Make it a hundred," the other guy said with a confident grin.

Paolo took the set again, but this time the guy took one game to deuce six times. It was slightly surprising to be held within a point of winning for quite such a long run, but then again, he wasn't as warmed up as the other guy, who'd been out awhile.

"You're very good," Darius said. He wiped the sweat from his forehead and neck, pushing back shoulder-length hair. Paolo noticed the back of his neck was covered with tattoos—the kind of Eastern mystic stuff people were so into.

"I'm a pro."

Darius rolled his eyes. "Aha. That explains it. I like to think I'm pretty good. But no one has ever taken a set from me by five games. Ever."

"Huh. You're taking it well. Very sportsmanlike."

"I knew you had to be good. Who else comes out here to practice early on a Saturday morning?"

"You?"

Darius laughed. "Busted! Listen, let me win my money back."

"Do you have it on you?"

Darius shook his head, smiling.

"Then I guess you better win. I tell you what, you win the next game and we're even."

To Paolo's faint surprise, Darius did just that. On the third deuce, Paolo felt his will fade. What did it matter to lose one game? He didn't know the guy, but he seemed cool. It had been a long time since Paolo had been forced to work so hard in any game that didn't count.

Darius was panting as Paolo went up to the net to shake his hand.

"Nice going, man," Paolo said. "You just beat the twenty-fourth best player in the USA."

"No kidding. Turned out all I needed was a real incentive. Care to see how I play for five hundred?"

Paolo stared for a second. "You're serious?"

"You've seen my game."

"Dude, it feels wrong."

Darius fixed him with a steely gaze. "I'm the one making the offer."

They played another game. Paolo won. Darius insisted on a rematch, double or nothing. In a few more minutes, Paolo had won a thousand dollars. Pretty soon it was two thousand. Each game was hard fought, until both players were straining at every point. When he was four thousand dollars up, Paolo realized that he hadn't been in a fight this intense since his last pro semifinal.

And then he lost. It was the kind of mistake that any player can make: a double fault on a deuce point. Darius punished him with a volley as fast as Paolo had ever seen.

Once again, they were even.

"You gotta let me go up. You've had me on the wire this whole time. You need to feel what that's like," Darius said, breathing hard.

Paolo stared at Darius. The guy had to be crazy. He'd gotten lucky enough to bring the score back to zero.

"Tell you what: If you're chicken, I'll let you go straight back to four thousand. One game. You'll be right back where you were."

Paolo shook his head. "I'm not chicken, man. But you got lucky."

"Yeah. I knew it. You can't face that I may be better than you. One game. I'll prove it. I'm wrong—you get four thousand. And then we stop. Word of honor."

"You want to play one game for four thousand dollars? *US* dollars?"

Darius plucked the strings of his racket like it was a guitar. "Yeah, US dollars. C'mon, man, out of the two of us, you're the pro."

Sweat was streaming down Paolo's back and into his shorts. He wasn't tired yet, but at this point he'd usually stop and take a short break. Darius, however, seemed to become calmer the more he played.

For the first time Paolo was beginning to sense some real doubts about his ability. He didn't like the way this whole scenario was making him feel. Walking away now would leave the doubts lodged deep within his psyche. What if they reared up again in some crucial competition? There were already games in his schedule that Paolo simply couldn't lose. He'd be haunted forever by Darius and this court.

Paolo felt his resolve solidify into something implacable. He had to beat Darius. Kill the curse before it took hold. The money would just be a bonus. What was at stake was worth a lot more than four thousand dollars to Paolo.

"One game?"

"One. Four large, winner takes all. We finish things here and go straight to the bank for the scratch."

Paolo looked around. At the mention of the bank, he'd suddenly wondered if Darius was part of some scam to express kidnap him. He'd heard of such things—people being marched to an ATM at gunpoint—but usually in tougher neighborhoods. And it was barely ten o'clock. There was still hardly anyone on the beach apart from the joggers and dog people.

Darius reached back, grabbed a foot, and stretched his hamstrings. "I can beat you, Country Club. You just don't want to believe it."

Paolo picked up two yellow balls and headed for the service line.

But it turned out that Darius was right. He beat Paolo, and this time with relative ease.

Three of his four serves blistered past Paolo at speeds that would have pleased any of the world's top ten players. As they shook hands at the end, Paolo began to wonder how to tell Darius that he didn't have four thousand dollars to spare.

MAYA

"Where's Paolo? And Candace?"

Lucy responded with a sullen glare. Maya wasn't sure if Lucy was taking a shot at Maya's whining or joining in with her implied criticism of the two housemates who'd escaped early enough to get out of cleaning up.

Maya found Lucy pretty difficult to read at the best of times. Neither girl was particularly sociable—they both preferred to watch TV or spend time on their computers. Maya guessed that Lucy was composing, watching videos, or even chatting. They'd both left friends behind in their previous schools.

It made sense for Maya to make an effort—she was a freshman at Our Lady. The school was popular with middle-class families of Latin descent who wanted to hold on to a precious aspect of Mexican and Central American religious life—plenty of the types of girls that Maya's family would love as friends for her. That way, she'd be invited to houses where Spanish was spoken and Mexican food served.

Maya loved Mexican food and she didn't mind listening to a bit of *cumbia* now and again, but she was far from fluent in Spanish. Worst of all, as far as her family was concerned, she couldn't remember the last time she'd been to Mexico.

Lucy, one of only a handful of black girls at school, was a junior. She didn't have much time left to bond with new people, and the older girls at school seemed like a cliquey bunch to Maya. Lucy spent a lot of time alone. Given the kind of haughty *señoritas* who went to Our Lady, Maya guessed that being alone didn't bother Lucy. It seemed pretty clear anyhow—Lucy preferred to hang out with boys.

Lucy stood up straight, both hands filled with trash she'd gathered from the kitchen floor and table. Finally, she replied to Maya's question.

"Candace had to go to the studio. She got the TV show. You don't remember?"

Maya gasped. "And I didn't even say anything about it. Man! I was so into my coding."

Lucy stuffed the party debris into a plastic garbage bag. She handed Maya a mop and brush set. "Floor disinfectant's in the cabinet under the sink. Make sure you use plenty. I'm sticking to this floor pretty bad."

Maya poured three capfuls of pine-scented syrupy fluid into a bucket and turned on the hot water. She lifted all six chairs onto the rectangular table that dominated the center of the kitchen and began to mop the wooden floor. It was alternately greasy and sticky with food residue and soda spill.

"So, do you know where Paolo is?" Maya asked.

"Well, he's not in my bed," Lucy said with a wry smile.

"Poor Paolo."

"Poor, nothin'. The boy needs to get used to hearing the word 'no.'"

Maya chuckled. "He's so cute. I bet he doesn't hear it too much."

"That kid's confused. He only wants me because I'm not interested."

Maya doubted that. Lucy was beautiful and exuded an almost intimidating level of confidence. Her musical talent was obvious to anyone who had ears. But Maya didn't say anything. Lucy would probably accuse her of sucking up.

At that moment the front door opened: Paolo. He seemed drained, his hair was slick with sweat, a racket in his left hand. He took one look at the cleanup operation and gave both girls a guilty look.

"Hey, I'm sorry. Totally slipped my mind."

"John-Michael's upstairs," Lucy said tartly, "cleaning the triple."

Paolo's face fell very slightly. "Oh. And Grace?"

"Cleaning up the backyard. I think it'd be nice if you helped John-Michael. That room's kind of bombed out."

Maya could see Paolo struggling to control some kind of impulsive response. She guessed he didn't feel it was fair to have to clean up the one room he hadn't even entered the whole party. He must really like Lucy because all he did was smile a little tightly.

Lucy hesitated. "Everything okay, Paolo?"

Paolo shrugged. "I . . . I guess."

"Where you been?"

Maya realized that Lucy was right. Paolo didn't look comfortable at all. Maybe his worries went beyond the mess that awaited upstairs?

"I was playing tennis down on the beach."

"Yeah, we got that, the whole racket and all. What happened?"

Paolo tried to smile, but it wasn't remotely genuine. Instead Maya caught a sudden, startling glimpse of something rather odd in his expression. For a second he looked like a frightened little boy.

"Well, I . . . I actually lost."

"To some guy on the beach?!"

Paolo nodded. He didn't bother to fake-smile anymore.

Lucy peered at him for a moment. "So?"

"I lost some money to him."

Maya said, "How much?"

"It doesn't matter. I couldn't pay. Most of my money's all locked up in long-term savings."

"You in trouble?" Lucy asked. "They gonna break your ribs or something?"

"No." Paolo seemed to choose his words carefully. "Dude said I could owe him a favor."

"That's cool of him."

"Yeah." Paolo was still looking at Lucy. Maya had the distinct impression that he wanted to be alone with her. She began to make her way to the stairs. Paolo followed after a few seconds, then disappeared into his own room.

Inside the triple room, John-Michael had just finished bagging the garbage. He was sweeping now with a dustpan and brush.

Maya crossed the room and opened her laptop.

"You mind if I take a quick break before I start again? Lucy and I pretty much finished the kitchen."

"No *problemo.*"

Maya added, "All the treats you baked got eaten, by the way."

John-Michael seemed pretty happy with that news. He started humming quietly to himself as he swept.

Maya gave him one final glance before she opened a second window on her desktop. It was a document named "school schedule." But the contents had little to do with school. She began to type:

> Paolo lost a tennis match to some guy he met on the beach. At least, I'm pretty sure he was playing tennis because he was wearing shorts and carrying a racket, plus, he was all sweaty and it wasn't all that hot outside. He said there was money involved. He seems pretty cut up about it. He told Lucy and me that the guy—whoever it was—isn't going to make him pay the money he owed. But now Paolo owes the guy a favor. He seems more freaked out than he's letting on. Maybe he didn't tell us everything that happened.

Lucy spent most of the party in her room with her friends from the beach. I already wrote most of their names in an earlier report so you can look them up, but from memory it was Darla, Mikey, and Luisito. There were a few randoms, too, friends of friends, but I didn't talk to them or get their names. They fired up a bong pretty early on and basically got wasted. At around midnight Luisito and Lucy came down into the kitchen to get the cupcakes John-Michael baked. They seemed pretty annoyed when I told them they'd been eaten already.

Maya's phone buzzed. Reading the text, she sniffed in irritation.

WHERE IS TODAY'S REPORT? YOU'RE SUPPOSED TO SEND IT BY 10 A.M.!

Stabbing at the buttons Maya typed back: Even weekends? So not fair! I can basically never sleep in.

DEAL WITH IT, BABY.

"Something wrong?"

Maya closed her laptop. She plastered a sweet smile onto her lips. "No, thanks, John-Michael. Just realizing that I have a lot of homework, more than I remembered."

"We'll be done cleaning soon."

She nodded. "I'm going to help Grace."

Candace and Lucy's bedroom, however, already looked fairly clean when she walked through the door. Grace was sitting on Lucy's bed, a photograph in her hand. When Maya walked in, Grace put the photo down in a hurry, embarrassed to be caught.

"Hey. Uh . . ." Grace stammered. "Someone pulled out a box of photos from under Lucy's bed."

Maya folded her arms, unsure of how to begin. "Grace . . . maybe you shouldn't, you know, be looking at Lucy's stuff?"

"Oh, I know, I wasn't trying to, I just found photos scattered all over the room so I was gathering them up. I found the box, too."

Maya moved closer. "I don't think I have a single photo. Who keeps actual, you know, snapshots?"

"They're pretty old. Lucy's a kid in most of them." Gently, Grace placed the photos inside a fabric-covered box and closed the lid.

Maya noticed that she didn't offer her any chance to look at them. She remembered how she'd caught Grace staring at the video of Lucy singing that Green Day song.

"Grace . . . is there something going on between you and Lucy? Do you have some sort of issue with her?"

For a moment it seemed like Grace was going to hotly deny anything. But when she looked into Maya's eyes, she began to shake her head. "I guess I should tell you that there isn't."

"But . . . there *is*?"

Grace's eyes filmed over without warning. "Maya," she murmured. "Why's he so crazy about her?"

"What? Who's crazy? About Lucy?"

A tear spilled over and Grace tried to smile. "Paolo about Lucy. She's not interested. But he doesn't care."

Maya could scarcely believe what was coming out of Grace's mouth. "You think . . . you think he should . . . look at someone else?"

Grace wiped a tear away with the back of her wrist. "God. I'm such an idiot. What's wrong with me?"

"You . . . you're telling me you like Paolo?" Maya didn't bother to hide her astonishment. "Whoa, Grace. You are one dark horse."

ARIANA CALLS CHARLIE

"Finally, you pick up your phone!"

"It's been crazy, Ariana. We had a party. There's a lot to clean up." Ariana could hear a guitar softly strumming in the background.

"I hear you," Ariana said. "That's why I had to get a place of my own. Too much temptation around my cousin and those college types."

"So it's working out for you? You're staying clean?"

"Eighteen months now." Ariana gave a short laugh. "Got my life down to Zen simplicity. Wish I'd lived like this when I was a kid. I'd be at Harvard by now."

"Well, things were pretty simple when I was a kid," Charlie said. "Mom and Dad. The TV show. A driver, a chaperone, the work. And I wound up with exactly the same problem as you."

"It wasn't a very normal life for a nine-year-old child."

"It felt normal to me. Remember, I was seeing the other kids in the show go through the same thing."

"But then everything changed?" Ariana probed.

"Yeah. When Tyson Drew drowned in that swimming pool."

"That's when you and your folks moved away, right? I thought you said you didn't tell them?"

"I didn't. The TV show wrote me out, remember? They didn't like the kind of coverage the Tyson Drew murder was getting. Just me being there was enough to throw off the vibe."

"And your folks were happy to move?"

The girl let out a sardonic laugh. "Are you kidding me? They were ecstatic. Not everyone likes LA. New city, new jobs for them. No more TV show for me. Their lives got a whole lot easier."

"How about you?" Ariana asked. "Were you sad to lose your job?"

"You'd think. And yet, by the time it happened, I was relieved."

"Relieved? I thought you loved being on TV."

"I loved acting. But then, my whole life became about pretending. I told the first cop that I hadn't seen anything. And after that . . ."

Ariana concentrated. Time to prod the kid again, see how much she might be hiding—even from her. After all they'd been through together in the meetings, Ariana wanted to believe that this girl trusted her. She was counting on that trust. "You had to stick to the story."

"Right."

"Were you scared? Afraid that the cops would call you a liar, say you were making things up?"

The guitar strumming stopped. The girl paused, thinking. "I was sleepy and I wasn't sure if I was awake. Because I was so convinced that I'd remembered things differently."

"That'll do it."

"Yeah. But now, after all these years, the image that dominates from that night is that hand on the back of his head. The person in the shadows holding him under. White knees. And fingernail polish."

"Fingernail polish?"

"Yes. It's a detail that's only really made sense lately. Someone in a dress or a skirt. And painted fingernails. A real pretty shade, I remember that. Like, flames and peaches."

Ariana laughed nervously. "You remember the color?"

She heard her friend pausing. "I guess."

"Wait up, wait up," Ariana said. "Are you telling me you're really sure now? Because you've talked about this a few times. And you never really believed it happened the way you say. You told me it was a dream."

"But I'm not sure now. I think maybe a *woman* killed Tyson Drew."

Ariana waited for several long seconds for the voice on the other end to start talking again. This was very dangerous territory. From the halting tone of her friend's voice, Ariana guessed that they'd both understood this. But only Ariana could possibly understand just how much the threat had suddenly increased.

"Ariana, if a woman killed Tyson Drew, then that guy they put in jail for the murder, the one they're going to execute . . . he's innocent."

Ariana began cautiously. "Lucy," she said emphatically, using her friend's name, not a term of endearment but to stress how important this was. "Lucy, seriously, think hard about this. I mean it. Just think about what you're saying."

"It's not easy to realize that things you've believed in for such a long time could have been twisted into a lie." Ariana heard Lucy give a heartfelt sigh. "I don't know how much longer I can take it."

PAOLO
BALCONY, SUNDAY, MARCH 1

Sunday morning, and Maya suggested that they all get up crazy early, rent some boards from the place on the beach, and go surfing. Paolo refused on account of *hello, tennis*, and he couldn't afford to get injured. Lucy refused on account of it was lame, but she'd still watch. Candace and Grace were eager—they'd hardly ever tried surfing. But most of all, they were curious. Maya surfed? Who knew?

In the end, Grace and Candace mostly wound up paddling on their boards and bodysurfing the waves, boogie-board style. Maya caught a couple of waves, which impressed them. But it was obvious that she was out of practice.

Afterward, Maya bought the whole house breakfast burritos and a blueberry cheesecake to celebrate finishing the beta version of her app. It was already being down-loaded at a healthy rate. Even though she wasn't making much money from it, which puzzled Paolo, she seemed relieved and happy.

The housemates all sat on the balcony, munching and

drinking coffee. It was another day of white clouds and haze but it didn't matter. The beach stretched wide in front of them: the faint roar of the ocean rolling in, the whisper of the palms. All this had grown familiar to them. Paolo felt as though he'd lived here for years.

But unlike the others, he couldn't relax. Paolo's eyes kept combing the sands, the path from the boardwalk and south, down to the tennis courts. He thought back to Darius's words when they'd parted the morning before. *"You shouldn't play for money you don't have."*

Paolo had privately doubted that Darius would have paid him had the outcome been different. What could Paolo have done about it? Nothing.

"Kid, people get their asses handed to them for a lot less," Darius had said.

"Don't be that way, dude," Paolo had replied. "You're not the type."

Darius had shot him a dismissive look, as though he had something far more serious on his mind and Paolo had interrupted his train of thought. "You think so?"

There was barely a hint of aggression; yet for the first time, Paolo had felt a little scared. Darius could be just about anyone. There was no way to know.

The guy had appeared out of nowhere. His body was covered in tattoos. Sure, that alone was no guarantee of toughness, but he'd proven himself the stronger tennis player. That final game, Paolo had felt it. Darius had played a different quality of game to what he'd produced up until that point. Almost as though he'd been faking it before that. Paolo hadn't even suspected—he was so used to winning against non-pros. By the time he and Darius had neared the house, Paolo had realized the truth.

He'd been hustled.

Darius had been serious from the start, looking to make real cash. It gradually dawned on Paolo that there really might be no painless way out of this.

"This is where you live?" Darius had said approvingly. "Nice."

Paolo had felt faintly sick. Probably not smart to let this guy see where he lived.

"You live here with your family, Paolo?"

He'd managed to limit his response to, "With friends."

"*Very* nice. I guess you're not short of a dollar or two. That's good. I wouldn't like to think you weren't good for the money."

Paolo had stopped walking. He'd turned to Darius, forced himself to look the guy in the eye.

"I gotta be straight with you, man. I can't easily get the kind of money we're talking about. And whatever you think about me living here, I'm not rich."

Darius had stared at Paolo then, a glare as pitiless as a granite wall. A lengthy silence had developed between them, long enough for Paolo's nerve to begin to falter. And then like sunshine after a rainstorm, Darius had broken into a grin. "You're not rich? I hear you. We could all use a little more, know what I'm saying?"

Paolo gave a tentative grin. Darius smiled more easily now, turned back onto the beach path, and put an affectionate hand on Paolo's shoulder.

"Now that I think about it, there's another way to work this out."

"Really? That would be awesome."

"A favor you could do for me."

Paolo hadn't answered right away. What if the guy wanted him to off-load a bunch of drugs or something? The cure might wind up being worse than the disease.

"I got a grudge match coming. A buddy who swears he can beat me in a doubles match. Only, I got no partner right now. But you, you're good enough to give me a shot at winning."

"You want me to play a tennis match with you?"

"Let the punishment fit the crime."

It seemed too good to be true. "And that's all?"

Darius nodded, slapping his back. "Not gonna lie to you, Paolo, it's a money game. But if we win, I keep the prize."

Here came the catch.

"Am I gonna have to come up with the stake?" Paolo asked.

"No, buddy, the stake is all on me."

"And if we lose?"

"I guess we'd better not lose."

And with that, Darius had stopped and watched Paolo veer off the path toward the house. He'd given a friendly wave and been on his way.

Since yesterday, Paolo had been waiting for Darius to reappear. He hadn't told anyone in the house what had really happened on the beach, and he wasn't about to tell them now. What kind of knucklehead got involved in a money game with some total stranger? He could just imagine himself trying to explain it all away, sounding more dumbass by the second. Paolo peeled foil from his breakfast burrito. Pensively, he took a bite.

Lucy looked across from the opposite end of the balcony, addressing Candace, who was sitting next to Paolo, her legs stretched out. "How was the first day of being a TV star?"

"Exhausting," Candace replied.

As she began to describe it, Paolo tuned out. His attention went back to the beach. Darius. Who *was* he? How could someone that good not be a professional?

The house was immaculately clean and smelled of pine from top to bottom. They'd toiled half of yesterday to straighten up after the party. The housemates were going to relax, do their homework, sleep. Paolo had about two hours of homework to do, and a tennis student at five in the afternoon. He decided to hit the shower.

He'd barely finished when he heard a knock on the outside door. As far as he knew, no one in the house was expecting a visitor. A horrible premonition struck him. In the pit of his stomach, something lurched. He quickly finished dressing and then opened the door. It was Darius. He took one look at Paolo and smiled broadly. "Heeyyy, pardner. You gettin' ready to come out with me?"

Paolo made to step outside, and ran straight into Darius's outstretched palm.

"Dude," said Darius. "Might wanna get your racket?"

Thirty minutes later Paolo was sitting next to Darius in a convertible Porsche Boxster, speeding past Malibu on the Pacific Coast Highway. The car felt very new, the silver blue paintwork gleamed with opalescence, the leather upholstery still had a squeak. Their rackets were tucked behind the rear passenger seat, in the shade.

Shortly after Leo Carrillo Park, they stopped at a diner and ate cheeseburgers.

"Now," Darius said with a warning grin. "What happens next is for your own protection. Unless you want someone to recognize you, that is." He led Paolo to the diner's bathroom, where Darius cut Paolo's hair short with a buzz-cut razor. Then he applied peroxide.

"Gotta love being blond. White hair. Chicks dig it," Darius told him smoothly.

Paolo kept his lips pressed tightly shut, fuming. But when they'd finished, he couldn't stop looking at himself in the mirror. Such a small change, yet such a transformation. He looked like Eminem. Not his best look.

They reached Montecito shortly after lunch—a little town just south of Santa Barbara. Paolo had only ever heard of rich people living there: movie stars and the like. The type that felt that Beverly Hills was too much of a zoo. Darius drove the Boxster down streets with their neatly manicured borders into a residential area. He stopped at the security gate before a complex of white, red-roofed buildings. There was no one around. Just a two-way speaker in the wall.

"It's Darius, yo, give my boy Jimmy a shout, okay?"

After a moment, the metal doors gave way. Darius drove through. He parked next to a red Corvette, sleek and beautiful. For a second, Paolo itched to reach out and touch it. "Nice wheels," he said.

Darius smiled. "That, my friend, is a 2012 Corvette convertible."

A young man approached. He didn't look much older than Paolo. He was very tan with shoulder-length, straggly blond hair. He wore nothing but yellow cotton espadrilles and a pair of white Billabong board shorts. There wasn't an ounce of fat on the guy, Paolo noticed. Plenty of lean muscle definition. This kid lived for sun and body worship, or else he was an athlete. And to judge by his house, very rich.

Paolo watched as the two other guys bumped shoulders lightly. Jimmy strode over to Paolo. "This the guy?"

"I picked him up playing on Venice Beach. He's the real deal, man. Closest I've come to losing for a year."

"A'ight, well it's gonna happen today, D. Because I got me a tennis pro. From Spain. He's buddies with Rafa."

Paolo interjected, "Nadal?!"

Darius winked at him. To Jimmy he said, "That's why I'm insisting on odds, bro. You put up your Corvette, I put up my Boxster."

Paolo took a sweeping look at the grounds. Two

cottages, a large two-story house, gardens. Between the pink and white bougainvillea, he could see the blue chink of a swimming pool. As they stood there a tall, slender, deeply tanned woman with shoulder-length, straw-and-sand colored hair approached along the path toward the pool. She wore only a turquoise sarong, dyed Balinese-style with a seashell pattern and wrapped tightly around her body, revealing her shapely collarbone and calves. The woman tilted her horn-rimmed Ray-Bans and flashed a smile at the tennis players.

"Hello, Jimmy's friends. You be sure and put on a good performance for me today. I'll be coming out to watch you once I've taken a swim."

Jimmy scowled. "Mom, don't."

Jimmy's mom pouted. Then she surveyed the rest of the group. Her eyes stopped on Paolo. He could sense her gaze sweeping over him, slowly taking in his entire frame.

"I may watch," she conceded, spinning on one foot. "And I may not. We'll see."

Paolo watched her go. He leaned into the back of the Boxster, picked up the rackets and handed one to Darius. "Where's the court?"

As they made their way around the back of the house, Darius whispered into Paolo's ear, "You know the Spanish guy?"

Paolo peered at the tall, well-muscled athlete who stood on the court, bouncing a tennis ball. "Oscar Cortada. He's number twenty in the world!"

"Good thing we fixed your hair."

But Paolo strongly doubted that the other player would recognize him. Cortada played on the international circuit. Paolo would be a huge nobody to him. Now he looked like a jerk and all for nothing.

The match turned into a tense, exhausting battle. The third set went to a tiebreaker. In the final set, Paolo finally understood why Darius had sought him out. While Darius and Jimmy were both flashy players with moments of brilliance, when it came to stamina, they just didn't have game. Paolo and Oscar dominated.

In the end, though, Darius's flashes of genius in combination with Paolo's power and technique eventually gave them the edge. And to Paolo's immense, exhausted relief, he and Darius won. And Jimmy's mom never showed up.

The two of them walked back to the cars. Fear had won it for them, Paolo realized. Darius had hurled murderous looks in his direction every time they lost a point.

In victory, Darius was surprisingly subdued. He handed Paolo the keys to the Boxster. Paolo closed his fist around them. "You want me to follow you home?"

"Hell no."

"Where should I leave the car?"

"I could give a shit."

Darius opened the door to the red Corvette, turned the key, and put down the top. Slowly, it dawned on Paolo what had happened.

"The Boxster isn't yours. You stole it for the stake."

Darius peered at him for a second. "I ever hear *word* from you, you're a dead man."

"Tough talk for a tennis player," Paolo responded softly.

For a second, thunder flared in Darius's eyes. Paolo tensed, ready to spring back if the man attacked. Then, abruptly, Darius relaxed. He took a breath. "You'll wise up, eventually. I was just like you once."

"In what way?" Paolo asked. "Honest? Or a tennis pro?"

"You just hustled a rich kid out of a forty-thousand-dollar car, homeboy," Darius pointed out. "So no, I don't think you're *honest* anymore."

The words sunk into Paolo like needles. Unsteadily, he backed away. Darius started the engine. As he reversed, Darius leaned out through the open window. A laconic grin was on his face.

"Get the Boxster off Jimmy's dad's driveway before they figure out it's hot. Don't let the cops catch you in that thing. And Paolo, before you go back to that country club, do something about your hair."

The keys to the Boxster felt strange and unwieldy in his hand. Paolo's fingers fumbled as he tried to find the ignition. In his mind, he was already being pulled over by some traffic cop, asked for his license and registration papers.

His future was looking precarious. Convicted felons didn't get licenses to practice law.

LUCY

"Miss Long, I'm going to pretend I didn't find you here."

Lucy glanced up, dropped her cigarette, and quickly stubbed it under her regulation black Mary Jane shoe. She tried to exude impassivity as she watched the young teacher stroll over to the water's edge and pick up the discarded cigarette butt.

"I'm not, however, going to pretend I didn't find *this*."

"Aww, shoot, Miss Ashcroft. That's not gonna help me. . . ."

The teacher silenced Lucy with a slicing motion across her own mouth. "Zip it. It's the third time I've found you in the water gardens. You know the water gardens are just for faculty and visitors. And smoking on top of that!" She paused. "It's almost as though you want to be expelled."

Lucy risked a pout. She was black, a punk, and she wasn't afraid of teachers—it was an unexpected combination that seemed to put most teachers on their guard. It was good to mix up the tough-girl act they expected with a bit of vulnerability.

She cast her eyes down and then glanced up from beneath her eyelashes. Normally, she would reserve the maneuver for a male teacher. But it seemed worth risking now. Ashcroft was one of those teachers who yearn to be liked by the cool kids. Lucy was fairly indifferent to her, but she'd made friends with teachers like her throughout her entire life. Without their protection, she'd have been expelled at least twice.

Miss Ashcroft was visibly surprised. Lucy watched the history teacher ponder the possible motives for the gesture. After a second or two, she clearly came down on the side of manipulation.

"I can believe that actually worked for you in Claremont, Lucy. But believe me, at Our Lady we get our share of princesses trying to give us the runaround."

"I'm no princess. Not here, not in Claremont."

Miss Ashcroft smirked. "Is that so? Well then, kindly report to the assistant principal's office. Do you remember where that is? You should, you were there only last week."

Lucy bristled. Time to drop the friendly act. She was fine with teachers being strict and bossy—that's what they were paid for. But when a teacher turned on the hostile sarcasm, it was time to check out of that relationship. She and Miss Ashcroft were not destined to be friends.

She could still feel Miss Ashcroft's eyes on her as she dawdled up the long rectangular pond and onto the sandstone staircase, toward the Spanish-colonial-style mansion that dominated Our Lady of Mercy Catholic High School for Girls. She climbed the stairs in the full glare of the midday sun. Reluctantly, Lucy pulled on her regulation blue blazer and straightened the collar of her white cotton blouse.

The assistant principal, Veronica Guzman, waved Lucy toward the chair in the middle of the room.

"I'm going to get directly to the point."

Her hair, Lucy observed, was solid, like a helmet—a monochrome block of glossy amber. Under a center parting and neat, narrow eyebrows, her eyes were large and solemn.

"There have been disciplinary issues with you since the day you arrived, Miss Long. Notwithstanding the minor issues of cigarette smoking on the premises, inappropriate use of the staff parking lot, and general backtalk to members of staff, all of which might conceivably be overlooked, there's the somewhat intractable matter of your attitude toward your academic studies."

Lucy smoldered in silence. The last grade she'd been given, which had been for music, was an A. In that subject—the only one that mattered to Lucy—she had never scored less than an A-minus. From school she planned to go on to a career in music: playing shows, recording. Maybe a college course or two in music technology. As far as Lucy was concerned, everything was on track. All in spite of her parents having thrown her out and robbed her of all her local friends and fellow musicians. In Venice, she was already managing to reconstruct something that might even be better. What had seemed edgy in Claremont was commonplace on the Venice boardwalk.

"I'm afraid I don't understand, Miss Guzman," Lucy said in her most carefully enunciated voice. It wasn't difficult to turn that on either—she simply imitated her mother. "I'm excelling in music. Isn't that the case?"

"Music, yes. No problems there, Lucy, I will give you that. I'm talking about English literature, chemistry, and Spanish. According to your teachers you are now overdue with papers in all three."

"I asked for extensions. I recently moved, and we had—"

"You moved at the beginning of January," interrupted Guzman. "Adequate time for any adjustments." She gave Lucy a hard stare. "I'd have expected more from you, Miss Long."

Here it came. The speech Lucy had grown tired of hearing—the one that simultaneously praised her for being smart enough to have been born to Robert and Anne-Marie Jordan, whilst bemoaning the poor efforts she'd made in upholding their undoubtedly stellar genetic standards.

"I don't know if you're aware of this, Lucy, but our principal, Dr. Keener, got her master's at your mother's college."

"I didn't know that." But it figured. How else could her parents have finagled a highly sought-after place in a snooty prep school like Our Lady with less than two weeks' notice?

"Dr. Keener is a tremendous admirer of your mother's. It's no mean achievement for a woman to be president of a private college. Especially a woman of color."

"Thanks, and yeah, I know."

"Dr. Keener would dearly like to be able to feel the same way about you."

Lucy wondered why Keener hadn't bothered to see her herself if that was really true.

"We'd like to see a marked improvement in your attitude toward your work. Please."

A nod. "Guess I'll try."

"It's easily within your ability to impress us. Mr. Steiner read me parts of your essay about Stravinsky's *Rite of Spring*. It was quite insightful, and very well written. I liked the section comparing it to *West Side Story*."

Lucy swallowed. Her voice became very quiet. "Thank you."

"There's another thing, Lucy." Guzman turned over her hand. In her palm was a half-smoked, hand-rolled cigarette. "I gather you sometimes smoke, out in the water gardens."

"That isn't mine."

Guzman managed a thin smile. "The trustees require that we keep that part of the school immaculate, for conferences and other events."

She dismissed Lucy then, with the firm suggestion that she head to the library. Since the library was housed directly opposite Guzman's office, albeit down a hallway, the request was difficult to ignore. Within a few minutes Lucy found herself in a part of the school she'd visited only once before, during orientation.

At the reception desk was a slim woman in her midforties, with long, dark brown hair pulled back in a ponytail. She looked up from the book she was reading, replaced the glasses that had been hanging around her neck, and signaled to Lucy to come over.

"I haven't seen you before, missy. You wanna tell me what kind of books you like? Or are you looking for something specific for your homework?"

Lucy was a little flustered to be put on the spot. The librarian was eyeing her with a kindly yet knowing air.

"Can I just use the computer?"

The librarian rolled her eyes melodramatically. "God help us, not you, too. Tell me you want some help with references at least."

Lucy began to smile. The librarian was having a bit of fun with her. "I just want to check the hits on my YouTube account."

"Well, hey, give me your username and we'll look you up."

When the Lucy Long channel came up, Lucy felt a rush of excitement. Ten thousand views of the original video posted by Paolo. And already over a thousand for the latest, a Rancid cover that she'd recorded during the party.

The librarian made a murmur of approval. "Looking good! Can't listen in here, obviously. I'll catch up with it later."

Ten thousand views.

ARIANA CALLS LUCY
SATURDAY, MARCH 21

"How's life on Venice Beach?"

"It's not like anywhere I've ever lived is for sure," Lucy answered.

"But you like it?"

Ariana could hear the smile in Lucy's voice. It was good to hear her so relaxed. When they'd spoken three weeks ago, she'd sounded impatient.

"I like it a lot," Lucy admitted. "The ocean. The light—this close to the water, there's so much sky. The air in the morning, how it tastes of salt. I can walk up to Santa Monica and get funnel cakes. I didn't even know how much I like them."

"Funnel cakes? Uh-uh. You'll get fat."

"Ha," said Lucy. "Good point. I should maybe run all the way back."

"How about the other kids? Are they how you expected?"

"How do you mean?" Lucy asked. "They're pretty normal."

"Are they like the people you worked with, back in the day?"

"Oh, not at all. Those guys were freaks. And me, too, now that I look back. TV is no place for a kid."

"It's okay for someone your age, though?" Ariana asked.

"Borderline. You mix with a lot of crazy people. You need to be pretty grounded."

Ariana smiled. "But you are grounded now, wouldn't you say?"

"Weirdly, I feel a lot better since coming here. The house is a good place for me. Nice mix of people."

"Tell me about them."

"Uhhhh. That feels a bit gossipy."

"It's not like I'm ever gonna meet them," Ariana pushed. "Besides, I want to hear about these people who make you so happy."

Lucy sounded hopeful. "You might meet them. It's only a few hours away."

"You think I can afford to be going out to LA?"

"Get the bus. You could stay with us."

Ariana gave a scornful laugh. "Sounds to me like your house is plenty crowded already. Aren't you three to a room?"

"Only in one room. We have a futon in the living room."

"Who's your best friend in the house?"

"I get along with everyone."

"Anyone you're into?"

"*Me?* You know I never like anybody."

Like always, Lucy said this as though it were a joke. And yet . . . Ariana smiled to herself. "Oh, sure, I forgot."

"Trust you to bring things down low."

"Honey, I'm just trying to stir up that rumor mill. I missed hearing all about your shenanigans."

"Maybe we'll just say that my folks might not be too happy."

"You partying?"

"Once in a while. But I'm not using nearly as much as before."

"Mm-hmm?" Ariana said a little dubiously.

"Sorta. There's . . ."

And finally, Ariana caught the hesitation she'd been waiting for.

"There's kind of something a little weird going on," Lucy confessed. "Just with a couple of people."

"Go on. . . ."

"This guy called Paolo. Cute guy, tennis player. Pretty sure I told you about him. He kinda flipped out, for, like, no reason. Got himself a radical haircut, the buzz-cut look. Started acting all nervous, working out a lot."

"People reinvent themselves all the time."

"I guess. What's odd is that it happened pretty much over a weekend, just after the party."

"Ah, that explains it. He met a girl."

Flatly, Lucy said, "Yeah . . . don't think that's it."

"A guy then? Maybe he's coming out of the closet?"

Lucy gave a wry laugh. "Highly doubtful. Believe me, I have some inside knowledge."

"Ah. Then maybe the change isn't in him," Ariana suggested. "Maybe it's in you."

"Meaning what exactly?"

Stifling a lazy-afternoon yawn, Ariana said, "Your boy there, shedding his Disney Channel. Maybe you like what you see. And it's taken you by surprise."

JOHN-MICHAEL
KITCHEN, SUNDAY, MARCH 22

"The first step is to prepare your oven. Ninety degrees, if it goes that low. That's the optimum temperature for yeast."

John-Michael watched Candace touch the control panel, discreetly checking that she set it correctly. "Done."

"Now we wash our hands and get started." He held up both his hands and grinned.

It had been a few weeks since the party. John-Michael had been fielding pleas to show his housemates how to bake ever since. Finally, John-Michael had caved. He began by weighing out flour and butter and pouring milk into a measuring cup. Meanwhile, Candace cleaned an area on the solid whitewashed pine kitchen table and sprinkled it with flour. John-Michael began to combine the ingredients in the food processor.

"Okay, now we switch to the dough hooks."

"So, John-Michael, this is your thing?"

He smiled. "No question."

"Who taught you, your mom?"

John-Michael stared into the food processor for a second. He reached into the bowl with a scraper and scooped up the sticky mixture. He dropped it onto the floured table.

Candace's question was natural enough. He'd heard it before. But it was never easy to answer.

"She started to. When I was seven or eight. But then she got sick."

"At least you have happy memories of her. She could have been a total pain, like mine."

There was an awkward silence. John-Michael took a large pinch of flour and threw it over the dough mixture. "Damn. We forgot to add the proofed yeast."

"Oh. Is it ruined?"

He tore open a packet of quick-rising yeast and emptied it into a bowl, then added a spoonful of flour and some warm water. He covered the bowl with plastic wrap.

"It's not ruined. But maybe we shouldn't talk about our moms. It's kind of distracting."

"Suits me."

He glanced at Candace sideways for a moment. He was itching to say something. Maybe it was wiser to stay quiet. But as he often did, John-Michael launched in anyway. "You know, 'total pain' seems kind of strong. Your mom is paying for you to live here. She checked in on us all the time at first."

But Candace seemed resolute. "The money means nothing to Katelyn. She's got plenty. And she was checking in on the *house*. We're convenient tenants for her. If she really loved me, she'd have let Grace and me live with her and the Dope Fiend on Malibu Beach."

John-Michael smiled gently. "Then I guess I'm glad she didn't. I like it here. And I like living with you guys."

Candace seemed to relax. "Yeah, well. I like it, too. I never had a friend as gay as you. It's pretty cool."

"As 'gay' as me?"

"You're what Tina—Grace's mom—calls 'literally gay.' Which means you're nice and clean and you can cook."

"Ugh. I sound like a dweeb," groaned John-Michael. "But Grace's mom sounds . . . interesting."

"I wouldn't be where I am without Tina. She moved in with my dad six years ago, married him five years ago. One big happy family ever since." When she saw his cynical smile, Candace flicked him with a tea towel.

"It's the truth! My dad is, like, this very mellow guy. He always wanted a big family, but my mom was obsessed about losing her figure. Tina and her little ready-made almost-soccer team, she made him really happy. Until they started to argue—over me."

"What happened?"

"Tina really got behind my career. A real stage mom. It kind of took over for a little while."

"Must have kinda sucked for Grace, to have her mom take such an interest in the new girl."

The idea didn't seem to have occurred to Candace, which John-Michael found surprising. Or maybe she just didn't want to face up to something that might have been a sore point of their childhood.

Candace merely shook her head. "Not really. You know Gracie. She's really cool."

John-Michael handed Candace a large ceramic bowl and a small bottle of olive oil. "Could you please oil this bowl?" He picked up a snack bag and a candy bar. "Dried blueberries or Reese's Nutrageous? For inside the roll."

"Both."

He emptied both packages onto a small wooden board and began with a sharp knife to roughly chop the blueberries together with the peanut caramel bar. "How's the TV show going?"

"The director seems to be happy. I don't get to do too much but what I do is pretty awesome. My character, Gina, is on the run. She kills a bad guy in the first episode, it's so cool. So now she's sixteen, on the run, and she's totally kickass. Half my rehearsal time is spent doing combat training."

"Real combat?"

"No, silly. Stage combat, of course."

"You couldn't actually kick anyone's ass then?"

"I can't hit or kick very hard. That takes a lot of training. I know a few moves now that might get me out of trouble . . . so long as the opponent was a wuss."

John-Michael removed the wrap on the small bowl and showed the contents to Candace.

She stared at it, her finger hovering just above the surface of the dough. "Huh! It's all puffed up."

"Don't prod it—you'll let the air out. We've kick-started the yeast." He spooned the mixture out and planted it in a hollow he'd made in the dough mixture. Then he folded over the rest of the dough and began to squeeze it through his fingers.

"Ewww," Candace said. "Icky."

There was a loud knock at the front door. John-Michael glanced at Candace.

"We expecting anyone?" he asked, a little nervous.

She frowned. "Not that I know of." She disappeared around the corner to the front door and returned a minute later with an attractive brunette in her midthirties, dressed in a dark blue pantsuit.

At the sight of the visitor, John-Michael felt faintly sick. He dropped the completed dough mix into the oiled ceramic bowl and slowly scraped the dough from his fingers.

"Hi, are you John-Michael Weller? I'm Detective Ellen Winter, Carlsbad police department." The woman's eyes twinkled slightly, gazing at his hands. "I won't offer to shake your hand, if that's okay."

He didn't answer, but took a moment to cover the bowl with foil. Unsteadily, he slid it into the oven and set the timer for forty minutes. He turned to the detective, his heart racing.

"Is there somewhere private that we can talk?" asked the woman. "I'd like to ask you some questions."

John-Michael felt his fingertips go numb. Candace squeezed his arm, gave him a reassuring look, and then left.

The detective examined the lined-up icing, sugar, milk, eggs, oil, and pastry brush. She seemed impressed by the neat preparations. "She's teaching you to bake?"

"I'm teaching her."

"Oh. That's nice. Did your dad teach you?"

"What do you want to know?" he blurted.

John-Michael regretted the outburst as soon as he'd made it. The tension inside him was almost unbearable. If only he'd had time to prepare. He'd vaguely expected this, the first few weeks after his father's death. But in the last week or so, he'd let the memory of that awful day slide. It was much less painful that way.

"Well, John-Michael, I've read your statement about your father's suicide. And I just had a few additional questions."

He leaned back against the kitchen table, steadying himself with both hands. "Okay."

"You've said that your father had made no indication to you that he was planning to end his life."

"No. He didn't."

"We've checked Mr. Weller's phone records. Seems that your dad called you about four hours before his death. You spoke for around ten minutes."

"That sounds right."

"Could you tell me what you talked about?"

John-Michael faked a shrug. It was hard to believe that she couldn't hear the heavy thudding inside his chest. "He whined at me for being a disappointment to him. Said I'd be sorry one day, that I'd regret leaving home. Same old, same old. What does your dad talk about to you?"

"Really—he was bitter to the end? No attempt to reconcile? No warning about what he planned to do?"

"No. Can I ask why you're asking?"

"It's just that if you were such a disappointment to him, if he was so desperately unhappy as to end his own life, then it seems a little surprising that he'd still make you his heir."

"I'm the only child," John-Michael answered. "Not much he could do about that."

"There are other ways of disposing an estate."

John-Michael felt his voice go up a notch. "And leaving your only son without frickin' anything to live on?"

"I'm not saying it's what I'd do." Detective Winter gave him a sympathetic smile.

"I don't get why you're asking me this. He took an overdose. I already told the police that I don't know where he got the heroin. It's not difficult to find out how to kill yourself."

"The autopsy shows that your father didn't die of the overdose, but rather from asphyxiation."

"Isn't that one of the ways you die from drugs?"

She nodded. "Unfortunately."

"I don't get it then, what's your problem?"

"John-Michael, I've got no problem, I'm just doing my job."

He swallowed, very nervous. "I know, I didn't mean

that. I just don't understand why you're asking these questions. The hospital said he committed suicide. He left a note saying he was going to do it."

"I agree; it all looks very cut-and-dried. But . . ." She broke off, picking up a teaspoonful of the chopped Reese's Nutrageous and dried blueberry mix. "Is this what you're putting inside the pastry? Can I taste?" Before he could reply, she'd popped them into her mouth. "Mmm. That's a great combination."

John-Michael took a moment to breathe deeply. There was no way she hadn't noticed that he was shaken by her questions. He could only hope that it didn't seem unusual for someone who'd just lost their only parent to suicide.

"Thing is, we've got one person saying that until recently she was also a beneficiary of your father's will."

"Dad's ex-girlfriend? I don't know what he promised her, but they broke up months back."

Detective Winter shrugged. Delicately, she wiped her fingers on a kitchen towel. John-Michael found himself looking at her shoes. Chocolate-colored suede ankle boots, very shapely, with an elegant heel.

"And then there's some footage—admittedly grainy—from a security camera of a nearby building. Showing someone crossing the yard behind your father's house, roughly at the same time as your father died."

John-Michael stared at her in horror. "Are—are you saying that my dad was killed?"

"I sincerely hope not, John-Michael. Because from what

we've been able to find, you're the sole beneficiary of his death. You don't have an alibi. If we really began to believe that your father didn't die at his own hand, things might start to look pretty bad for you."

"But . . . but . . . the suicide note!"

"That's what's reassuring me," conceded the detective. "Still, it would have been helpful if you'd been able to tell me something a bit more enlightening about your last conversation with your father."

He said nothing, but felt the sensation of numbness creep ever close to his heart. The detective seemed to be satisfied—for now. He saw her out of the house and onto the path toward the boardwalk. When he went back inside, he was trembling. Candace appeared at the doorway to the kitchen.

"John-Michael! What the hell did she say to you?"

PAOLO
BALCONY, MONDAY, MARCH 30

"Look at you, Muscle Beach! What's next, a tattoo?"

Paolo merely looked amused, continuing with his thirty-five-pound bicep curls. Lucy dragged a chair into position opposite him, dropped herself into it, and peeled the wrapper from an ice-cream sandwich.

He blinked in mild surprise. "You just gonna sit there and watch me while you eat?"

"Mm-hmm, yes I am."

Closing his eyes, Paolo allowed a dreamy smile to spread across his lips. He imagined Lucy taking the opportunity to get a good look at him wearing nothing but board shorts, his arms and shoulders glistening with sweat. When he opened his eyes though, Lucy was looking straight into them.

"You sure think you're fine, Paolo King."

"Not so. I'm working out here because there's more space than in my room. And I like the sun."

"You do have a nice body," she conceded. "Some extra decoration couldn't hurt."

"So I'll get a necklace."

Lucy nibbled the corner of her ice-cream sandwich. "Seriously though, why did you buzz your hair? Although—I have to say, good call on dying it black, again. The bleached look?" She shook her head doubtfully. "It's not you. And what's with all the working out?"

Paolo shrugged and kept pumping the dumbbells. It had been almost a month since his radical "makeover" by Darius. The shock of it had worn off—especially once he'd restored something like his natural hair color. He'd started to adjust.

"I got tired of looking cute."

Lucy burst out laughing. "And now what—you're gonna become one scary mofo?"

With great care, Paolo placed both weights on the decking. He took the chair opposite Lucy's and picked up a small white towel that he used to wipe his upper torso. When he was done, he put both hands on his thighs and gave a tight smile. "You've got the wrong idea about me."

"Really?" She sounded skeptical. Paolo could partly understand why. His first approach had been way too flippant. The country club women had spoiled him for the chase. He was supposed to exert a little energy—use guile and wit; Paolo was beginning to understand that. Lucy was going to be a challenge. The more he accepted that, the more he embraced it.

"What was I supposed to do," he said very softly. "Ignore that you're hot? Pretend I don't find you attractive?"

"We're living together, so yeah, you could try."

He shook his head. "The slow-burn thing? No. I'm not up for that."

"Me either. That's how I know this isn't gonna work. But I'd like to be your friend."

"A female friend. Huh. Could be cool."

"You say that like you have any other kind."

"Okay, you got me."

They shared a smile.

Paolo closed his eyes, enjoying the feel of the sun on his face. "How's the music going? I saw your YouTube stats are wild."

"I wouldn't say 'wild.'"

"You're getting some good comments. How about those guys who want you to audition?"

"Yeah, I saw that. Seems a little, I dunno . . ."

"Like a discount item at the jerkstore?"

"Sounds about right."

"Their music sounds okay, though."

"I didn't listen."

"You should. Check out the videos they posted. There are some good songs. One especially that I think you'll like. 'Sweet Child o' Mine.'"

Lucy stared, incredulous.

"No good?"

"That's not punk, it's Guns N' Roses. Man, you don't know anything about music."

Lucy shook her head, clearly disappointed. Paolo wasn't sure whether in him or in the song. Maybe she was actually more interested than she seemed?

"You want to be in a band, right?"

"Sure I do."

"So, try out for these guys. Maybe after school? They're in Inglewood."

"I should mosey on down there, all Catholic school-girl?" Lucy leaned back in her chair.

"Couldn't hurt."

"If they're a bunch of fools like you, maybe," Lucy teased. "On the other hand maybe they're looking for someone who can sing and play the damn guitar."

Paolo opened one eye, peering at her. "They already know you can do that—they've watched your videos. Which are getting better and better, by the way. They flipped for that Rancid song."

"Yeah," she murmured. "It's my favorite."

"If they want to meet you it's about, you know, the chemistry. Bonding. Look at me; when I wanted to get students at the country club, I went in there all clean-cut, nice hair, pristine tennis whites and sneakers. Looking the part."

"I should show up there like a black Avril Lavigne, that what you're saying?" Lucy gave a sardonic chuckle. "Yeah, right. Says it all, Paolo."

"Quit being so down on this. There's a time for sitting in your room making videos. And then there's a time for getting your ass out there." Paolo leaned forward in his chair. "Play some gigs. Look, every Sunday on the beach, right outside the house. People playing, people watchin' 'em. That could be you. That *should* be you. With a great big crowd around you going, *Yaaaaaay! Lucy! Lucy Long, I love you, I wanna be your boyfriend!*"

Despite herself, Lucy was laughing at Paolo's high-pitched voice and waving arms.

Paolo stood up and stretched out a hand to her. "Well then, let's go."

"Now?"

"Why not? I emailed the guy, said we might drop by this afternoon. The band's rehearsing."

"You did that?"

"Someone had to. Get your guitar. You can finish your ice cream in the car."

Paolo held her gaze just long enough for Lucy to realize that he was serious. Then he headed off to his room to grab a sweater. But he wasn't certain that she'd follow. When he found Lucy on her way down the spiral staircase, he breathed a quick sigh of relief.

They arrived at a community center in Inglewood to find the members of the band in the middle of an impassioned argument. It seemed pretty intense and from what Paolo could tell had something to do with the music. He turned to Lucy, on the verge of making a sour comment.

Yet it was obvious that the tension in the band's dynamic didn't upset her—rather, the opposite. Enthusiasm shone through her usually reserved grin.

"Who's right?" Paolo whispered. "Can't say I know the difference between 'pentatonic' and 'Mixolydian.'"

"They're both right. How cool is it that they care so much?"

With that, she strolled up to the stage. Three guys in their early twenties turned to her. They were far more toned down than they'd appeared in their videos. Paolo noted the appreciation in their eyes as they watched Lucy. Naturally. Who wouldn't want a Beyoncé look-alike for their band?

"You should do both," Lucy said. "Go from G minor pentatonic to Mixolydian over G7." She laid her vintage Fender Telecaster guitar case down on the stage and popped it open.

Then she was playing, fingers dancing over the strings. She finished with a flourish and looked up. "Like that."

A guy with a raggedy mop of sun-streaked fair hair nodded his grudging approval. "That could work."

"I'm Lucy Long, by the way," she said, suddenly shy.

Two of the band members slid off the stage and bumped fists with Lucy.

"Ruben."

"Tommy."

Slowly, the third guy, the blond, joined them in greeting her. Paolo noticed this one seemed far less friendly. Almost wary. "I'm Bailey." He indicated Lucy's guitar. "Nice

Telecaster. It's from the fifties, right? Kind of a bluesy sound for us." He glanced at his colleagues before adding, a touch archly, "We're pop punk. You're aware of that, right?"

Lucy's manner became defensive. "I play it all. Blues, punk, rock."

"In that case we're honored, Lucy Long." There was definite sarcasm in his reply. "Won't you please play something for us?"

Without a word, Lucy plugged her Telecaster into an amplifier and launched straight into a dazzling guitar solo, which after a few minutes turned into shredding. Paolo watched the band members. Two of them, Ruben and Tommy, seemed impressed and were happy to let their appreciation show. Only Bailey remained unmoved.

When Lucy finished, Ruben and Tommy burst into applause and noisy approval.

Tommy was nodding. "Good enough for me!"

Bailey scowled at him. "It's a group decision."

"Ruben votes yea, I vote yea. Hell, Lucy's better than all the others. By a 'Long' way," Tommy chuckled. Paolo noticed Lucy managed to smile at the joke. She must be trying hard; Paolo would never get away with anything that lame.

"I write songs, too," Lucy said.

"Not necessary," Bailey said quickly. "Tommy and Ruben write the songs."

She shrugged, but was obviously disappointed. "Okay."

"I'd be happy for you to pitch in," Ruben added a little anxiously.

There was an uncomfortable silence. Ruben pulled two drumsticks from his back pocket. "Shall we play something together? Let's try that Rancid song from the video. Lucy, you can play lead."

It was obvious, watching them, that Bailey was a gifted front man. He had strut and swagger, as well as a pleasingly rambunctious tenor voice. Tommy and Lucy meshed nicely on the guitar sounds. Ruben sounded like a pretty good drummer, too, to Paolo's fairly inexpert ear. Paolo had the vague impression that he, not Bailey, was the dominant member of the band. Musically, these guys seemed to know what they were doing.

When they were done, Ruben glanced at Tommy, who gave him a single nod. Then he turned to Lucy. "If you'd like to join, that'd be awesome."

Lucy took one look at Bailey. "Bailey. That good with you?"

He glared at Ruben. "Like the man said. Band is a democracy."

"Still—better for me if you all agree, no?"

Bailey paused. "Truth is, you're okay."

"Thanks."

"It's just that we're kind of an all-male band."

From behind his drum kit, Ruben spoke up. "That's because he's talking garbage. We *were* an all-male band.

Now we can have a girl, too."

"The labels aren't gonna like that," Bailey protested. "Think Blink-182 woulda been so big if they had a girl on lead guitar?"

"Don't give two shits about Blink, bro. This girl is in."

Lucy played three loud chords on her guitar. They were still ringing around the hall as she announced, "Well, okay. I'll let you guys know."

MAYA

Maya met Lucy at the bus stop after school the next day. Lucy acknowledged Maya with a toss of her head. "No ride home today? What happened to Cadillac Lady?"

"You mean my auntie?" Maya shrugged. "Now that I don't live with her, Venice is kind of out of her way. She tried to keep it up but . . . you know how it is."

"Sucks to be rejected, doesn't it?" Lucy said with a sly grin. "Candace, Grace, Paolo, and John-Michael—they're all in the house because they wanted to leave home. But you and me? We were forced."

"I wasn't exactly forced."

"You know what I'm saying. There were good reasons for them. Us? Nuh-uh. I was happy at home. Didn't want to end up at a preppy-assed Catholic school."

Maya was silent. It had been hurtful, being asked to leave home. But she'd been surprised and rather delighted with the outcome. Our Lady was the best school she'd ever attended. And living with other teenagers on Venice Beach was like being suddenly handed a free pass to Disneyland. You'd think it would get boring, that you'd get used to it, but so far, no sign.

"Maybe. Who knows?" Maya eventually said.

Lucy seemed intrigued by her answer. As they boarded the bus, she asked her to elaborate.

"Look at Paolo, for example," Maya said. "He told us he's this up-and-coming tennis star, okay? Then one day he goes out, loses to some random guy on the beach. Next thing we know he's cut his hair short and turned into a bleach-blond. Next day he's colored it black, then he buys a set of weights and a punching bag and starts working out."

"Yeah, so?"

"You don't call that strange?"

Lucy pulled a face. "Dude's got issues with me, Maya, so what do I know? Paolo's been behaving different, yeah, maybe."

Maya began slowly to smile. "You think he's into you?"

"Maybe, maybe not. He did me a big favor yesterday, anyhow."

"Oh yeah?"

"He drove me to an audition."

"For a band?"

"Lead guitar in a band."

"Oh, cool! Did you get it?"

"Ehhh. Maybe. Yeah, I think so."

"Whoa, Lucy, that's amazing!"

Maya detected the tiniest hint of a bashful smile. It was gone after just a second, replaced by Lucy's more usual cool blast of don't-cares. "We'll see. Coupla those dudes were pretty jerkish."

"It's great that Paolo gave you a ride."

"More'n that, it was his idea. Those guys had been leaving comments on my YouTube and yeah, Paolo decided I should meet them."

"So—anything happen between you and Paolo?"

"Me and Paolo?" Lucy shook her head. "No way."

"You're not even a little attracted to him?"

"Sometimes I think, maybe, just a little."

"And?"

"And, nothing. He's too vanilla for me."

Maya raised an eyebrow. "Don't be so sure. Sudden changes in behavior can mean he has something to hide. Could be something interesting. People can surprise you."

Lucy gave her a curious look. A few thoughtful nods. "Seems you've given this some consideration."

Maya felt herself blush. She'd almost slipped before, when Lucy had mentioned Cadillac Lady. And now she'd drawn attention to the fact that she was quietly observing and pondering the lives of the other housemates. Inside the house or out of it, Maya had to be more careful.

"You're probably right," she reflected, trying to sound nonchalant. "Love makes people do strange things. You weren't into him when he had the floppy, dreamboat hair. Maybe now he's testing out the tough-guy look."

"I swear, that boy could tattoo half his body and double the size of his biceps, and I'm still not falling for him. Wanting someone—that's instant. It happens in the first few minutes or not at all."

Lucy seemed totally confident. But Maya wasn't convinced.

The bus dropped them off on the boardwalk near their house. Maya spotted Lucy's friends Mikey and Luisito on the corner near Andy's Fish Tacos. They were both pointing triumphantly at Mikey's new hairstyle—blue with a razor cut at the back. Maya left Lucy to her friends and headed inside.

Maya went straight to the kitchen. John-Michael was there, alone, fixing himself a turkey club sandwich, slicing pickles with a paring knife. It took him a few seconds to notice that Maya was standing less than five feet away. When he did, John-Michael barely muttered a greeting. He had an air of urgency about him. He hastily cut the sandwich in two, wrapped one piece in aluminum foil and stuffed it in his backpack while taking a bite out of the other. He managed a quick nod to Maya before he was out of the kitchen, and then the front door of the house.

Maya surveyed the mess he'd made. She decided to clean it up. John-Michael was usually pretty careful about kitchen hygiene. She guessed he'd come straight from school, hungry, and was in a hurry to get out of the house. As she picked up the packets of sliced roast turkey and bacon, Maya reflected on how unusual that was. From what she'd observed, John-Michael didn't really enjoy going out. Of all of the housemates, he was the biggest homebody. He was often the first one home after school and rarely went out in the evenings.

And yet, he had the best car. Paolo and Candace had cars mainly so that they could get to work. But John-Michael didn't have a job. He didn't even drive his car to school. An amazing car like that Mercedes-Benz. What a waste! If Maya had a car like that, she'd drive into the hills, or along the Pacific Coast Highway, maybe as far as San Francisco.

Sometimes being fifteen was a huge pain. Sixteen couldn't come fast enough.

She was just about done cleaning up when Candace got home, dumped her school bag on the kitchen table, opened the fridge, and poured a glass of filtered water.

"Man, it's starting to get hot out there! I saw John-Michael leaving. Seemed like he was in a hurry."

Maya nodded. "He was acting kinda weird, too."

"Like how?"

"Like pissed off."

Candace raised an eyebrow but said nothing. She took a large cake tin from a shelf and opened it. Inside were neat rows of tightly rolled sweet buns with a pale white glaze. She offered one to Maya and then took one herself. Each girl bit into the roll. Maya sighed. "Omigod. It's like a bite of heaven."

"I know, right? Incredible. John-Michael made them."

They were silent for a while, chewing the pastries.

"I'm gonna get some work done on my app," Maya announced. She took out her laptop, placed it on the kitchen table, and sat down. Within a few minutes she was lost in a screen of green, blue, and red code.

Then Candace said something that totally snapped Maya out of her code-building reverie.

"Did you hear about the detective who was here the other day?"

Maya caught her breath. She swallowed and took a quick breath. "Really? What day?"

"I think you were out with your aunt."

"Sunday? She made me go to Mass with her. This happened *Sunday*? Man, no one tells me anything."

"What a brat! I'm telling you now, aren't I?"

"It was the evening, right?" Maya asked.

"Yeah. This lady cop wanted to talk to John-Michael about his father's death."

Maya felt herself begin to relax. "Huh! That's odd."

"I know. He didn't seem very happy when she left," Candace said. "Didn't John-Michael tell us that his dad killed himself?"

Both girls shared a puzzled frown. "Poor John-Michael," Maya said. "He's had such a lousy time lately."

Candace agreed. "That's true. But do you ever . . . ?" She paused. "Do you ever get the idea that he hasn't told us the whole story yet?"

JOHN-MICHAEL
CARLSBAD, SUNDAY, APRIL 5

Returning to Carlsbad was easier than he'd expected. In his mind, John-Michael had made the trip more than once. The drive south on the 5. Zooming through neighborhoods where he'd tried to find a way to exist, alone, homeless and stone-cold broke.

At first, he'd stayed with friends. It was too painful to admit he'd been thrown out, so he'd made excuses. His dad was away on business and refused to leave him alone in the house. The house was being bug-bombed. None of his options were good for more than a few days. He had left every house cheerfully, head held high, thanking his hosts, all the while certain that the next few nights would be a terror compared to the comfort he was leaving behind.

There'd been days when he was too tired and hungry to go to school. He'd gravitated to the beach at first, for the soft bed of sand it promised. Not all beaches were swept at night. One night he'd woken to find a couple of methed-up bikers ripping away his sleeping bag and then going for his jeans. They'd been too wasted to chase him for more than a hundred yards, but the experience had been terrifying enough.

After that, John-Michael had avoided beaches.

At least back in the urban sprawl food was plentiful. There'd be people with whom to trade favors, such as watching your back. And under the freeway bridges you could always find a dry, warm, if noisy place to sleep.

Free from the geographical constraints of being in school, he'd started moving around Southern California. He'd become opportunistic. Life was more enjoyable that way. Eventually, John-Michael had made friends with Felipe, a twenty-four-year-old Guatemalan guy, a hustler. He was a heroin addict who had lived on the streets for three years. Rail thin, tattooed, and scarred from a knife attack, Felipe had presented such an enigmatic aura—vulnerability wrapped inside a knowing, cynical air. John-Michael had fallen in love almost instantly.

Felipe had noticed and taken pity on him. "You don't love me," he had told John-Michael. "You want to *be* me. I'm too old for you, *hermanito*. These eyes," he'd said, touching a finger to his temple, "what they've seen, what this brain has thought . . . are too much for one so young. God has placed you here, *'mano*, to learn from Felipe. And a good teacher doesn't take advantage of his students. No, baby, I'm gonna take *care* of you."

Felipe had sheltered John-Michael for three weeks in the luxury Santa Monica beach apartment he'd been sharing with a rich black guy. His new "boyfriend" also had a wife and a kid up in Portland, so had been anxious to avoid scandal. Felipe had been very clever about that—never threatening, always charming and yet provocative. The truth was, John-Michael had learned from Felipe. How to hustle, who to hustle. How to stay safe.

But John-Michael wasn't like Felipe. He'd realized that more than anything what separated them was the heroin.

John-Michael's luxury stay had ended when the boy-friend had offered to pay for Felipe's rehab. As soon as Felipe had packed up and said his good-byes, the boyfriend kicked John-Michael out. "Hey, now, Felipe's little brother," he'd said. "No room and board for you here any longer. Time to get back to Mom and Dad."

It wasn't that John-Michael couldn't go back. A grovel-ing apology, a promise to keep all traces of what his father referred to as his "fag lifestyle" out of the house. He'd thought about doing it, too. Judged from the outside, it probably looked a lot easier than some of the things John-Michael had done to survive. Yet he couldn't do it; not for a man who despised something so fundamental to his nature. Even the thought of it grated.

Sometimes John-Michael reflected that his one mistake in leaving home was that he hadn't done it soon enough.

The day his father had called to ask him to come back had come entirely out of the blue. The one expense that his father had continued to pay was his cell phone. John-Michael hadn't understood this, had asked for the cash instead. But that last day, his father had told him why.

"I've never given up hope that you'd come home." There'd been a long, considered pause. "Some things are only for family."

He hadn't told John-Michael the whole story on the phone. Just enough to ensure that he hopped on a bus and made his way back to Carlsbad. A three-hour trip, all told.

That time, he'd taken three buses to get back to his dad's house—with one crucial stop-off on the way. If anyone ever found out about that five-minute meeting, if anyone ever identified the guy he'd met with, John-Michael's life could go nuclear pretty much overnight.

He'd spent just under an hour with his father, talking, arguing, crying. All for nothing. Things would never be right between them. He should have known that the minute he answered the call.

Today, the wind was in his hair as the Benz rode the freeway back to Carlsbad. John-Michael forced himself to focus on the positives. Dad's car, a monthly allowance, cash from the sale of the house, too, eventually. Even if his dad's will had permitted it, John-Michael didn't want to live there after what had happened. A shared room in Venice Beach beat living in Carlsbad any day. Take all that into account and life sure was better without the old coot.

Quite the contrast to when his mother had passed away.

John-Michael reached his father's place around four in the afternoon. A car was parked outside the house, but there was no sign of anyone inside. He listened at the door, then let himself in, went to his old bedroom to fetch his one suit. He took a suit bag from his dad's room and left the suit inside, hanging on a coat peg near the front door.

Then he did what he'd really come to do.

His father's bedroom wasn't a place where he'd spent much time. He didn't have any idea where to look. Yet what he was looking for couldn't be in the drawers or cupboards. If it were, the cops would have found it.

He pushed aside the nightstands and began to shift the bed. Then he stopped. Was there someone at the door? For several seconds John-Michael stood still, waiting. He went to the front door and stood behind it, listening. Nothing. He moved to a window at the front of the house and checked outside. There was no one there. The car was still parked, but empty. After a final quick check at the periphery of each window he returned to the bedroom.

This time he moved the bed out by a few feet. He stood in the gap between the wall and the bed. His eyes searched the wall carefully for any sign of disruption. Nothing. He looked underfoot. The hard oak floorboards fitted together neatly, no gaps. But at the edge of one board he could see that the varnish was chipped. A neat rectangular block about half an inch long was missing, as if it had been snapped off by a tool. John-Michael opened his father's nightstand, searching for something that he knew very well would still be there.

His father's Ranger Swiss Army Knife. He picked it up almost reverently. The last time he'd been allowed to touch it, John-Michael had been nine years old.

He opened several tools, in the end going with the sturdiest blade. He jammed it in the sliver between two boards, one of them the chipped one. Then he slid the blade down, working the board free. After a second or two, he felt the board buckle. The blade had found a large dent, a section where the board was narrower. He levered the board up and felt it lift out. John-Michael looked at the board. It had been carefully filed down in one section.

He leaned back to shift his shadow away from the hole in the floor. There was a cardboard file box underneath. He grabbed the edge of the box and jimmied it out through the narrow gap. He pressed the side studs to release the catch. Inside was a thick wad of papers and images of medical scans.

The evidence was all here.

Then he heard a car door slam shut. His heart rate shot up. For a couple of seconds he couldn't think straight. He almost dropped the box, but managed to catch it before it slid down his knees. He shut the box and replaced it, hurriedly, under the floor. He pushed the floorboard back into position.

Then a sound that almost froze his blood: the front door was being opened. With the side of his shoe, he hurriedly brushed dust from another part of the floor to cover the boards he'd disturbed.

He heard casual footsteps as someone strolled around the front of the house, opening doors.

John-Michael slid back out to the edge of the bed and

pushed it as painstakingly slowly as he could, not daring to make more than the tiniest noise.

When he was done, he realized that he'd been holding his breath. His heart was pumping hard. The footsteps were approaching his father's bedroom. He was about to replace the Swiss Army Knife. Then he had a change of heart.

The door opened. John-Michael looked up in shock as an Asian American man in jeans and a black T-shirt approached him. He brandished the knife, flailing. "Get away from me, man, I got nothing worth stealing."

The newcomer just folded his arms and looked askance. "Slow down, pal. I'm a police detective. Put the knife down."

For a second John-Michael was confused. And then fear swept through him. If he didn't get that box, things were going to get pretty damn horrible for him. His only chance now was to play dumb. He gave the cop a sullen stare. "This is *my house* now, dude."

"Put it down or I'll arrest you."

John-Michael dropped the knife. Petulantly, he said, "At least you could show me some ID before you fleece me."

The detective picked the knife up without taking his eyes off John-Michael. He checked the knife, folded it up. Then he took a badge from his back pocket and showed it to John-Michael. "Detective Shawn Leung. Where'd you get the knife?"

"My dad's nightstand."

"You came all the way back from LA for a lousy pocketknife?"

"I came for my suit. I got a job interview coming up." As he said the words, John-Michael was praying that it wouldn't occur to the cop to cross-check.

"Where's the suit?"

John-Michael walked him to where he'd left the suit in its carrier. The detective unzipped the suit carrier and peered inside. He stared hard at John-Michael. "Next time you want to go inside, call the station. We'll send someone to escort you."

"Why?"

"Didn't anyone tell you? This is a murder scene." The cop handed back the Swiss Army Knife. "Don't go waving that at folks now."

John-Michael took the knife, picked up his suit, and left, aware of the detective watching him all the while. He got back into his car. He drove four blocks away to a Pollo Loco, ate some chicken taquitos, and drank a Diet Coke. He put up the top of the car and prepared to let the hours pass until dark. The box of medical records under his dad's floorboards would have to wait.

GRACE
CULVER STUDIOS, TUESDAY, APRIL 7

"Go ahead, take something from the breakfast buffet. Just don't make me look like someone with a bunch of freeloading friends."

Candace tried to smile. She looked somewhat less confident than when she'd first promised she could get her stepsister and maybe a couple of housemates into the TV studios as visitors.

Grace watched Candace take a piece of cantaloupe and another of pineapple. "Aww," she said, pouting. "Stuff like this is wasted on you, isn't it?"

Paolo grabbed a plate. Eagerly, he loaded it with slices of Swiss cheese, baloney, and crispy bacon. "You gotta love Hollywood." He turned to Lucy, who was picking out a muffin from a tray with six different types. "So, your rock band buddies. You're going to say yes eventually?"

Lucy took a nibble of her poppy seed muffin. "To the band? Eh. That Bailey guy seems like kind of a jackass."

Paolo sighed. "Lucy, the guy wants to be a rock star. Of course he's a jackass."

Lucy narrowed her eyes to slits. "Hmmm."

Grace poured a glass of milk to go with her powdered donut. She felt uncomfortable around Paolo when he was sharing cozy little moments like this with Lucy. It could have been worse, she reflected; she might have wound up sharing a bedroom with Lucy. At least she had the possibility of getting away.

Jealousy was something she hadn't expected or welcomed. It had simply appeared in her life one day like a stray dog. Difficult to avoid, insistently reminding her that things were not quite right in the world.

She stole a surreptitious glance at Paolo. If he'd been gorgeous with the boyish, thick mop of hair, he was even more arresting now. She'd even caught the director of Candace's TV show eyeing him with interest.

At first, Grace had been shocked by the bleached-white scrub Paolo had presented one evening, a month ago. It had made him look like one of Lucy's crazy friends from the beach; a bunch of junkies from what Grace could tell. But Paolo had changed his mind almost instantly and gone back to a darker look. Now he looked like a soldier. Or a cop, or an investment banker—something serious. As cute as he'd been, that haircut, together with his toned, slightly muscular body, made him look like a man. Every time Grace saw him, she felt herself fall a tiny bit more under his spell.

Meanwhile, Paolo remained oblivious. All he could see, all he'd seen since the day she moved into the house, was Lucy.

The assistant director was calling actors to take first positions for the scene they were about to record. With a cheery wave, Candace left them at the buffet and headed off with her actor colleagues. Every one of them was skinny and pretty, but Candace aside, none of them quite had the head-turning presence of either Paolo or Lucy.

Maybe Candace had invited the housemates precisely to show her actor buddies just how cool her friends were?

The director announced, "Action!"

For a moment they all watched the actors. It was a scene set in a dingy back room where the characters were engaged in a little "underground" poker. The characters were sitting around a table. They picked up cards and threw down chips. One of the older females was smoking a cigar. Grace guessed that her character was meant to be "edgy" or even bad. After a few minutes, the director called cut. Then he began asking each actor to repeat their line, this time in a close-up.

Ten minutes in and Grace was bored. Her thoughts turned back to Lucy. With that girl's history, her background, talent, and looks, there was simply *no way* to compete with her. No boy was worth that. The attraction was mostly physical, anyway. The kind of idiotic thing you read about in romance novels. She wasn't going to let herself behave like a moron to get his attention. She wasn't going to do a thing. Whatever she felt for Paolo would eventually fade.

If Grace had let Maya in on her secret, it was because she'd had no alternative. How else was she going to explain going through Lucy's things? Now Maya probably thought she was a crazy, jealous psycho. Well, that couldn't be helped. At least Grace hadn't needed to invent anything about her feelings for Paolo.

She watched the two of them drift back toward the buffet table.

"I didn't think it would be so boring," Paolo said. "They're just saying the same thing over and over in slightly different ways!"

"It's called 'direction,'" Lucy said with a smile.

After a few seconds, Paolo and Lucy went back to talking about the band she'd been invited to join. She was vacillating, but, of course, she'd end up accepting. There was no point in Grace sticking around to be invisible yet again. She poured potato chips into a plastic bowl, picked up her glass of milk, and left them to it.

Eventually the scene finished. The director called Candace to him. He spent a few seconds talking. Grace watched the expression on Candace's face go from polite to disbelieving. Wide-eyed, she nodded vigorously at whatever the director was telling her. After he'd moved on, she practically skipped over to where Grace was sitting in the catering area. She snatched a large potato chip out of Grace's fingers and took a solid, crunching bite.

"All right, sis, spill," Grace said firmly.

Candace grinned with delight. "I'm actually getting lines in the next episode."

"I thought you already had a line."

"That was in the pilot. *So long, sucker.* As I snapped the neck of one of the bad guys."

"Ooh. Pithy."

"It would be so amazing if they developed Gina into a bigger character."

Grace gave a sage nod. "It could only improve the story."

"I'm only thinking about what's best for the show."

"You're all about the selfless concern."

Candace gave her stepsister an affectionate kick. She glanced across the studio toward a set that wasn't being used just then—the disheveled bedroom that was shared by Gina and another character on *Downtowners*. Lucy and Paolo were sitting on the edge of the bed, engaged in what seemed to be an intense conversation. "Hey, what's going on with Paolo and Lucy? They seem awful snug over there."

"He's trying to get into her pants," replied Grace. "And she's reviewing her options. Just a wild guess."

"Cynic."

"Independent observer."

"You don't think he's, like, actually into her?" Candace asked.

Grace considered. "I think he's under the influence of

his hormones, shall we say. If Lucy really decides she's not into him, he'll be after you next. Or Maya."

"Or you."

"No," Grace said with vehemence. "Not me."

"Yes," Candace said, beaming. "Definitely you. You're gorgeous. Do you realize I've never seen anyone with eyes like yours? People comment, you know."

"They do not." Grace felt her cheeks heat up.

"Do too. *Your sister has the bluest eyes I've ever seen. Ooh, they sparkle like crystals. Your sister's eyes! They're like blue icicles.*"

"Liar."

"Self-absorbed geek. Stop feeling sorry for yourself," Candace said. "And I think you're being hard on Paolo, too."

"What do you mean?" Despite herself, Grace found she was staring hopefully at Candace.

"He's not seeing anyone right now. As far as I know, he's never had a girlfriend. Not a steady one."

Grace said, "All the better to stay available for his tennis students."

"Or maybe he's looking for the right girl."

"If that's true, then why go for Lucy?"

Candace frowned. "Are you kidding? She's amazing."

"Yeah, but *he's* not exactly her type. Come on, he's practically preppy."

"Yet ironically, Lucy is the one at a prep school." Candace smiled.

"Not by choice. And you know what I mean."

"Opposites attract," suggested Candace.

"But they don't last."

Grace could feel herself growing warmer. Candace was starting to regard her with amused suspicion. "You like him," she concluded after a few seconds.

Grace couldn't reply.

"Yep," Candace said blithely. "You like Paolo. I shoulda seen it coming. What does it for you? He's so *blah*."

Grace was torn between defending Paolo's blah-ness and denying the accusation. She hesitated to go down the route of denial. She knew herself well enough to know she probably wouldn't be convincing enough. Not to Candace. Then there was the matter of having someone to confide in. Grace preferred to keep thoughts as private as these to herself, but with Paolo sharing space with them, it was getting harder and harder not to feel her resolve crumble and crack.

She could see the time coming when she'd need someone to understand her tears. It filled her with a kind of horror to picture herself on her bed, surrounded by Maya, Candace, and John-Michael, weeping like a pathetic whiny tween because some lame-ass guy wasn't giving her any attention.

Distraction. She opted for distraction.

"He said he might join Amnesty International at school," she said, hopeful.

"Project Death Row?" Candace snorted. "Yeah. That's gonna happen."

"Why not?"

"Paolo? Sure. A real man of letters, that one." Her sarcasm was thick.

"He's not just a jock. He wants to be a human rights lawyer, remember?"

"And he told you this when?"

"At the party," Grace said, indignant. "You were there, for chrissake."

"When we were *smoking*? You think that was for real?"

"*In weed-o veritas.* Don't you think?"

"Huh?"

Grace glanced sideways at Candace. "Are you saying it wasn't?"

"We were getting high. He was doing his Mr. Deep-and-Mellow schtick. How did you not see that?"

"I think he meant it. We talked about it more after you left."

"Whatever floats your boat."

Candace began to slide off the folding chair.

"Candace." Grace grabbed her arm before she could walk away. "Don't tell anyone."

"About you liking Paolo?" Candace said, raising her voice a little. "Fine."

"I mean it."

"Don't worry, sis. It's in the vault."

As Candace returned to the set for the next scene, Grace wondered if she could trust her own stepsister. She glanced at her smartphone. An email had just arrived.

He called. Says he needs to see you soon. He sounded
awful lonesome.

San Quentin State Prison. This weekend. She needed to
get up there. It had to be possible. But how?

PAOLO
VENICE BEACH, SATURDAY, APRIL 11

"Hey, Paolo. You're certainly braver than me, swimming this early."

Grace was outside the house by the spiral staircase, waiting for a taxi, when Paolo got back from a bracing early-morning swim in the ocean. Normally he didn't swim until June, when the sun was hot enough to make the water bearable without a wet suit. But he was tired of waiting. Plus, he needed the exercise, and the memory of Darius had made him wary of the public tennis court farther along the beach.

He patted his head with the towel. "It's cold. But there's nothing like it. Although you need to watch out for the surfers."

Paolo watched her for a moment. Grace seemed anxious, even agitated. He suggested that she call another taxi.

"They're all busy."

"Where do you wanna go at this hour?" he asked.

"Just to the bus terminal."

"And then where?"

Grace hesitated slightly. "To San Quentin."

Paolo stared. Then he remembered—Grace wrote to death row prisoners. "The prison in San Francisco? That's . . . that's like a zillion miles away!"

"I can't afford to fly."

"You staying overnight?"

"My cousin Angela usually comes along with me to these visits, on account of me being under eighteen. She lives just outside of San Francisco. I usually stay with her."

Grace wasn't giving much away about the reason for her sudden visit, but Paolo assumed that she was going to say good-bye to one of her prison pen pals. "That's a tough trip," he admitted, with grudging respect. He thought about his schedule over the weekend. It wouldn't be hard to move things around. He felt instinctively that someone shouldn't have to do such a noble thing without support from one of the housemates. It would be good for him to get out of town for a while. It might even make Paolo feel good to help Grace—less like the kind of a loser who helped crooks take luxury cars off idiot rich kids.

"I'll drive you."

Grace looked gratifyingly amazed. She stared for a second and then laughed. "Are you serious?"

"Yeah. We'll make a weekend of it," he said.

"Sure, of course, that would be incredible! And I'll pay for the gas, I absolutely insist."

"We could swing by San Francisco," Paolo suggested. "I haven't been in years."

Grace nodded, utterly delighted. After a pause, she leaned in for a tentative hug. Paolo was a little surprised at her awkwardness. Girls were usually all too ready to hug him. Grace didn't strike him as someone who had issues around personal space, either. Somewhere in the recesses of his mind, the tiniest hint of suspicion flared into life. But within a second Paolo had dismissed it.

They both went inside. Grace hung out in the kitchen while Paolo dressed and packed an overnight bag. John-Michael was loafing on the couch, staring at the TV, and eating Reese's Puffs straight from the box. When he heard about their plan he sat up.

"Why don't you let me drive you both? I've got the Benz. It's a seriously cool ride up the PCH. And you know what—I've never been to San Francisco."

Half an hour later, Paolo found himself in the passenger seat of a convertible, driving up the Pacific Coast Highway with the sun beating down. Grace sunned herself on the backseat while Paolo glanced across at John-Michael and remembered his fateful ride with Darius.

He'd tried not to think about it, to dismiss the memory, to simply move past it, but the sense of powerlessness, of being manipulated, wouldn't quite go away. In retrospect he'd folded so easily.

Maybe the only thing to do was to put the whole experience in a box marked *history*. Everything he wanted to do lay in his future, after all. The insistent little digs at his conscience were easier to dismiss when he stopped looking back, only forward.

The housemates decided to take the scenic route along the coast, up the 1. With the sun shining, they stopped briefly, at an In-N-Out just outside the city. John-Michael and Paolo shared the driving—an unexpected bonus.

But as they approached San Quentin just after two in the afternoon, the gravity of the situation seemed to hit Grace. She became even quieter than before. In the visitor parking lot, Paolo turned to her.

"You need us to come in with you?"

Grace smiled a quick, artificial smile. "No. My cousin just texted me—she's already in the waiting room. Death row, guys. It's . . . it's really not very pleasant."

John-Michael said nothing. He'd made no bones about his reasons for wanting to come along—he wanted the excuse to visit San Francisco. But Paolo hesitated. Having come all this way, he felt that he ought to escort Grace into the prison. All that *talk* about how he wanted to be a human rights lawyer. If he backed down, he'd look like a wuss. But right now, faced with the grim reality of a lookout tower manned with snipers and the somber reception buildings beyond the high walls and razor wire, Paolo felt a sudden revulsion. He tried not to think about Darius and what they'd done together.

Grace began to climb out of the car. Paolo leapt out of the driver's seat and opened his door for her. Impulsively, he said, "I'm coming in with you."

John-Michael looked at him with a mixture of surprise and disappointment. He slid over to the driver's seat and plugged in his earbuds. "I'll watch the car."

"It's a high-security prison, man. You think anyone's gonna risk stealing a car from here?"

John-Michael didn't budge. "Watch out in there."

As Grace signed in, Paolo hung back, watching. The waiting area was pretty full, a mixture of regret-laden, middle-aged women and a few tough-looking adult men; shaved and even tattooed heads seemed to be the norm. For the first time since the encounter with the Spanish tennis pro when he and Darius hustled Jimmy, Paolo was glad of his austere new haircut.

Paolo was careful not to look anyone in the eye. The atmosphere was cold and sterile. He'd imagined it would be like a hospital, but it was much worse. An undercurrent of despair ran through the place. He could barely even look at the few prison guards who wandered in and out. Paolo sank into a molded plastic chair, rifled through the magazines, and picked out *Entertainment Weekly*.

Grace waved at him from the security gate. She seemed so young and fragile compared to almost every other visitor. Then she was gone.

Paolo waited. When he was done with *Entertainment Weekly* he flicked through a *Smithsonian*, and even took a shot at *Harvard Law Review*. He didn't want to be alone with his thoughts for even a minute so he concentrated hard on every article. Finally, when he thought he'd really just about had enough and was thinking of returning to the car, Grace emerged. She looked tearful and drained. At her side was a woman in her late twenties, pale and blond, with a visible family resemblance to Grace but not nearly as pretty.

Paolo stood up. He took her into his arms without a word. This time she didn't hesitate. For a few minutes he just hugged her. Grace's cousin Angela stood by, watching discreetly, a weak smile on her face.

Paolo murmured into Grace's hair, "Was it rough?"

She nodded, brushing away a tear. "I don't like to let him see me cry. Guess I store it up for after."

Grace's cousin stepped forward. "Hi, I'm Angela." Paolo shook the hand she offered and gave a polite smile as the cousin said her good-byes to Grace and left the prison grounds as quickly as possible.

Paolo watched Angela leave, then turned to Grace. He didn't know quite how to phrase his next question. He'd avoided asking it during the drive but now it seemed only fair to give her an opportunity to talk.

"Was that the last time?" Paolo asked. "You know . . . that you'll see him?"

Grace stared in confusion for a moment. Then she shook her head, clearly upset. "No, *no*. What gave you that idea? No! He's going through an appeal."

"Hey, that's good, that's great. It must be real important to him to have you show support like this. Does he know how far you came to see him?"

She nodded, glancing at the front doors. "Of course he knows." But she didn't seem eager to talk about her pen pal. "Can we go? I don't like to stay any longer than I absolutely have to."

"Sure, I totally understand."

Back in the car, John-Michael had put up the top and was nodding his head along to some music on his phone. He squinted at them through the open windows.

"Hey, buddy," Paolo called. "We're ready to leave."

John-Michael acknowledged them with a couple of nods. "Ready to see San Francisco by night? Get some chocolate at Ghirardelli, hang out on Fisherman's Wharf?"

"Dude, shouldn't you be hitting the Haight?"

"Oh sure, walking homosexual cliché that I am, you mean?"

"I'd be happy to go to the Haight," Paolo said. "Except I'd get more dates than you."

John-Michael laughed, shaking his head. "No way, King. Although you do give off an I'm-So-Not-Gay vibe that's so powerful, it's practically gay."

Paolo laughed, too, a bit harder than was sincere. Grace was finally smiling a little. He was glad they'd been able to distract her a bit, although she seemed less relieved and more wistful than he'd have expected. If he'd been visiting someone on death row, he guessed he'd be happy to get the "good deed" over with. But obviously, after a while of writing letters, you came to care—maybe too much.

Paolo wondered if it was like that for the prisoners'

lawyers. Could he ever bring himself to defend someone on death row? It had to take a huge amount of courage and resilience. Their visit had made this fact painfully clear.

Paolo held open the car door so Grace could slide in. "I think what you're doing is seriously, seriously cool, Grace."

"It's . . . it's not all that special," she said with a sad smile.

"Yeah. It really is."

John-Michael nodded in fervent agreement.

"I'd kind of like to try it myself," Paolo said. As he said the words, he realized that he sincerely meant them. He wasn't just saying it to impress his friends. Maybe good deeds were missing from his life. And it couldn't hurt to start learning the terrain he might one day choose as his professional field.

"You want to write letters to guys on death row?" Grace asked. She seemed more than a little surprised.

"Maybe I'll start with just one. How do I do it?"

Grace took her seat in the rear of the car. She was still acting a little dazed. "I can get you the details."

"Okay. Let's do it." Paolo nodded firmly. "I'll reach out to some guy in San Quentin. Then we can do the visits together."

Grace hesitated. "You might . . . it might be nicer if you wrote to a woman. Most guys prefer to have women write to them."

"I'll bet."

"It's not necessarily sexual. Just that there's less sense of competitiveness than with another guy. At some point, they might compare their life to yours and get envious."

"Okay, a woman then."

"There aren't many women on death row. But there are plenty of lonely lifers who need people to write to them."

Paolo felt the situation slipping from him somewhat. If Grace could handle the emotional roller coaster of a death row pen pal, then he wanted the same challenge.

"We'll see," he said. "Maybe I'll hang in there for one of those tough ladies on death row."

LUCY

I need a favor. Can u call me?

Lucy pressed the button to return John-Michael's text with a call. The bus was pulling up to her stop in Venice. She gripped the rail as she waited for him to pick up.

"Where are you?" John-Michael's voice sounded urgent, almost aggressive.

"I had detention."

"Oh. Bummer."

"What's up? I'm on the bus . . . be home in a few minutes."

"Stay at the bus stop. I'll come pick you up in the Benz."

"Dude, I'm in my uniform. Let me come home and change first."

"I have an appointment, Lucy. I need to go right now."

"Right now?"

"Yes. I want you to come with. I *need* you to." He paused, then added in an anguished tone, "Please, Luce."

"What kind of appointment?"

"At the health clinic." Another pause. This time she could sense the anxiety in his voice. "I'm getting some blood tests done. Routine stuff, but . . ."

Lucy dropped her resistance. "Got it. I'm here for you, JM."

John-Michael drove by a little later and Lucy hopped into the Benz. They just looked at each other for a second.

Impulsively, she leaned over and hugged him. "Try not to worry. It'll be okay."

He managed to nod. John-Michael looked paler than she'd ever seen him. His eyes had a haunted look.

Lucy leaned back into the thick leather upholstery. She guessed he was going to some kind of STD clinic. Lucy didn't like to ask people if they did drugs or had a risky lifestyle, but someone like JM who'd lived on the streets might be at risk from hepatitis or even HIV. In which case, he'd have to get tested every three months. That had to suck. Even though there was a treatment nowadays, HIV was still a dangerous, troubling condition.

She felt honored that John-Michael had asked her to come with him. They'd had a brief period of intense friendship two years ago at rock camp, but since then, their friendship hadn't gone much beyond the superficial. It was good to know that he still felt some kind of bond.

Lucy missed the thoughtful, intelligent, and surprisingly well-read boy she'd met when they were both fifteen. He was just coming to terms with his sexuality back then and wasn't openly "out." He'd come out to her one night as they wrote a song together. It had been an intense love song, what she'd taken to be a girl's lyric. But when John-Michael had sung it back to her, he hadn't changed the line, had sung of aching love for a boy. Suddenly, all the pieces of a puzzle had fallen into place. And very gently, she'd asked him if he was gay.

Yet the John-Michael she lived with now seemed, in some ways, completely different. He was still occasionally as sweet as he'd once been, especially when he decided to bake for the housemates. But he could be brusque, even belligerent, when he didn't get what he wanted. Grace and Maya, who shared a room with him, often commented that he wasn't as neat and organized as Lucy had led them to expect from her memories of him at camp. His corner of the triple room was as slovenly as Maya's. Most of all, he wasn't nearly as chatty as she remembered. He resisted being drawn into long conversations, especially about their childhoods. Now that Lucy thought about it, John-Michael often made an excuse when the conversation got even remotely personal.

He hadn't been that way at all when she'd first met him. She could remember hearing all about his mother, who'd died when he was nine. About his father, whose girlfriend drove John-Michael crazy. About his school, his friends.

In all the time they'd been living together in Venice, Lucy couldn't remember John-Michael saying any more than the bare facts about his dad. How they had hated each other, how the old guy had killed himself. How John-Michael didn't really know why and didn't really care.

Lucy suspected that despite what John-Michael said, he did care. Something had changed him—she guessed it was his father's death, together with the experience of spending most of last year living on the streets. There had to be all kinds of stories he could tell about that life. Any of that would have been instant fascination for Lucy and the other housemates. Like a kind of dread fantasy. But he never talked about it. Hardly told them anything, in fact.

Maybe it had all been so awful that he simply preferred to move on?

Lucy was glad to see that at least he took his health seriously enough to get a checkup. She was sure he must have put himself at risk at least once while living on the streets. She never asked, but she'd often peered at his arms looking for track marks. Mikey used heroin. She'd been startled by the evidence it left on his body. Mikey had lived in a squat for three months. He'd told her about some pretty messed-up stuff. It seemed likely that John-Michael had lived that life, too, at least for a while.

She decided to test the waters.

"You ever live in a squat, JM?"

He glanced at her quickly, a little suspicious. "Yeah. Why?"

"I was just thinking about my friend Mikey."

"The junkie?" John-Michael said, a tad warily.

"Yeah. Mikey gets checked for HIV every three months.

Says it doesn't even scare him now."

"HIV?" John-Michael was pensive for a few seconds.

"This your first time?"

He shook his head.

"So what, you only get tested after you've been exposed, or annually, or what?"

"Something like that," he answered cagily.

"But you're still nervous?"

John-Michael seemed to take his time before answering. "I think medical tests are always heavy. I mean . . ." For some reason he seemed reluctant to continue.

"Isn't it better just to talk about it, JM?"

He continued hesitantly. "It's just that some of it is, like, irrevocable. You get the diagnosis and that's it. That's your label. For the rest of your life. A horrible destiny. Just as well that I don't plan on having any kids." He spoke with an air of finality, turning the car into the underground parking garage of the clinic.

Lucy was still pondering that statement as they walked into the clinic and rubbed their hands with squirts of sanitizer gel from a dispenser by the front door. Surely only pregnant women could pass HIV on to their baby? She wondered if John-Michael had his facts straight on the subject.

As John-Michael was led into the consulting room, she decided to pick up a leaflet: *HIV and AIDS—The Facts*. After a few minutes, Lucy was no clearer about why John-Michael had said that thing about not having kids. Because it was pretty clear from the leaflet—men rarely passed on the virus "vertically" to their babies. Why was he so worried?

He emerged about ten minutes later, expressionless.

Lucy stood up. "So . . . ?"

"So what?" John-Michael handed his credit card to the secretary.

"So—do you have HIV?"

"Oh. No. I don't."

Lucy began to smile. "Aren't you happy?"

John-Michael gave an impatient sigh. "Sure. I guess." He took the receipt that the secretary offered to him and turned to leave. Lucy followed him. She was beginning to feel pretty baffled.

"It's just that . . . on the way here, it seemed like a big deal. And now you don't seem that happy is all."

John-Michael beeped open the doors of the Benz. "I'm happy, okay?"

"Sure, John-Michael, if you say so."

He didn't respond. Lucy fastened her seat belt. John-Michael seemed even tenser now. There was absolutely no sense of relief. If anything, he looked as though he'd received bad news, not good.

It was odd, and gave Lucy an unsettling vibe she just couldn't shake.

LUCY

It had been three days since John-Michael's blood test and still the good news didn't appear to have sunk in.

Lucy had been on the verge of talking to him about it a couple of times since then, but he'd been even more reclusive than usual. He hadn't even been in the mood to bake. Lucy knew that at least a couple of the housemates were quietly pleased by the recent lack of temptation.

It was beginning to dawn on Lucy that something else had to be wrong with John-Michael. He'd been behaving oddly ever since the police detective had visited. No one knew exactly what the cop had said to him. Candace had been hovering upstairs, but she hadn't been able to hear properly. All she could confirm was that the cop had told him something about the way his father had died. Whatever it was had come as news to John-Michael.

The following weekend, he'd hightailed it out of there in his car. He'd been gone all day Sunday. Since she'd returned from the clinic with John-Michael, Lucy had asked Maya and Grace separately what time he'd come back that day. Grace didn't remember that he'd even been away all day. Maya, on the other hand, had known precisely what time he'd left and what time he'd gotten home—around two in the morning, she reckoned, because he'd woken her. "I'm a light sleeper," she'd confessed.

Weirdly though, when Lucy had commented that Maya seemed pretty clued in to her housemates' movements, Maya had become evasive to the point of retracting what she'd originally said. "Maybe it was two? Maybe it wasn't. I looked at my phone and saw a two, is all I know. It could have been midnight. Eh. I don't really remember, I guess."

Something about that cop's news had jolted John-Michael into action. He rarely left the house apart from going to school and the grocery store. Sometimes he walked along the beach, alone, but there hadn't been one day in which he'd been out of the house all day—until after the cop's visit. Then the mysterious day out. And the following weekend, too, when he'd taken off to San Francisco with Paolo and Grace. Just like that. A recluse one minute and the next, on some kind of road trip kick.

And then, after San Francisco, he'd decided to take the blood test.

It was as though there was a connection between his father's death and his fears about HIV.

Could his father have died of AIDS? He'd hated his father and had been thrown out of his home, forced to live on the streets. Somehow, John-Michael seemed to worry that he'd been infected, too. But how? Lucy's mind began to go somewhere very dark before she pushed the thought away. God, no. It couldn't be anything that horrible, could it? The thought was simultaneously sickening and pitiful. Was it possible that John-Michael could be hiding such an agonizing truth?

Lucy paused on the threshold of John-Michael's room. She needed to choose her words carefully. You didn't just blurt out a question like that. One of the guys she'd befriended on the beach, Luisito, had been sexually abused by an uncle. He'd run away from home rather than admit the truth to his parents. Lucy remembered very clearly how Luisito had resisted talking about it at all. He rarely spoke about it unless he was wasted; even then, he was cautious, wary. But most of all, sad.

Inside the triple room, John-Michael was sitting on his bed, back against the pillows, his knees folded up. Propped up and laying across his lap was a surf-green Fender Stratocaster. He was just staring at it. The sight of John-Michael with his guitar was such a nostalgic hit—it took Lucy's mind clean off the issue with his father.

"Hey, JM. You gonna actually play that thing?"

"I was wondering if I even remembered how."

Lucy leaned against the doorjamb and folded her arms. "If you brought it over when you moved in, I'm guessing you wanna play. And of course you remember how."

John-Michael's fingers tightened around the fret board.

He flexed them a couple of times. Lucy could see his throat tense.

He was open and vulnerable—a rare thing for John-Michael. This could be her cue. Lucy moved over to his bed and perched at the other end. John-Michael seemed suddenly uncomfortable. He couldn't look her in the eye.

The words froze inside Lucy. Abruptly, she changed the strategy and said, "Come to my band practice with me."

"I don't know."

"Come on. Bailey brings his girlfriend all the time."

John-Michael looked away, shaking his head. "Nah."

"You just gonna sit home?"

"Yeah."

Lucy tried to catch his eye. "Seriously, dude, I'd really like it if you came."

"I'm not feeling sociable."

Lucy sighed. "Okay, whatever."

She stood up and turned to leave. It wasn't going to be easy to raise such a delicate matter with him. Maybe she should stay out of his business. Whatever had gone down between John-Michael and his father, it was over now. Maybe dragging this particular pond would do nothing but dredge up the rotting corpse of something best forgotten.

The traffic on the 405 was insane. The taxi was easily going to cost twice what she'd expected to pay. The studio where they rehearsed was in Inglewood, where Ruben lived; a densely residential neighborhood, largely Latino and African American. It was pleasantly relaxing to go somewhere a little more ethnically diverse than Venice Beach, she realized. The main ethnicity around their beach house could be loosely classified as "white weirdo" or "trustafarian."

She wound up being late for band practice. It didn't go down well. Under his breath, Lucy was certain she heard Bailey mutter, "Lazy—"

For an instant she froze. The insult cut surprisingly deep. It made her blood run hot.

"What's that now?"

Bailey smiled craftily and half turned to adjust his microphone stand. Louder, he said, "Hey, Lucy, glad you could make it."

Lucy could see Ruben adjusting his drum kit. Tommy was busy tuning his bass. They showed no sign of having heard Bailey. Lucy gave him one final glare. He'd shown his true colors from the outset. She could already begin to see how this might play out.

Well, okay. Game on. She could handle Bailey. She'd handled worse than him.

The rehearsal went on for two hours. There was very little chance for chitchat. Lucy had agreed to learn four new songs, two of Tommy and Ruben's as well as one by Green Day. Bailey's girlfriend showed up after an hour; a skinny cutie pie of a white girl dressed in a tiny skirt and a tight leather jacket. She immediately sat down and proceeded to ignore the band, transfixed by her cell phone. Studiously, Lucy ignored her back.

At the end of the session the four new songs were beginning to sound competent. Ruben wanted to do at least two more rehearsals before they risked a live set. Tommy urged him to reconsider. "We need to get it tight, man. Only way to get that is *live*."

Ruben flared up. "No. Rep is everything. We don't go out there and do okay. 'Yeah, I heard this new band and whatnot, they're okay you know? They're a'ight.' *Forget* that shit. We go out there and we *own* it. First time. We totally kill. That's how we get people talking. That's how we build a reputation."

Lucy couldn't help smiling. There was a kind of thrill in seeing Ruben's passion. It was always positive. Unlike that scuzzball, Bailey, who was mainly what Candace would call a "whiny brat."

"Is that our name then?" Lucy said.

"What?"

"*Whatnot*?"

Ruben shrugged. "Maybe."

Bailey looked incredulous. "Are you kidding me right now?"

"I like it." Tommy nodded. "Yeah. *Whatnot*."

Lucy glimpsed something close to hatred cross Bailey's face as their eyes briefly met. He had the sense to tear himself away, stomping off to where his girlfriend was still engrossed with her phone.

But Ruben just grinned. "Ignore him."

"I do."

"Front men. What are you gonna do?"

"You know it."

"But you, your Tele was sounding *sweet.*"

She chuckled a little. "Thanks, man. You too."

Ruben opened his mouth as if to say something, and then seemed to think better of it. She watched his eyes move to a point somewhere behind her and realized that someone had just come into the room. She turned to see John-Michael.

"Hey, Lucy. Did I miss it? Jeez. I'm sorry." John-Michael approached and took her elbow, speaking in a whisper. "I only just figured out that you might need a ride. I'm sorry, Luce."

"No problem. I got a taxi."

"Why didn't you tell me you needed a ride?"

"You had to want to be here, dude," Lucy said. "Hey, it's all good."

"This your ride home?" Ruben asked. Lucy watched him look John-Michael up and down. "Hello. I'm Ruben."

John-Michael nodded hey. "Yeah. I'm the ride."

From out of the corner of her eye, Lucy caught Bailey's malevolent stare as he pulled a yellow beanie hat over his streaky-blond hair. His resentment seemed to extend to John-Michael, too. Lucy wondered if Bailey was homophobic as well as sexist and racist or if he just automatically hated all her friends. He might as well go for comprehensive knuckleheadedness.

The traffic on Santa Monica Boulevard hadn't eased up

much on the way home. Lucy and John-Michael drove with the top down, Lucy's Telecaster stowed across the backseat. John-Michael drove with an earpiece in one ear. Partway home, his cell phone rang. He checked the number before he hit the answer button. Lucy was certain she saw his hand shake as he repeatedly jabbed at the touch screen.

His breathing became shallow. He nodded a couple of times, barely audible in his replies. After a minute or two he said very quietly, "Thank you." His right hand dropped the phone into his lap. The traffic had completely stalled. He peered through the windshield as if confused.

"John-Michael."

He didn't answer.

"John-Michael."

Still he was silent. Lucy could sense the pressure building up inside him. It seemed to explode from within, hitting his chest, throat, and then his face. He broke into a loud, single sob.

She stared, didn't know what to do. She didn't dare touch him, not when he was trying to drive the car. Tears began to roll down his cheeks. He dabbed at them absently with the sleeve of his hoodie. After a few long, horribly awkward minutes, he turned to Lucy.

Through his tears a smile of pure astonishment transformed his face.

"I'm okay, Lucy. I'm completely, totally clear!"

ARIANA CALLS LUCY

"What's up, doll? You sound kind of frosty."

Lucy resisted the friendly tone. "We're about to have a big-deal dinner."

Ariana kept her voice calm, friendly, inviting. She had to keep the girl talking. That information *had* to flow. "We?"

"The housemates. John-Michael got some really good news yesterday so he cooked us a fancy dinner. We're all dressed up. . . . I gotta go."

"You, dressed up? Now that's a picture. You wearing a pretty dress?"

"As a matter of fact I am."

"Sugar, take a photo and send it across."

"Maybe later. Sorry, Ariana. I really got to go. John-Michael made Cajun snapper and some fancy French strawberry cream cake for dessert. We got wine and everything."

"Wine! That boy sure sounds like a talented fellow. What's his news?"

Lucy's tone seemed deliberately dismissive. "Oh—a health thing. He had a blood test and, well, he's got the all clear."

Ariana didn't miss a trick—whatever was going on, Lucy was playing it down. "Poor kid. He been hooking up a lil' too much?"

There was an awkward pause. "Ariana, he's calling me. I got to say good-bye."

"I'm glad you're getting along so well with those guys. You don't miss home, your folks?"

"We message our moms all the time. Except John-Michael—his mom's dead."

"Poor kid. He's the one whose dad died?"

"Yeah. Killed himself. . . ." Lucy took a deep breath.

"Ah! That why the police were at your house?"

"I guess."

"Least now you know his secret."

"What secret?"

"Last time we spoke," Ariana said, "you said he had some kind of secret? He must have been thinking about the blood tests."

"Oh. Yeah. Maybe so."

"Well, Lucy, honey, you have a nice night with your buddies. We'll talk another time."

GRACE

"Wow. Really. Just, wow." Lucy held up both hands in help-less amazement as Maya gave a shy little twirl, showing off the first dress anyone in the house had ever seen her wear.

Candace arched an eyebrow. "We're gonna have to look out for you."

Grace watched as Maya turned red. She guessed Maya wasn't used to getting this kind of attention. Grace would have blushed, too. Sometimes people stared at Grace and made comments about her eyes being like blue crystals or some other hyperbole. Comments like that always made Grace feel uncomfortable. Candace was the opposite, she seemed to revel in any attention. Maya's response felt very familiar to Grace.

Only Lucy had actually said anything but Paolo's appre-ciation was pretty blatant. His eyes couldn't get enough of this sexy new version of Maya. Grace and John-Michael restricted themselves to nods of approval.

"So," Candace said with a little toss of her head, "where

have you been hiding those curves?"

"Under my jeans," Maya answered, a little tightly.

"Well, geek girl, you got it going on."

Grace picked up her napkin, a burgundy linen folded into a swan. Next to it, the place setting was immaculate; the wineglasses, out of their boxes for the first time, were filled with red or white wine. The kitchen ceiling lights had been dimmed and three brand-new steel candlesticks were placed along the table, each with a bloodred candle.

"The table looks beautiful, John-Michael!" Grace said. "Did you really do all of this yourself?"

He tried to brush off the compliment. "I wanted everything to be just right."

"It's beautiful. And everyone is dressed so nice."

"Yeah, yeah, we're all fabulous, darling," Candace said, sipping from a glass of Viognier. "Now let's eat! I've got a math test tomorrow morning."

John-Michael went around the table, serving each of them a portion of blackened snapper. Then he did another round, offering Moroccan couscous salad and roasted red and yellow bell peppers. Finally, he went around a third time, this time topping off everyone's wine. It was all done in such a slick, professional manner. Paolo commented how gracefully John-Michael did it all.

"Thanks, man," John-Michael said. "I used to wait tables in a conference center."

"Your year off?" Paolo asked.

"'Year off'?" John-Michael laughed. "You make it sound

glamorous. I was homeless for most of the year. Had to take work where I could find it. I got that job toward the end. A guy I knew got me hooked into the hotel where they did the conferences. I was working there until a little after my dad died."

"It must have been awful," Grace said softly. She hadn't really taken time to get to know John-Michael. He gave off a friendly vibe, but she sensed that was all surface. He was surprisingly quiet for a young, good-looking guy. She guessed he could easily be out every night partying. But mainly he stayed home, watching TV, baking, and doing his homework. This was the first time she'd had a chance to hear him talk about his missing year.

John-Michael took his seat at the head of the table and picked up his fork. "A lot of it was bad. If I'm honest."

Paolo chewed thoughtfully. "You ever get attacked?"

"A few times."

"Raped?"

John-Michael kept his eyes down low. "Almost. On the beach, one time. But they were outta their heads on crystal meth. I managed to get away."

"Jeez."

"It wasn't good."

Paolo seemed determined to continue the line of questioning. "How about drugs?"

"Weed. Coke, a couple of times."

"You ever inject?"

Grace reflected that John-Michael seemed very calm,

almost blasé about all these revelations. As though he'd come to terms with the entire experience. Or perhaps that he'd suffered something even worse.

He shook his head. "Hard drugs scare the bejesus out of me." John-Michael's willingness to talk about his life on the street seemed to be running thin. He glanced across to Maya, who sat on Paolo's left. "So how's everything with you?"

"I'm working on my app, you know . . ."

"An app?"

Maya gave a bashful smile.

It looked to Grace as though Maya was about to speak, but Candace interrupted her. "Hey, Lucy," she asked, "you hooking up with anyone in that rock band yet?"

Lucy's reply was ice cool with sarcasm. "No, young lady, I'm not *hooking up with* anyone."

"That's what I thought. Is anyone here getting any? 'Cause I know I'm not."

Paolo chuckled. "Looks like it's going to be that kind of evening." He winked at Maya.

But instead of joining in with the joke, Maya replied innocently, "What do you mean?"

"Perhaps you're all virgins," Candace said. There was a brief pause, then Paolo laughed.

Maya looked at them in turn. "What's funny?"

"Oh, nothing," Paolo said, smiling. "I've just had too much wine. Yeah. Virgins. That's it."

"I lost mine when I was fifteen," Candace remarked. "Grace was sixteen—just."

Grace sighed. She gulped down some wine. "Thanks, sis. Now I don't have to worry about keeping that private."

Candace set down her wineglass, hard. "Oh, please. We're all friends here. Aren't we? Paolo, how old were you? I bet you were young. A hottie like you."

Paolo gave a bashful grin. "I was fourteen. Not proud of it. A girl who used to be my babysitter."

Candace guffawed. "Tramp."

"I know."

"Man whore."

"Okay, okay." Paolo turned to John-Michael, clearly reluctant to share any more about his own experiences. "How about you, John-Michael? When did you first get some sweet gay action?"

Eventually, John-Michael replied, "I was sixteen. A guy at school. We'd known each other since middle school, but we didn't have any classes together until my freshman year. We were lab partners in chem and bio."

"Classic. The Bunsen-burner meet cute. Who came on to who?"

"I did. He was so gorgeous. Tito, from Costa Rica. I really love Latino boys," he said with a shy glance at Maya. "The caramel skin tone, the chocolate-colored eyes, the accent."

"So," Candace said coyly. "How was it?"

"Your momma never told you?" John-Michael replied archly. "Nice boys don't kiss and tell."

Grace found herself blushing on behalf of the two boys, neither of whom seemed eager to say any more. She guessed that it might be different in front of other guys. But Candace's slightly mocking tone was pretty off-putting, even to Grace.

Grace broke in: "So how come you couldn't go live with Tito when your dad kicked you out?"

"His family didn't know he was gay. No one knew, only me. I was stupid enough to come out to my dad."

"Can't have been easy," said Grace.

But despite Grace's efforts to alter the direction of the conversation, Candace seemed determined to bring it back to sex. "What about you, Lucy?" she said. "What's your number?"

Lucy merely smiled. "As in, how many guys? Sugar, you think I'm gonna give up that particular piece of information?"

"I'll show you mine if you show me yours." John-Michael grinned.

"I'll take some of that action," Candace said. "Mine is easy to remember—two. Lame and lamer."

"Who's lame—them, or you for choosing them?" Grace said. "Okay, I'm in, too. Mine is a one. And he was kind of sweet. I liked him a lot."

Maya asked, "What happened?"

"Oh, you know. Possessiveness, clinginess, whining."

"True," Candace said. "You *were* kind of unnecessarily mean to him."

Paolo said, "Okay, so we'll assume Maya is a zero, on account of her extreme youth—"

"Hey!" Maya interrupted. "I'm only a year younger than you!"

He turned to her. "Am I wrong?"

She shrugged. "Ehh. Okay, it's true. I'm a good Catholic girl."

"Okay, so I'm on a two," Candace said. "Grace has one, Lucy isn't telling, and John-Michael . . . ? How many guys have you ah . . . serviced?"

"A few."

Candace said insistently, "Be specific."

"Maybe twenty? I don't remember."

They were all a little shocked by this, although Paolo pretended otherwise. "You *rascal*."

John-Michael followed his lead, putting on a posh English accent and shaking his head with mock regret. "I know. I'm an absolute cad."

Candace laughed with delight at their performance. Grace watched for a moment as Candace drained her glass and filled it up again, almost to the brim. It was at least her third glass. No wonder she was being so outrageous. She already sounded drunk. And it was just getting worse. Candace turned to Paolo. "What about you, Cougar Boy?"

Grace flinched at the nickname. It was easier to forget how dumb it was to have a crush on Paolo when she wasn't reminded of his popularity with those women at the country club. "Candace, let's drop this."

Her stepsister turned to Grace with a look of amused disbelief. "Come on! We're finally getting somewhere interesting with these bozos."

Grace replied, "Maybe they don't want to go there?"

Maya added, "Plus, some of us don't have any stories to share. It's kind of one-sided."

Paolo merely leaned back, took a sip of wine, and raised his glass with an enigmatic smile. "Like our boy John-Michael says, a nice guy doesn't kiss and tell."

"But methinks thou liest," Candace said, slipping into her best Shakespearean English. "The word on the street, Master Paolo, is that thou art nothing but a goatish knave."

Amid the laughter that ensued, Paolo smirked and mimed picking up a phone. "Hey, Candace, the British called. They want their accent back."

"Ha, bloody, ha," Candace replied with a dramatic flounce. As if in a mood of reconciliation, she raised a glass. "So now we know about everyone—except Lucy. To Lucy giving up her number."

To Grace's irritation, the rest of the housemates cheered. Lucy shook her head in resignation, smiled a drowsy smile. "What a bunch of sex-obsessed children."

"Guilty," Paolo said emphatically, his hand on his wine-glass. "Now, Lucy, 'fess up."

Grace shook her head. "Come on, guys. Some people don't like to talk about this."

Candace stuck out her tongue. "Jeez, what's with all the prudery?"

Grace replied quickly, "You didn't enjoy doing it, so now you have to make it all into some big joke?"

Candace laughed in a way that struck Grace as cynical, an imitation of Candace's mother, Katelyn. "Well, if you can't laugh at stuff like this . . ."

Lucy sighed. "I don't mind telling. It's not like I'd be the only blabbermouth around here. . . ."

There was another cheer for Lucy's being a good sport. "Are we counting *everything*?" she asked. "Or does it have to be the all the way?"

"Fourth base," Candace confirmed with a satisfied nod.

"Okay. In that case," she said very slowly. "My number . . . is zero."

They all gasped. Maya began to grin. She held high her right palm to Lucy. "Yeah, baby! Virgins unite!"

Lucy high-fived Maya. She threw the others a defiant stare. Candace and John-Michael joined in with some good-humored, if ribald jeering.

Paolo, however, seemed transfixed. He couldn't look away from Lucy. Grace couldn't tell if he was appalled or enthralled. She felt the familiar stirrings of jealousy once again.

LUCY

"Candace and I are gonna go up to the room," Lucy said. "Maybe take a couple of hits on the bong. Grace, you want in?"

"But there's all that food left over." Grace hesitated, but walked with them up the stairs. "We'll just wind up eating even more."

Maya lagged behind them a few steps. John-Michael was dozing in front of the TV, while Paolo had gamely volunteered to clean the kitchen. Maya kept glancing at Lucy, hopeful, expectant. Lucy guessed that she wanted an invitation to hang out with the older girls. When that didn't happen, Maya seemed to give up and tapped Grace on the shoulder. Lucy could just make out Maya's words, spoken very softly. "Could I talk to you? About that thing we were talking about . . . the other day."

Grace's eyes widened for a split second. Then: "Oh! Yeah, sure."

The two girls disappeared into their room.

Candace turned to Lucy. "Grace doesn't really like to do drugs. If it weren't for me, she probably never would have."

"You're the bad influence?" Lucy said with the beginnings of a grin.

Candace said lightly, "I'm the bad sister, the bad student, the badass."

"Yeah?" Lucy's grin widened. "Oh, I like that."

The two girls settled into their room, sitting cross-legged at opposite ends of Lucy's bed. Lucy busied herself with prepping the bong, cleaning out the residue of previous smokes and refilling from the small stash she kept under her mattress in a brown paper bag.

"We probably shouldn't do this."

Candace shook her head mournfully. "No-oh."

"You have that math test tomorrow."

Candace gave a slow nod. "Algebra."

"You, me, and a myster-ee." Lucy smirked. "Solve for x."

"What mystery?"

"Are you kidding?" Lucy asked. "John-Michael."

"So?"

"Blood test? Throwing us a party 'cause of the all clear? He knew two, three days ago he didn't have HIV."

"He said he was waiting for news on other STDs," Candace pointed out.

"Yeah, I heard that. But it doesn't square with the facts."

"What 'facts'?"

Lucy put down the bong for a moment. "Lookit. Our boy John-Michael gets a visit from a detective. He freaks, starts riding out in that car of his. Gone all day, one day. Doesn't say where he's at. Another day, he goes to San Francisco."

"He was giving Grace a ride to visit her Dead Man Walking."

"Yeah, sure, I'm not saying there's no reason. I'm saying it was new. You ever see him go anywhere but school until last week?"

"His dad died, Lucy. I'm sure he was depressed."

"He hated his dad. Dude was a big fat homophobe. Threw John-Michael out for being gay."

Candace sighed, a little impatient now. "Yeah, boo-hoo. What's your point?"

"He told me that he was worried about passing something on to his kids."

"Is he planning on having any?"

"That was the thing," Lucy said. "He was glad he wasn't. So he wouldn't pass it on."

"Maybe he meant the gay gene?"

Lucy gave her a stern look. "Gay isn't as simple as that."

"Then what?"

"Guys hardly ever pass on HIV to their kids," Lucy said, recalling the leaflet she'd read when John-Michael was being tested. "So it can't have been that."

"Did he ever say it was?"

"No. Now that I think about it, it was me who mentioned HIV first."

"Do you even know if he got the test?"

Lucy pondered this for a few seconds. Slowly, she said. "Clever."

"I try." Candace blinked, as if acknowledging applause.

"Not you; John-Michael."

"Huh?"

Lucy took out her Zippo lighter. "He let me believe he was checking for HIV. I bet it wasn't even an STD clinic."

"So what was he getting tested for?"

"Whatever it is, he didn't want me to know anything about it."

"What's more scary than HIV?"

"Cancer, for one," Lucy said. "Leukemia."

"It would majorly suck to get cancer at our age."

"But it couldn't have been cancer."

Candace frowned. "Why not?"

"Dude, did you ever listen in bio?"

"No, I already told you," Candace replied, pouting. "Bad student, remember?"

"You can't pass cancer to your kids."

"Are you sure? None of the cancers?"

Lucy paused, thoughtful.

Candace seemed to warm to her point. "Maybe there's, like, a kind of cancer that's inherited. And John-Michael was going to get a DNA test to see if he's got the gene."

Lucy took out her smartphone. Inherited cancer? It was news to her. She thought it came from smoking, drinking, and eating unhealthily. Toxins in the environment, not genes. After a couple of minutes tapping on the screen, she sat back, staring. "Well, I'll be goddamned. You *can* pass cancer to your kids. All kinds of cancers."

"Really?" Candace seemed surprised. As though she hadn't actually believed her theory would turn out to be true.

"Yeah. But mostly it just increases your risk. Having the gene doesn't definitely give you the disease."

"Still. That's a scary thing, to have that in your DNA."

"Yeah. I don't know, though."

"What d'you mean?"

"John-Michael seemed awful scared. Like if the news was bad, he's *definitely* getting sick. That's why I thought HIV. I assumed he'd been injecting drugs, or having unprotected sex."

"Well, he did say he'd been with a lot of guys."

"Yeah, but he also said—did you notice?—that he never injected. And he refused to admit if he'd actually had full sex."

"True. But you can get HIV from oral."

Lucy fired up the bong, inhaled the cloud of smoke, held it in for three seconds, and then slowly exhaled. She gazed glassily at Candace. "Maybe, but it's much less likely. HIV ain't it, Candace. He wasn't worried because of what he'd been doing. He was worried because of what his *dad* was doing."

Lucy was already blissing out as she passed the bong. Candace took a quick hit and then tipped the mouthpiece away from her for a moment, considering. She was finding it harder to follow the thread.

"His dad?" Candace asked. "Where'd you get that?"

"Because that detective sparked all this. I'm sure of that. Something she told him made John-Michael freak. And he started to worry that he had a disease. Maybe . . . maybe he went on those road trips to get the bad thoughts out of his mind? But he couldn't put it off any more. So he took the test."

Candace inhaled a second time, sighed, and breathed out. Lucy's theory was impressively mysterious. John-Michael did indeed seem to be concealing something. But on the other hand, was it even relevant now? Her thoughts were already drifting toward the remains of the strawberry cream cake that John-Michael had baked for dessert.

Sleepily, she commented, "Great that he's got the all clear."

Lucy drifted into a world of her own. "Uh-huh."

Candace's mouth was beginning to water. "I'm getting some more cake. You want some?"

MAYA

"I told my mom about my problems with dyslexia. She wants to get me extra tutoring."

Maya watched Grace trying to wrap her head around this sudden adjustment from the group's alcohol-fueled discussion to what was clearly going to be a more angst-ridden exchange, and not about sex.

It seemed like Grace was going to try to blow it off. "So?" She waved a hand. "Get some extra tutoring. And move on."

"Gracie, I don't have time."

"Because of the thing you're writing?"

"Because of my app, yeah."

Grace asked, "Didn't you finish it already?"

"Doesn't work like that," Maya said. "The version I released was just a first version. With software, you've got to keep improving it. Like a shark. Keep moving or die."

"You tell that to your mom?"

"Are you mental? No, I didn't. She'd go nuts if she

thought it was eating into my study time."

Grace thought for a moment. "So where is your mom these days?"

"Back in Mexico City with my dad. She's . . . ah . . . she's flying out to see me in a few months. She has to stay away for a little while before they'll let her back in. Even on a tourist visa. But when she does, we're going to go to Disneyland. Can you believe it? All the time they lived here we never went."

"Your mom wants you to live the American Dream?" Grace asked. "Because she can't?"

"I wish. What's more American Dream than writing a piece of software and getting rich and famous for it? She's got something more traditional in mind."

"Like what? Marriage and kids?"

"She's not from the Stone Age, Grace. She's thinking more along the lines of a college degree. Something respectable like premed, pre-law. At the very least, business."

"You into any of that?"

"What do you think?" Maya asked. "Business, yeah, maybe. I can see how it could be useful. But no; I want to get into a computer science program. Do this stuff properly."

"Seriously? Isn't that an all-male, all-geek program?"

Maya smiled sweetly. "Imagine how popular I'll be with the admissions boards."

"It's true. You'd tick every box."

Maya rummaged under her pillow for her pajamas. In

the bed next to Maya's Grace was halfway into her own by now, neatly folding her clothes as she discarded them. She was under her sheets a moment later, eyes closing with relief. "Oh man," she moaned. "How is it that wine makes you so wretchedly drunk so quickly? I'm sure I didn't drink more than four glasses. But I feel like I'm going to be so hung over."

"Drink water," Maya advised. "My mom always told me that. One glass for every glass you drank. It hydrates you."

"So I have to be up all night dying to pee?"

Maya shrugged. "I'm just telling you how to avoid a hangover."

Grace stretched both arms until they hit the headboard. "I heard that a good bacon and eggs breakfast is the solution. Lots of fat and protein."

"Sounds good. First one up fixes that for everyone?"

Drowsily, Grace replied, "Sure. But only if I can have the bathroom first."

Maya thought for a moment. They'd left Paolo and John-Michael downstairs, sitting down to watch some *Banshee*. They'd probably be there for an hour at least. Grace looked and sounded as though she was headed pretty swiftly to sleep. And Lucy and Candace had disappeared upstairs to smoke.

There was a solid chance that Maya would be undisturbed for the next half hour. She plucked her toiletries bag from their shared nightstand and grabbed a toothbrush, floss, and makeup remover. A quick glance at Grace confirmed that she was almost out. When Maya returned from the bathroom, Grace had rolled onto her side, facing away. She didn't reply when Maya softly called her name.

Satisfied that the time was right, Maya sat at her desk and switched on her laptop. She released a shallow, regretful sigh. After the buzz of the dinner party, she was plummeting back to the miserable deceit of spying on her housemates.

There was no question of refusing the assignment. There'd been enough at stake before she moved into the beach house. But now? It would be like getting fast-tracked out of paradise and straight to the back of the line.

And those were just the consequences for Maya. She didn't need reminding that it wasn't only her own future that was at risk.

She stared at the screen for a full three minutes before she could bring herself to type a single letter. The familiar nausea had already begun. Self-loathing. Who knew it was an actual, physical thing?

Lucy is getting more serious about her music. That's all she really talks about. Very little info about her life before coming to LA. She's even been getting John-Michael to take his guitar out. They were friends years back, in rock camp, and now she's trying to get him to start up again. I get the impression that Lucy worries about John-Michael. She's been having issues with school, too. They can be pretty strict at Our Lady. She's been in detention some. She doesn't seem at all interested in Grace.

Grace.

Maya hesitated. She was finding it hard to get a handle on the girl. She didn't seem to do anything but read books, watch TV, and do her homework. Oh—and write the letters to the death row guys. Maybe if Maya could read the letters she'd have more to tell. But Grace was intensely private about them. Maya hadn't been able to hack into her computer, and the box where she kept the handwritten ones was locked with an eight-number combination padlock.

Grace has a crush on Paolo but she won't let him know. It's like a point of pride. She even pretends to be into other guys, like, we'll all be watching TV and that *Deadbeat* show will come on with that cute actor—the one who married your *inglesa*—and she'll say she likes him, too. Or she'll talk about boys at her high school. I finally got the name of her death row guy out of her: Alan Vernon. I looked the guy up online but I couldn't find any news stories about him. No murderer with that name. Maybe he's really old and was put on death row before the internet, I don't know. I'd say that of all the people in the house, Lucy is the one that she gets along with the least. This probably has something to do with the fact that Paolo is obsessed with Lucy. It's also because they

don't have many interests in common. Lucy is creative
and kind of a beatnik, into smoking weed and all. Grace is
thoughtful and quiet and apart from the fact that she's not
a virgin, (allegedly), I'd say she's a bit of a goody-goody.

She stopped typing, read the final paragraph back. The
wine had made her sloppy. She shouldn't be making references to the star of *Deadbeat*, or to the *inglesa*—the British
movie A-lister, Dana Alexander. She deleted both. Then
read, with a pang of guilt, the bit about Grace not being a
virgin. After a few seconds' thought, she deleted that also. It
almost sounded catty, and Maya didn't think of herself that
way at all. Who was she to discuss her friends' sex lives,
to cast doubt on their confessions? It might make someone
who knew her wonder whether Maya herself was truthful
about such things. She didn't want to open that particular
can of worms.

Not when she considered who was going to read the
report.

LUCY
OUR LADY OF MERCY CATHOLIC HIGH
SCHOOL FOR GIRLS, THURSDAY, APRIL 23

In the corridor outside the assistant principal's office, time stretched. Lucy shuffled her feet. She avoided the glances of students who passed her on their way to the library. It wasn't possible that Guzman was actually held up this long. No, she was keeping Lucy in the corridor to intimidate her.

Twenty-two minutes after Guzman had summoned Lucy, she cracked open her door. There was no hint of apology, no sign that she realized the meeting was late. She called Lucy inside. Lucy sat opposite Guzman in silence for a few minutes while the teacher apparently studied the relevant paperwork.

Then she glanced up. "Looks like it's go time, Miss Long."

"I'm sorry?"

"You've had three detentions since we last spoke. I wasn't messing around when I told you that your work was under review. Well, from these notes from your teachers, you're finally drinking in the Last Chance Saloon. Which I imagine for you is probably accurate, not metaphoric."

Lucy bit her lip. She loathed it when the dumber teachers like Guzman tried to be witty.

"I've never done anything illegal."

"In school—maybe. You're too intelligent for that. Outside though, pardon me, Lucy, but I have my doubts."

"I've never been arrested. Not one time."

"Never been caught? Quite the achievement. I'm sure your folks are very proud."

Lucy fought back a wave of resentment. Guzman had absolutely no evidence for her accusations. If she repeated them in front of anyone, it was borderline slander. There was nothing Lucy could do, though. Even her mother would probably take Guzman's side.

"What did I do now?" she asked in a low, sulky voice.

"As I'm sure you're aware, your parents have asked for regular reports concerning your progress. Following the latest, I'm afraid they've issued something of an ultimatum."

Lucy's jaw tightened.

"To achieve a satisfactory overall grade, your next three term papers will have to average an A-minus. You could get an A, A-minus, and B-plus, or three A-minuses. That's the minimum; I advise you to aim higher."

Lucy couldn't suppress a sharp intake of breath. She hadn't gotten so much as a B-plus in a year. What Guzman was asking for was basically impossible.

"Could I maybe just get three Bs? I'm having problems

with studying. The work is much harder than I'm used to."

"That's nonsense"–Guzman showed a thin smile–"and you know it. Your essay on Stravinsky wasn't the work of a beleaguered learner. I've seen your grades from middle school. You were a straight-A student. Even in ninth grade. A students only become C students for one of three reasons: the three Ds–disease, drugs, and demotivation.

"You, my dear, are suffering from the latter two," Guzman continued. "Demotivation is partly the school's responsibility. I accept that. Clearly, we've failed to motivate you."

Lucy didn't like the assumption that she had a problem with drugs. Okay, so she smoked pot now and again, maybe snorted some coke when someone else was buying. But how could Guzman possibly know that? It meant that her parents must have shared details of Lucy's personal life. That idea made her so angry that she felt like walking out right then.

Yet, she didn't. The house in Venice was the best place she'd ever lived. She was forming a bond with some of the housemates. John-Michael and Maya were becoming like her brother and baby sister. Now that she stopped to think about it, Lucy had to admit that she even thought the two Texas girls were pretty cool, especially Candace.

Her parents were capable of canceling her lifestyle and she knew it. Despite her annoyance, it wasn't worth bleating about Guzman's superior tone, her smug implication of a drug habit.

Especially since she was right.

"Your parents have made it clear to the school that we need to step up our efforts to motivate you. So—those papers need to average out to A-minus. If not, your parents' ultimatum comes into force and they exercise the right to pull you out of school."

Unlikely. Lucy knew how careful her parents were about money. They'd paid the fees for a full semester in advance. She couldn't imagine them taking her out until they'd gotten their money's worth.

It was as though the assistant principal had read her mind.

"Now financially, as it turns out, we're able to offer you and your parents an alternative. The trust that owns Our Lady also owns a small girls' boarding school in Santa Barbara. It's a lovely place. I gather you live near the beach now, is that right?"

"I live on Venice Beach," Lucy replied, still sullen.

"Well, the Sisters of Mercy have their convent very close to a beach. The school shares the same grounds."

"Boarding school? I don't think so."

"It is the solution that would best accommodate both your wish to live away from home and your parents' commitment to your education."

Lucy rose to her feet. It was getting harder to contain her anger. "What if you just expel me? I'm *emancipated.* I get to *choose* where I go to school."

Guzman forced a smile. "Insofar as your parents are

happy to continue to fund you, maybe. If they withdraw financial support, you would presumably become home-less."

"They wouldn't do that," Lucy said. Untrue, she realized, but it was at least worth a try.

"Lucy, let me assure you, there is only so much a parent can do for a child. At a certain point, at a certain age, you have to let your children go. You are seventeen. You were well on track to qualify for the Ivy League or Juilliard as of ten months ago. Or so your mother assured me. It's on that basis that we accepted you at Our Lady."

"Never said I wanted to go to an Ivy League school."

"Nevertheless," Guzman said dryly. "You want some kind of tertiary education, don't you?"

"Not necessarily."

Guzman sighed, resigned. She leaned across the desk and handed Lucy a folder.

"I don't like fighting with students. It's unseemly. Inside that folder you'll find an evaluation from each teacher who is missing work from you. As well as a deadline and a reminder of the task they set. You can find the supporting documents on the e-learning platform. Now, I have phone calls to make."

Guzman stood, and pointed at the door.

Lucy rode the bus home wrapped within a tense silence. When she reached the house, Grace and John-Michael were on the couch watching TV, while Paolo fixed himself a protein shake with strawberry-flavored whey powder. She paused, reviewed her plan to go to her room and light up a joint. Maybe she should try to resist. Paolo beamed at her as she wandered into the kitchen. She dropped her school-bag to the floor and reached for the Wonder Bread. Only a grilled-cheese sandwich could attack this despondency.

As they prepared the snacks, Lucy updated Paolo. He listened, looking serious.

"That sucks," he said when she'd finished.

"It really does."

"Can you get the grades?"

"I don't think so. I haven't paid much attention in class, if I'm honest."

"Writing songs or thinking about me?" Paolo asked, straight-faced.

A wry smile. "Oh, it was all you, baby."

Paolo slid across the kitchen counter, positioning himself between Lucy and the living room. He glanced swiftly over his shoulder at the others, engrossed in their TV show, then back at Lucy.

"There is another solution."

"Like what?"

"Like, if you're going to get a low grade this year, why don't you drop out? Go into a public school, but in the grade below."

"Do-over?"

"Yeah. Think about it—what your parents save in school fees could pay for an extra year of rent. You've had a disruptive year. John-Michael's doing it."

A smile began to appear at the edge of her mouth. "An extra year here? Any idea which school I should move to?"

"Van Buren is okay, I guess."

"Van Buren, huh? Isn't that your school?"

"And John-Michael's." Paolo gave her a mischievous grin. "Rides to and from are guaranteed."

"And in August, what, start the year over again?" She shook her head with a bemused smile. "Same grade as you?"

"And John-Michael," he added softly.

Lucy pondered. "Interesting idea . . ."

"I thought so."

". . . Now to try to convince my folks to keep paying for me to live here, even if I don't go to the school they chose."

He watched her eyes for a second, and then leaned in and softly kissed her lips. Lucy didn't move or respond. When he moved away, she shook her head.

"Not very cool, bro." Her tone was faintly admonishing.

Paolo just shrugged. He was trying brush it off. Just the same, an angry response flared in his cheeks.

"The offer stands," he told her. "For now."

PAOLO
VENICE BEACH, FRIDAY, APRIL 24

"Dude, you do not look happy."

Paolo wrenched his thoughts away from Lucy for a few seconds and focused on Candace. Her Prius was parked in the spot next to his. He'd have to wait for her to get inside before he pulled out. He tried to smile but it came out a little flat, so he changed the subject.

"You recording tonight?"

" 'Fraid so."

"You got any lines today?" he teased.

Candace gave a knowing smirk. "Not today. How 'bout you; pimping yourself out at the country club?"

He smiled. "You'd better believe it. Two lessons. Another hundred bucks."

It was a lie. He didn't have any students tonight. It was months since he'd stayed after a lesson with a student. Lucy's brush-off, though, had been the last straw. He'd been nice to her, he really cared, and he'd shown it. Okay—she wasn't into him. Fine. But to let himself stay in some kind of hypnotic trance, unable to even think about seeing another girl? He was starting to look pretty dumb.

There was *whipped* and then there was *total friggin' control.* The girl didn't even have a clue what she was doing to him.

Paolo waited for Candace to leave and then set off for the Malibu Lawn Tennis Club.

Forty-nine minutes later he was dressed in dazzling tennis whites and cruising the bar. This was how he'd found his first student. One week later, they'd wound up in bed—at her suggestion. That time was exciting, but not as much as with the former babysitter who'd seduced him after they'd bumped into each other at a local coffee shop. Even with the third girl, it had been pretty thrilling. Only with the fourth, Allegra, had Paolo started to wonder if this was all there was—some excitement, a few laughs? And then what?

In his mind, he'd felt nothing. He'd even tried broaching the subject with some guys at school. They'd either misunderstood or pretended to. One guy, with total frankness, had said, "Maybe you're just not that into women?"

It was this thought that ate at Paolo. Six women and he hadn't cared about any of them. Surely, surely he should have felt more—even for one of them? That guy's comment had made him wonder. Could he be right?

Then he'd met Lucy and that theory had crumbled. Lucy turned him on like no one he'd ever known—a smile from her was enough. She was like a virus in his blood, circulating, omnipresent. A mania.

He was wound tighter than a clock. He couldn't take this much longer.

From across the room, Talia Kravic smiled at him. She was recently over from the Czech Republic. At eighteen, she was the second youngest coach in the club. Talia was taking her seat at one of the outdoor tables, placing two glasses of ice and lemon on the table, and chatting to her companion, another woman. When the woman turned around, Paolo noticed that she was quite a bit older than Talia. At least forty. She had the kind of permatan you saw on some bleached blondes. Not one of Talia's typical students. He'd noticed that Talia took on a higher-than-average count of the aggressive young banker types. They probably fantasized about beating her in a match.

Darius would wipe the floor with all of them.

The fleeting thought caught Paolo unawares. He thought he'd finally managed to put Darius out of his mind. But apparently not.

He peered at the woman with Talia. She was about five feet eight with a slim, toned physique, straggly, overtreated hair, her eyes gray and flinty. There was something familiar about her. Had he taught her once? He hated when he ran into a former student, the type who moved on after one lesson. Invariably, he'd forget their name. They always looked kind of annoyed when he admitted it. There had to be a way to get them to tell him their name without looking like a jerk, but he hadn't thought of it yet.

Talia waved him over. Paolo began to make his way to

their table very slowly, all the while racking his brain for the elusive name.

"Hello," he said, smiling at Talia and her companion. The older woman remained seated, giving Paolo a rather calculating look. She sipped from her drink, a gin and tonic to judge by the small bottle of tonic water next to it. He'd certainly seen her before, and not all that long ago. When it came to a name, though, Paolo drew a total blank.

"Hi," said the woman. "I didn't catch your name."

Relief flooded him. She didn't know him, either.

"I'm Paolo."

She just nodded. Paolo sat down. He had to suppress the urge to stare at her in open curiosity.

So familiar. Yet apparently not one of his students. How did he know her?

Talia began to chat. She'd been applying for tennis scholarships. Things were looking good. She'd been accepted at USC and Irvine, but what she really wanted was to go to Duke. Her boyfriend from the Czech Republic had just started a doctoral program there and she was dying to join him. Paolo wondered quietly if the boyfriend was as eager for Talia to get an offer from Duke. She was pretty good-looking, with all that fine, ash-blonde hair and toned arms and thighs. But she talked nonstop and she wasn't even funny. He'd been sitting there for seven or eight minutes and she hadn't let him get one word out apart from his name. Meanwhile, the older lady was silent, smiling a knowing smile at Paolo, barely acknowledging Talia at all. Paolo avoided looking at the companion as much as was barely polite, but it wasn't a sustainable strategy.

Then she spoke. "Talia, sweetie, would you go get me some pork rinds?"

"Pork rinds?"

The fortysomething woman blinked calmly. "Let's give that Lipitor something to work on."

Talia turned toward the bar with a vaguely puzzled air.

"Lipitor?" Paolo gave a quizzical smile. It was something to say.

"I'm not taking Lipitor."

He shrugged. "Honestly, I don't even know what it is."

The older woman smiled. "I just wanted to get rid of Talia."

Paolo froze. He recognized her sudden predatory grin.

"You looked cuter as a blond," she said, her voice silky smooth. "I almost didn't recognize you."

He stared.

Very softly she said, "Do you remember me now?"

Paolo glanced around. Talia had struck up a conversation with the bartender. She didn't seem in a hurry to return.

"You and that Darius fellow made a pretty big fool out of my son."

He felt his heart lurch within his chest. When eventually he spoke, his voice was barely audible. "Jimmy's mom?"

"Answer me one thing—why'd you leave the Boxster so near to my house?"

Paolo began to murmur an excuse, but she interrupted him.

"Jimmy found it. But do you think he thought of going to the police? No. Darius—or whatever his real name is—was long gone by then. So Jimmy told me and his father that the deal from your silly game had been to swap the cars. The police picked Jimmy up in that Boxster about two weeks later. Took a lot of fast talking from an expensive lawyer to get him off the hook."

"I didn't know the car was stolen."

"Oh, I see. You just abandoned it as an act of charity?"

Paolo said nothing, lowered his eyes. She nodded as though he'd confirmed her suspicions. She took a sip. "You're the honest type?"

"I try."

"But not very hard, at least not that day."

"Darius didn't give me a lot of choice."

"No. From what Jimmy says, I imagine he can be fairly persuasive." She gazed at him intently. "Can you be persuasive, Paolo?"

"Ma'am . . . I'm really sorry."

"I'm not interested in your remorse. What I want is an answer to my question. *Can you be persuasive?*" She let her words sink in for a moment. "I'm open to persuasion, Paolo. I could be convinced to develop a *very* short memory. Maybe I'll forget the forty thousand dollars we spent on

Jimmy's Corvette, and the extra ten we spent on his lawyer. Maybe I'll forget all those questions the cops asked me about the mysterious tennis players who showed up at my house that time."

She placed her hand gently on his leg. Paolo forced himself not to flinch, forced himself to return her stare.

"Just before you came over, Talia told me you have something of a reputation here."

He didn't dare say a word.

"Are you teaching tonight, Paolo?"

His throat felt like sandpaper. "No."

The sharkish smile returned. "I'll be outside in my car. Look for a silver BMW."

PAOLO
CLARION INN HOTEL, FRIDAY, APRIL 24

Paolo pulled his tennis shirt down over his head. Awkwardly, he asked, "Are we good?"

Jimmy's mother hadn't moved. She wound one end of the sheet around her fingers, eyeing him lazily. After a moment she said, "We're good. Just one thing. Did you have a good time?"

"It felt amazing," he said simply. It wasn't a total lie. He'd imagined he was with Lucy and any inhibitions he'd had simply vanished.

He took it slow on the drive back to the house. Allowed himself time to think. It didn't help matters. Paolo arrived home just as shaken as he'd been with Jimmy's mother. He'd sunk pretty low tonight—having sex with a stranger in a hotel to cover up a crime. Not much that was more wretched, by conventional standards. John-Michael, hustling for food and shelter, was a paragon of virtue by comparison.

Yet Paolo felt strangely at peace. It had been a more

than fair transaction the way he saw it. Jimmy's mom had seemed pretty satisfied. And now, hopefully, the whole Montecito tennis hustle was a thing of the past.

Any other judgment, he decided, was simply society planting its moralizing fingers where they didn't belong.

In the Venice house, only Lucy and Candace's light was still on. Paolo showered in the second-floor bathroom. He was still thinking about Lucy. Damp from the shower, he pulled on some jeans and a T-shirt and climbed the stairs.

To his surprise, Lucy was at her desk, working on her laptop, her books open on the floor and on her lap. She glanced at him with a clear expression of relief when he walked in. She placed a finger over her lips and jabbed a purple-polished fingernail in the direction of the bed where Candace lay, peacefully asleep.

"Aw, she looks so sweet," Paolo chuckled. "Are you *studying*?"

Lucy nodded, frowning.

"Take a break?"

She seemed hesitant. "Maybe a little one."

In the kitchen, Paolo offered to scramble up some eggs. What he wanted now was to eat and spend time with Lucy. He'd already decided on a couple of eggs; no toast, just a little ketchup and hot chili sauce. But she wasn't hungry, just poured herself a glass of skim milk. As he tended to the eggs, Lucy told him that she planned to spend the entire weekend studying and writing term papers in chemistry, Spanish, and literature.

Paolo shook his head, stunned. "Don't you have a gig this weekend?"

"Our first one," she agreed.

"You're ditching?"

"Don't see I have much choice. Little enough chance I'll get the A-minus average even if I study all weekend. And then I'd be out of the band, no matter what."

"Lucy, didn't your folks already throw you out? They don't get to tell you how to spend your time anymore."

She looked at him sadly. "Sure they do. They pay the piper, they call the tune."

"Is their tune so bad?"

Lucy gave a soft laugh. "Their tune is a boarding school up near Santa Barbara. With nuns. I don't much like the sound of a boarding school. Kinda like it right here in Venice."

"Oh. Man, their tune *sucks*."

"I know. To be avoided at all costs. But it means missing the gig this time."

"The guys are okay with that?"

"You mean Whatnot? I didn't ask yet."

"Lucy. You'd better tell them."

She sighed, turned to leave. "I know."

Paolo watched her go. He'd have to think of something he could do to help. He was pretty good at Spanish and okay at literature; how hard was it really, just read a book and spout some opinions. But chemistry—he'd be useless. And right now, he was tired and hungry.

He took the plate of eggs to the couch and switched on the TV. He found a channel airing an episode of *Dexter* and began to eat. After about five minutes, Grace appeared at the door.

"That's really loud, Paolo. Could you turn it down?"

He muted the TV, trying to gauge if she was angry. But Grace didn't seem it, just sleepy. She stayed in the doorway, wearing nothing but a long, green T-shirt. She glanced in the direction of the kitchen. "Don't you wish John-Michael would quit baking?"

"But it makes him happy."

"Yeah. But when I know his cookies are in the house, I can't sleep."

"Just take one."

"Really?" She gave a sardonic laugh. "Don't ever apply to be Jiminy Cricket."

A moment later Grace was sitting beside him on the couch. He watched curiously as she shimmied a little closer, tucked her legs underneath her, and lay back on the cushions. If they weren't friends, he'd be wondering if she was flirting with him. She grinned widely and took a bite of the oatmeal-and-cranberry cookie.

"What have you been up to tonight?" she asked.

"The usual: an hour on my own training, then a tennis lesson. And then a couple of beers with the coaches."

Grace commented, "How very energetic. I've spent most of the day sitting on my ass."

"Lucy's gotta do that all weekend."

An expression of irritation crossed Grace's face. Then it was gone. "She's screwed, by all accounts."

"We should help her," said Paolo firmly.

"Why?" Grace's question surprised him. "It's not like Lucy ever offered to help boost my grades."

"She's a housemate. If she doesn't get the grades, her folks are going to make her leave."

Grace said, "So what? She had the same chance as any of us. She's no busier than Candace, and Candace is still making the grades."

"Oh yeah?" Paolo walked over to the kitchen to get a cookie, still talking. "What's Candace's average?"

Grace called after him, "She's a strong B."

"Huh. Well, Lucy has to get an A-minus or she'll get kicked out of school."

Grace said, "Only 'cause she's been getting Cs all semester. Whose fault is that?"

Paolo arrived back at the sofa, a cookie in each hand. "Man, you're tough! And yet you don't seem the type."

Grace moved aside so he could sit down. "I could be out having a lot of fun like Lucy," she said. "But then I wouldn't get good grades."

"Maybe so, but still . . ."

"You think I'm harsh?" Grace smirked playfully. "Maybe you have a vested interest in Lucy staying."

He didn't reply.

Grace said, "I'm sure you'll help."

"I have a hunch I'm not as smart as Lucy."

"Well . . . I didn't want to be the one to say it," she teased. "Maybe you can do the typing."

Paolo gave a slight shake of his head. "You know, I underestimated you. Or overestimated."

"Which is it?"

"I thought you were, you know, a sweetheart."

"Oh, you mean a pushover."

"No, I mean, a kind person who goes out of their way to be good and helpful."

"Yeah, you do mean a pushover."

They shared a laugh. "Okay," he conceded. "Maybe. Maybe I thought you were a bit of a do-gooder. But can you blame me? You write to all those poor bastards on death row. You drive hours to go see one of them. You talk me into joining Amnesty International."

"You and John-Michael drove me," she said quietly. The line of questioning seemed to be making her uneasy. "And you offered to come along. Anyhow—" She hesitated. "I only write to one death row guy."

"Really? I remembered more."

"You might have got that impression," Grace admitted carefully.

"How come?"

"I may have exaggerated."

"Why?"

"Isn't it obvious?"

He didn't answer because it wasn't. "Candace thinks you write to more than one guy, too."

Grace lowered her eyes. "What can I tell you? I embellished. First to Candace. You can imagine why. And then I had to be consistent."

Paolo felt like it might be obvious after all: Grace had been trying to impress him. Surprising, actually. It was already impressive enough to write to one person on death row. But once Candace was brought into the equation, it made more sense.

It had to be tough, having such a talented, gorgeous stepsister. Candace was the glamorous one. She represented "cool" in the Deering family. Grace was just as beautiful, he realized as he looked at her. Less overtly sexy than Candace, possibly, but definitely attractive. Her eyes were more intense, more suggestive of the intelligence that lurked behind them.

Candace must cast a long shadow. No point trying to outdo her in the same arena. Grace's interests in human rights and activism must have stemmed from a wish to carve out her own niche. Something super-distinctive. But she'd obviously underestimated how absorbing it could be, to get involved in the life of someone under threat of execution.

"So there's *just one* guy?"

"Don't tell anyone."

"Are you into him?"

Grace's calm veneer vanished for a second, replaced by a flash of something like anxiety. "Heck, no! You're as bad as Candace."

"You can't blame us. You're very pretty. He's very doomed."

Grace paused, staring at him for a moment. "Did you mean it about joining Amnesty?"

"Sure, why not?"

"You still thinking of studying law?"

"Are you crazy right now? Of course!"

Paolo didn't feel as confident as he sounded, but he'd lied and conned and had sex to keep that ambition alive. It wasn't something he was about to drop.

MAYA
KITCHEN, SATURDAY, APRIL 25

"Never thought I'd see the day when you and I were the first ones up."

Maya smiled at Lucy's languid expression of disappointment. She dropped two pieces of bread in the toaster and waited for it to pop up. She spread it with peanut butter and strawberry jam and sat down at the table. Lucy poured herself some Cheerios and milk and took the chair opposite Maya's. Maya checked the time on her cell phone. It was just past eight o'clock. Pretty early for anyone in their house to be awake on a Saturday, let alone Lucy or Maya.

"Whole world's gone crazy," Lucy said. "It must have: I actually studied for six hours last night. And I'm down for more today."

Maya had heard all about Lucy's school ultimatum, naturally. Her system for keeping tabs on what was going on in the house was working okay from what she could see. "Major aggravation," she said, trying to show some sympathy.

Lucy hesitated. "Kinda hate to admit it, but . . . they have a point."

"The school?"

"My folks. I was an A student. And yeah, okay, I've slipped to a C average. Truth is, that doesn't feel so great."

"I guess. But I thought good grades weren't very punk rock?" Maya took care to hide the tiny shred of smugness she was feeling. When you worked as hard as she did, it was galling to see party types like Lucy cruise through a battery of A grades.

"They aren't. The music is one thing. And I'm another. I thought that it didn't matter to me. I thought nothing mattered but the music."

Maya was genuinely taken aback. "But it does?"

"Yeah. It does. I like my life here." She smiled a rare, sweet, and friendly smile. "I like you guys. I don't want to leave. And—don't tell this to the others—but I liked being an A student. I liked knowing things and being smart."

"You're still smart."

"Yeah, but not like you, Maya."

Maya felt the blood rush to her cheeks. "I'm not all that smart."

"Don't be a sap. You're real smart. How many other kids have developed apps?"

"God, tons. Honestly, I could show you."

"There's a difference. You're gonna get somewhere with yours."

"With Cheetr? I'm gonna need a hell of a lot more

people to download it before I get any serious advertising revenue."

"You'll see. This app, or one you'll make in the future. You're a hard worker. In your business, that pays."

Maya managed a grin, but didn't mention all the cases she'd heard to the contrary. Of code monkeys working all hours on their apps and getting precisely nowhere. It was just nice, for once, to have someone as cool as Lucy express her admiration for someone like her.

"So you're gonna ace those grades? Good for you, Lucy."

Lucy sighed. "It'll cost me. Bailey sent me this text last night." She plucked a cell phone out of the pocket of her hoodie, pressed a few buttons, and then passed it to Maya.

You made a commitment, idiot girl. A gig is a gig. This counts as a no-show. You're out.

"What an A-hole!"

"Oh, significant A-holery."

Maya watched Lucy thoughtfully. She seemed resigned, defeated, sad. But not angry. Maybe she hadn't really liked being in the band after all? Or maybe she was just more chilled out a character than Maya had initially thought.

"So that's it?"

Lucy shrugged.

"And you're going to study all weekend?"

"I'm going to rock those term papers. It's worth it just to

wipe the smirk off Guzman's face. She so wants me to fail. I can feel it! She's already imagining me up in Santa Barbara, saying novenas and rosaries all the livelong day."

Maya chuckled. "I don't think the convent school is all that holy."

"They're such hypocrites. You know when my family last went to church? It was my confirmation. I was fourteen."

"I guess they're outsourcing the religious instruction."

"Maybe. But I'm not going to a boarding school. I'm not going back to Claremont. They gave me a taste of freedom—big mistake! No way I'm giving that up."

Both girls were silent for a few moments. Maya offered to make them all smoothies. The suggestion went over well. She broke bananas and dropped strawberries and blueberries into the blender, poured in some milk and a scoop of strawberry frozen yogurt. She let the blender churn away for a couple of minutes and poured the mixture into two glasses.

Lucy took a sip. "That's good!"

"My mom used to make them every day just to get me out of bed."

"Nice mom! Mine got the housekeeper to do it."

"You had a housekeeper?" Maya asked. "Gee, I guess you did. I keep forgetting that you're basically rich."

"Good thing, or they sure wouldn't let me live here."

In Lucy's eyes, Maya caught a sense of the question that was probably in the minds of all her housemates—how could the daughter of poor immigrants afford to live in this house?

"I'm lucky that my dad has a good job in Mexico City," she ventured.

Lucy became noticeably quieter, obviously waiting to hear more.

"What does he do?"

"He works for a pharmaceutical company."

"And he couldn't get a green card?!"

"It's gotten a lot tougher."

Maya's phone buzzed, jangling across the wooden table. She grabbed it, pressed the button under the name that flashed up: AUNT MARILU.

"Hi, Marilu," she said briskly, before switching into Spanish. She flashed a friendly grin at Lucy and began to walk with the phone to her head, moving out of Lucy's earshot.

"*Hola, mi reina*, just calling to check in."

"Well. Everything's cool."

"Maya—about the last report."

Maya tensed. "Yes?"

"There . . . there wasn't too much about Lucy in your latest report. Everything okay?"

"Lucy's fine. She's just busy with schoolwork. There was talk of her being sent away to a boarding school. But I don't think that's going to happen."

"Oh. That's a shame."

Maya didn't agree, even though it would certainly make

her life a hundred times easier. It was refreshing to discover that Lucy, for all her chilled-out rock-chick attitude, might be a closet geek. It made her feel like someone in the house really "got" her.

"And what about Grace? Have any of the other housemates figured out who she is?"

Maya sighed. "You mean—do they know her name used to be Grace *Vesper*? No. What's the deal with that anyhow?"

"Maya, you think I care? It's enough that you have to be sure to write about it if the subject ever comes up. What about Grace herself—does she suspect that *you* know?"

"Why would she? I try to avoid the topic of her family."

"Good! Well, you keep it that way and we'll all be happy. *Adiós, mi amor.*"

Maya stared out to the ocean, pale and gray that morning, the same color as the sky. She longed to fling her cell phone far away, onto the sands below. This spying arrangement was seriously beginning to get on her nerves. It wasn't just scuzzy, having to report back on the people you lived with; it was eating into her time and focus.

She didn't know if she could put up with this much longer.

ARIANA CALLS THE WEST COAST

"Honey, I'm getting awful tired of leaving messages for you. It's been what, a month since we last talked? Guess you've grown tired of ol' Ariana. If you're going through some-thing, I wish you'd tell me. Maybe I could help? Anyhow, if you're too busy to talk, at least send me a text, will you?"

Ariana hung up. She paused for a moment, debating her next move. Reluctantly, she dialed again, another West Coast number.

"It's me. She's still not picking up. Girl got some attitude right now."

The crisp voice on the other end of the line said only, "Ah." Then: "Not to worry. Things are under control."

"Good. You gonna tell me how you're doing that?"

The woman drawled, "I don't think so. Let's stick to what we agreed. Sometimes the right hand prefers not to know what the left hand is up to."

"All right, but just so you know, I don't enjoy being ignored. That girl needs a lesson in manners. Rehab buddies are supposed to check in with each other. I could be using again!"

"You're not, are you?" the woman asked sharply.

"Of course not. But Lucy should give a damn."

"Given where you met, one can see why she'd have certain reservations about staying friends."

For a moment, Ariana felt resentment bubbling within. She'd always envied the interest people showed in the oh-so-adorable "Charlie." But Lucy had turned out to be just another confused teenager, not too different from Ariana herself, only a little younger.

Ariana grumbled, "I'm almost two years clean. Not everyone in rehab relapses."

"Well now, that's true. Some people find religion. How's that working out for you?"

Ariana's mood was quickly shifting into anger. She'd have to get off the phone within the next thirty seconds or risk losing her cool.

Her cell phone piped up. "Oh, look, Lucy just sent me a text."

"There! That's something positive, isn't it? What does she say?"

"'Ariana, I'm okay, sorry, having some issues, but mainly okay. Let's talk, maybe next weekend?'"

"Lucy is distracted just now . . . I happen to know that."

"By what, exactly?"

"Ah-ah. Right hand, left hand, darling! All right, Ariana, we'll talk again. *Ciao.*"

GRACE
KITCHEN, WEDNESDAY, MAY 20

"Omigod. This is sooo much harder than it looked when John-Michael was doing it."

Paolo glanced over Grace's shoulder at the printout of the recipe. "Strawberry and apple turnovers?"

"I know. Puff pastry, right? What was I thinking?"

"You have to make your own jam!"

"Yeah, well, obviously I'm skipping that."

Paolo put a finger on the liter-sized tub of chunky applesauce. "You're not making the applesauce, either. Why even bother making the pastry? You could have just bought it."

"You can buy ready-made pastry?" Grace looked awed.

"You can buy ready-made apple *turnovers*."

"I'm running the bake sale, Paolo. The stuff's got to come out of our own oven."

Paolo looked at the tray of burned turnovers, black and shiny with caramelized jam and applesauce that had spilled beyond the loosely crimped edges. He picked one up and took a bite. The carbonized sugar crunched between his teeth.

"Tastes good."

"Boys will eat anything," Grace said dismissively. "We can't sell them like this."

He took another, larger bite. "Mmm. *Real* good!"

Grace just frowned. "Could you try to be actually helpful?"

"Why don't I drive you to the store; we'll buy some pastry dough and you can try again."

He picked up two more of the burned pastries in his left hand and dug the keys to his car from the pocket of his board shorts. Grace followed him out of the kitchen mumbling, "I overfilled them. That was the problem."

The air-conditioning in Paolo's Chevy Malibu took several moments to get properly going. The day was cloudy and overcast, but still hot enough to make Grace begin to sweat the moment they were inside the car. She opened the window and let the breeze ripple over her.

"I think it's so great that you're organizing this fundraiser for Amnesty International," he told her with a warm smile. "First time I'm ever going to one as a member."

She beamed at him. "One day maybe you'll be one of their lawyers."

"That would be cool," he agreed. "It would be so great to get to fly all over the world, meeting people who'd stood up to corrupt governments and all."

"How's it going with your letter writing?" Grace asked.

"I requested a woman, but they said they really needed more people to write to guys. So I got this one, Harrison Coyle, a black dude, twenty-six years old, on death row for a year now. Double homicide, including one police officer. And I wrote him just the way you said, with some friendly questions and some generally supportive stuff. . . ."

Now he turned to her with a quick grimace. "But."

"But?"

"But bad news, is what. Turns out his appeal just got turned down. So I guess it doesn't look good."

Grace sat calmly in her seat. She turned on the radio. After a moment, she realized that Paolo was staring at her with a kind of appalled expression.

"Oh," she said. She reached out reassuringly to touch his arm. "It's okay. Don't worry. This is all part of the experience."

"Really?" His eyes went back to the road. "The thing is, I'm kind of freaked about supporting someone through an execution."

She couldn't stop herself from smiling a little. She squeezed his arm harder. He reacted with a brief, puzzled glance. Then back to the road. He was frowning now, confused and anxious. Grace couldn't stop thinking about how cute he looked. Once in a while Paolo still had that little-boy look. It made him even more irresistible. She felt a sudden tug inside her chest.

She realized he was scared.

Grace remembered well what it felt like, that fear. The first time she'd written a letter, she'd felt a sickness deep within her belly. It had been hard to put pen to paper. The image of the death chamber, the gurney inside, a man strapped to it waiting to die before the watching eyes of the press, the victim's family, his own family. And in one of those viewing galleries: herself.

She'd seen the schematics of that part of San Quentin. She'd memorized them. If Grace didn't do something, one day for certain everything she had imagined would come true.

Paolo might be luckier. Although if his guy was a cop killer, probably not.

She loved that Paolo wasn't afraid to seem vulnerable in front of her. Some guys were just so terrified to lose any kind of face in front of a girl, they turned into complete dolts. Grace wondered if Paolo had any idea how attractive it made him—and not just to those country-club cougars he'd confessed to sleeping with. She decided that he probably did. More reason to keep her own feelings in check.

"You have to stay positive, Paolo. He's only been on death row a year, yes? This is probably his first appeal. If there were grounds for one appeal, there are probably more grounds. If he has a good lawyer, they can keep appealing. Maybe one day they'll change the law."

"You really think?"

"Hey, you could be one of the people to defend him."

"I hope he'll be out of jail by then. I read up about him.

Harrison said in his testimony that the guy he killed died by accident, he didn't mean to kill him. And he shot the cop in self-defense."

Grace wasn't sure self-defense was allowed if it was a cop shooting at you, but she didn't mention that. "All I'm saying is that it's a long haul. You have to steel yourself. My guy has been through three appeals so far. All turned down. But his lawyer keeps starting up the process."

"Must be, like, majorly grim. I bet some of those guys just want it to be over."

Grace said doubtfully, "I'm pretty sure they prefer to live."

"Than be killed by the state? Of course. But they gotta get depressed."

"They get *horribly* depressed."

"I guess. Hard to tell—Harrison doesn't write too well."

"That's often the problem," she agreed. "Smarter guys, guys with good educations, they have a way with words, contacts; they usually get reduced sentences, or if they can really make the case for self-defense, they might even walk."

"What's your guy like? What's his name?"

Grace hesitated. "I didn't tell you the day we went to San Quentin?"

Paolo seemed to consider. "Nope, don't think so."

"Alan Vernon."

"And he's in for murder?"

"Yes," Grace said. "But he didn't do it."

"You believe that?"

"I'm sure of it."

"Really? Because when I joined the program it said that you had to allow yourself some reasonable doubt. Doubt with sympathy, that's the idea."

Grace said nothing for a moment. Maybe it wasn't safe to keep talking about this. She didn't enjoy having to deceive Paolo. Better to keep the lies to an absolute minimum.

"You know what, I feel like we talked a whole lot about me and Alan when we were up in San Francisco. Your experience is valid also. We should talk more about that."

Paolo laughed. "Hey, don't worry about me. Look, it's good to know that Harrison might get another appeal. That makes me feel better. I'm really not ready to go into the viewing gallery."

"You don't have to do that, you know."

He shook his head, eyes firmly on the road. "If you're there for them, you're there for them. Least, that's what I'd want. If I was on the other side of the bars, I mean."

He didn't speak for a while, turned up the volume on the radio station that Grace had selected. Eventually, he turned to her with a gold-plated smile. "Let's get *a lot* of pastry dough."

JOHN-MICHAEL
VAN BUREN HIGH SCHOOL, THURSDAY, MAY 21

John-Michael leaned against the side of the Benz, one hip knocked against the window. The match flared in his fingers, he lit the cigarette, put it to his lips. That's when he caught first sight of her.

She was marching along the sidewalk toward him, pushing past the huddle of students who'd paused to smoke on the boundary of the school grounds. Some of them, John-Michael could tell, didn't take too kindly to having a bony, middle-aged woman shoving them aside. In some parts of the city she'd be risking a knifing. But these kids were too occupied with looking cool to make a big deal of it, however they felt. They parted like a human Red Sea, with nothing more than a middle finger waved at her departing back.

John-Michael took another drag on his cigarette and waited. He was glad of the nicotine spiking in his blood right now. He'd never been good at handling Judy. It had been a happy day when she'd skipped out on his father's life.

Somehow, he wasn't surprised to see her. In fact, he wondered what had taken her this long.

"There y'are, you little piece of shit." She was a little out of breath, her thin lips quivering. He could just see a sheen of moisture on her upper lip. Since they'd last seen each other, John-Michael had grown another two inches; tall enough to look down and notice the graying roots of her chestnut-colored hair.

"Hi, Judy."

"Didn't think you'd ever see *my* ass again, didja?"

"Jeez, Judy, could you not mention your ass? I'm a delicate homosexual, didn't you hear?"

"Shut up, you lousy *father killer.*"

"The correct term is 'patricide.' And I hate to disappoint you, but I'm not."

Judy laid one hand on the edge of the Benz, her fingers caressing the bodywork. She smiled at him, then watched his eyes follow her hand.

"So you took his car."

"His pride and joy," he agreed. Her fingernails were long and painted the color of a flamingo.

"Bet you enjoy riding along in this, sonny. Thinking about what a clever boy you were to get rid of him. Got him off your back and all his cash, too. Nice going, kid."

"Watch your mouth," John-Michael warned.

"You know, you might not enjoy the Benz so much if you knew what me and Chuck used to do in it." Judy paused, enjoying the look of revulsion that flashed across his face. Then she smirked. He could see the row of sparkling veneers that his father had paid for. John-Michael had asked for a car that year, but, of course, Chuck had just laughed and told him to *get a friggin' job*.

It was time to drop the pretense of amiability.

"Judy, what do you want?"

"I want what's coming to me. Fifty percent of Chuck's estate. That's what he left me."

John-Michael snorted in derision. But Judy just continued to stare at him with all the righteous verve of a protestor on a march.

"Not according to his will."

"That's because you used an old will," she said, baring her teeth. "You thieving bastard."

"The will was legal. Don't blame me if my dad hadn't updated it in ten years."

"He made a new will when he was with me. I know, I saw it."

"He did? Then where is this mysterious new will?"

"How the hell do I know? All I know is what I saw."

"Who knows what he showed you? Did it ever cross your mind that he showed you something nice to keep you sweet? To keep you . . ."

But John-Michael couldn't bring himself to complete the vulgarity. Even the thought of his father and this woman together was disturbing. She'd looked better then, but even so she'd been a daily drain on his father's temper. The woman in front of him now looked about ten pounds lighter, which was okay for the way the clothes hung on her frame. But it had taken something from her face—the slight chubbiness, the surprisingly cherubic look that she'd sustained well into her late thirties. Now she looked angular and dilapidated, permanently sour.

"I saw a will, goddamnit. Fifty percent to you. More'n you deserve, lazy faggot. And fifty percent to me. To thank me for all the years I looked after him."

His laughter was short and hollow. Even her insistence on using homophobic insults barely touched him now. "You didn't look after *nothing*. You made him miserable. Apart from that first year when you were sinking your claws in him, all he wanted to do was to get rid of you."

"Is that what Chuck told you, mama's boy?"

He went quiet. A cold rage began to chill his bones. She caught the scent of his distress but mistook it for fear. Her sneering tone intensified. "Things looked pretty different from where I was looking up at your dad."

John-Michael began to experience something he'd rarely felt: an itch at the base of his wrist, the impulse to ball his hand into a fist, to swing for the woman. The cigarette fell, forgotten, as he fumbled for his car keys. He had to get out of there before she said much more to enrage him.

Judy leaned against the driver's-side door. She put her face close to his and whispered.

"I know you've got the original will. But I've got a *draft*. My lawyer says it'll be enough to give you a motive. They've already placed you at the scene. You've got no alibi. He died with his veins turned white with heroin, and we all know what good buddies you are with the junkies. Face it, John-Michael. I take that draft of the will to the cops and you're looking at juvie until you turn eighteen and then—well." She pretended to wipe away a tear. "Gee, I just don't know if you're gonna get along with those prison types. Maybe you can find yourself a big ol' sugar daddy to protect you?"

John-Michael put the keys in his jeans pocket. His back firmly against the door, he pressed both hands against her shoulders and lightly pushed. She sprung backward, obviously shocked. He followed through, gave her a second push.

"You believe I killed my own father?"

"Put your hands on me again," she spat, "and I'll lay a lawsuit all over your goddamn face."

He crossed his arms, stifling a glorious urge to punch her. "You think you got a hope of persuading anyone that my dad left a skank like you a single dime? Good luck with that."

"Goddamn evil little . . ."

He turned, opened the door, dropped into the driver seat, and inserted the key. She was at his side, leaning over the door, two seconds later.

"Give me my fifty percent, John-Michael. And I'll pretend I didn't just hear you call me a skank."

Very deliberately, he said, "I met some lousy people when I was living rough. But you, you're a real class act when it comes to lowlife. Never understood why Dad got mixed up with you. It's no wonder he killed himself, probably to get away from you."

He revved the engine, watching Judy struggle to contain her fury. Her eyes became as narrow as a snake's before the kill. "Fifty percent. That's my offer. In a week, it's going up to sixty." She stared pointedly at the car. "Enjoy yourself, twerp. It's later than you think."

CANDACE

THIRD FLOOR, THURSDAY, MAY 21

Candace stood outside her room barefoot, her feet absorbing the sun's heat from the warm cedar decking. She was transfixed by the music within. Lucy's acoustic guitar had stood in the same place since she'd moved in, untouched, as far as Candace was aware, until today. Now this: the sound of an astonishing, virtuoso performance resonated throughout the house.

She noticed Maya and Paolo gathering at the base of the staircase to listen. One by one, they caught her eye and mouthed a silent, wide-eyed *wow*.

Lucy's playing continued for several minutes. It wasn't a short piece, but the mood switched every few minutes. As spellbinding arpeggios gave way to a more contemplative melody, Maya and Paolo edged back toward their own rooms. Candace's hand hovered over the doorknob. It seemed like sacrilege to burst in on Lucy, like interrupting a private moment between her and the guitar. Very quietly, she turned the handle and slipped into the room with an apologetic glance.

Lucy acknowledged her with a nod, then continued playing, her features stern with utter concentration. Candace perched on the edge of her bed and watched until the final chord. When it was over, she burst into heartfelt applause. Lucy smiled slightly, shifted a little uncomfortably on her chair.

"Sorry, didn't mean to keep you waiting."

"Are you kidding? Lucy, you can really play!"

Lucy shot her a look of thinly veiled derision. "I know. I got picked to play lead guitar in an up-and-comin' band."

"No, I mean, like, really, you know, like, classical."

"I trained to play that. Only really started with the rock about three years ago."

"Is that why your parents threw you out?"

Lucy's answer seemed guarded. "Had something to do with it, yeah."

"Well, you know I love rock music, but seriously, Lucy, wow!"

Lucy shrugged. "You think so?" She didn't seem convinced. "That was going to be my audition piece for Juilliard."

"You should still try out. You're amazing."

"Not so much. I'm still playing too slow in the arpeggios."

"You don't want to go to Juilliard . . . ?"

A beat passed. "No."

"Why ever not?"

"It's . . . not what I want. You think I'm good but, truth is, I'm not good enough. Do you have any idea what kind of talent is coming out of China and the Far East these days? There are twelve-year-old kids that play that Bach Chaconne better'n me. The only way a guitarist can make it in that world is as a soloist. You don't see many guitars in orchestras. And I'm not good enough to cut it as a soloist."

Candace hesitated. There seemed to be a degree of regret to Lucy's tone. Maybe rock music wasn't her first love after all. Candace shook her head. "Seems pretty screwed up to me, throwing your own kid out because they don't want to go to a particular school."

"Wasn't only that. Wasn't that at all, matter of fact. Just that me deciding that I didn't want to try for Juilliard led to . . . a lot of stuff, actually. The rock music. And I fell back into some behaviors that . . . Ahhh. What's the point talking about it? What's done is done."

"You seem sad. Are you?"

Lucy shook her head, staring into Candace's eyes. "No. I'm really not. Maybe once, but not now." She leaned forward and picked up the soft instrument case, which lay discarded at her feet.

Candace wandered over to the music stand and stared at the sheet music. She'd taken piano lessons until she was eleven and never reached a high standard, even for that age. Lucy's music was covered with an impossible tattoo of black notes. Candace's own tiny experience playing an instrument made her realize that to play as well as Lucy did meant that at some point she must have been completely dedicated. To be able to perform as well as she just had, without having practiced the piece at least since they'd moved into the house, meant that Lucy's talent was prodigious. It was hard to believe that Lucy couldn't go just as far as she wanted with the guitar.

There had to be something Lucy wasn't admitting.

"You just love to rock, right?" Candace prodded.

Lucy allowed the beginnings of a grin. "I sure do."

"How'd that happen, seeing as how you were this little goody-two-shoes classical player?"

"My big brother, Lloyd. He took me to see Green Day when I was fourteen. Told me there was a chance, if I could swear I could play, that Billie Joe would invite me on stage to play with him."

"No kidding."

"I looked online and he was right. Every big concert they did, some lil' kid would get hauled up on stage to play guitar."

"Amazing. So did you, like, study the songs before the concert?"

"Please. It was like three chords."

Candace's mouth stalled in mid *O*.

"Anyhow, we went to the concert. Lloyd made me get there real early so that we could dash for the front row when the doors opened."

"And did . . . ?"

"Did he pick me? A black girl outta all those pasty white-boy faces? You bet your ass he picked me."

"Damn! That's so awesome."

"He picked out three of us. We played 'Knowledge' by Operation Ivy. Not the most challenging thing in my repertoire but . . ." She gave a nostalgic sigh. "Looking out over that crowd. A sea of upturned faces, all expectant, waiting to be entertained. The energy of it. I can't explain. It was like the energy flowed from them to me and back again. In this incredible feedback loop."

Candace grinned in appreciation. "I have some idea of what that's like. Our Shakespeare youth theater group used to play to fifteen hundred people sometimes. You're right, there's nothing like that feeling from a crowd."

"Take that feeling and multiply it by at least ten—'cause there were, like, seventeen thousand people in the crowd that day. I was buzzing for weeks. Went to sleep with the bass lines pounding in my veins."

"You got the bug."

"That was me bought and sold. Never could feel the same way about classical music again. When I play a piece like the Chaconne, I'm lost inside myself. Which is good, too, don't get me wrong. It's just not how I wanted to connect with music. Being on that stage was like being a lightning rod, collecting all this energy and transmitting it. I didn't tell my folks, didn't even tell Lloyd, but I knew it from the day of that concert. So that's how I started on my third attempt at a career at the age of fourteen."

Candace frowned in contemplation. "Don't you mean your second?"

Lucy shook her head. Candace had a vague sense of some reluctance in Lucy's manner. She put the acoustic guitar back onto its stand near the door. Then Lucy flopped onto her bed, eyes fixed straight on the ceiling. She fumbled under her pillow for her cell phone and reached for some earplugs. It seemed that the conversation was over, but Candace wasn't ready to let it drop.

She had an idea and turned on her laptop. "Where was the Green Day concert?"

"In Oakland."

She searched for a few minutes until she found the video online. She hit play and leaned back to watch. Sure enough, there was Lucy, young, slightly chubby and wearing blue jeans and a black *American Idiot* T-shirt, strumming the chords, eyes facing the audience, Billie Joe Armstrong singing along, his face wreathed with delight.

"Dear God, there's a video!"

"There's more'n one," muttered Lucy.

Candace looked over at Lucy. "That *would* be a pretty tough experience to top."

"My folks didn't agree."

"So—how come it was your *third* career? You did something before the classical guitar?"

Lucy hesitated. She eyed Candace with what looked almost like suspicion.

"Since you ask, I used to want to act."

"Honest to God?"

"Yeah." Lucy paused again and then admitted, "TV, actually. Kinda like you."

"You wanted to act on TV?"

There was a too-long pause. "I did it, for a while."

"Are you being serious right now?"

She felt sure Lucy might have said more, but John-Michael poked his head around the door at that point and asked if Lucy wanted to go with him to get some burgers from In-N-Out. He didn't extend the invitation to Candace, which didn't surprise her. Every now and then those two seemed only too eager to fall back into their older friendship.

Candace watched them go. Then her eyes wandered back to the computer screen and fourteen-year-old Lucy Long, strutting her stuff with Green Day.

Now *that* was inspiration.

GRACE
BALCONY, THURSDAY, MAY 21

"Come look, it's gorgeous out."

From the balcony of the beach house, Grace announced her invitation to anyone within hearing distance, and then turned to watch a peach-and-magenta sunset flare against the horizon. The beach was largely empty, just the occasional dog gamboling along, owner and pet stark silhouettes in the sand. Out in the water she could see the lights of a few boats being rocked in a light offshore breeze.

The evening bar crowd was just beginning to arrive. Slightly more than the normal weekday buzz, fairly standard for a Thursday. After a moment, Candace appeared on the threshold of her bedroom, laptop in hands.

"I gotta finish this civil rights essay."

"You still haven't finished?" Grace asked.

"I got distracted by the ol' 'Tube."

"Hamsters playing the piano?"

"No," Candace said calmly. "Lucy playing with Green Day."

Candace placed the laptop on the balcony's drinks table and played the video. Grace watched over her shoulder, marveling at the young Lucy's supreme confidence.

"Well, I'll be. . . ."

"I know. She's got major stage presence," Candace said. "You know what's even more surprising about her past?"

Grace hesitated for a moment. There was a gleam in Candace's eye, the air of someone on the verge of divulging a juicy secret. Did Grace really want to risk where this conversation might lead?

"More surprising than Lucy playing live with Green Day?"

"Yeah," Candace said. "You'd think she'd have mentioned something huge like that before, right? But I'm talking about something else, something bigger."

Grace began looking for some kind of distraction. She swung around, toward the sunset. "Whoa. I never get tired of looking at that view."

"It is awful pretty."

"Your mom's so lucky to have this place. What made her buy out here?" Grace risked a sidelong glance at Candace. But she didn't seem remotely suspicious of Grace's apparent lack of curiosity about Lucy. She leaned forward on the rail, shoulders hunched, and allowed a dreamy gaze to fall over the golden beach.

Good ol', laid-back Candace. Grace faintly wished that she could be just as relaxed when the time called for it. Her own languor was studied by comparison.

"My mom always dreamed about living with artist types," said Candace. "Such a boho wannabe. Until she got her hands on some real money. Now she does all her shopping on Rodeo Drive. A real hipster, ha."

"Her loss, our gain." Grace smiled at Candace. "You wanna walk down to Santa Monica? We could go to the boardwalk. I'm kind of in the mood for a banana split with a lot of hot fudge. And a fairground ride."

"Banana split?" Candace frowned. "You have any idea how long I'd have to run to burn that off? I'm not allowed to gain more than a pound or two."

"Maybe it would be more fun if we went with the others."

"Yeah. You know, when we moved here, I thought we'd be there every couple of weekends."

Grace grinned. "Me too. It's because it's so close. We can do it anytime."

"So we do it never."

They both laughed. Candace straightened up. "God, I love living here. I don't know what I'd do if anything happened, and we had to move out."

"We have to make sure that doesn't happen," agreed Grace. The distraction seemed to have worked—Candace had gone quiet, probably thinking about food, which wasn't surprising since she was usually hungry.

"We could just walk along the boardwalk," Candace suggested. "Maybe grab some fish tacos. Or a chicken salad. My treat, little sister," she said, wrapping an affectionate arm around Grace. "And then I can tell you this amazing news about Lucy."

"Are you sure it's something Lucy wants everyone to know?"

"Why not? It's nothing bad. She didn't make a big deal out of it."

Grace gave up. Clearly, there was no discreet way to prevent Candace from indulging in gossip. "Okay, so what is this big secret?"

"Well, guess what? Our Lucy, rock guitar goddess, used to be on TV."

"Seriously?"

"Yes, she was on some show."

"Regularly?"

"Didn't say."

"On network TV? Or some crummy cable channel?"

"What, you mean like me?" Candace said, smirking.

Grace frowned. "Yours is hardly one of the crummy cable channels, Candace."

"She didn't say what channel it was on."

"So maybe she was on a show *one time*."

Candace shrugged. "Hey, getting any kind of a spot on a TV show is major. Especially for a kid."

"Huh."

"Why are you so down on this, Grace? I thought you'd be psyched like me."

"I don't get why it's a big deal."

Just then, the yellow-painted spiral staircase began to

shudder with the rhythm of someone ascending the steps. Maya's face appeared in the stairwell. She seemed tired, with gray shadows under her eyes.

"Did I miss the sunset?"

Candace said, "Almost."

"Darn," Maya said. "I promised myself I'd catch one this week."

"We were just talking about that," Grace said. "All the cool things we said we'd do but never actually do."

Maya nodded. "There's just so much schoolwork. With all the shopping and the cooking and cleaning, and the coding on top, I swear, I haven't had more than an hour to myself these past two weeks."

There was definitely more work involved in simply keeping a home going than Grace had expected, too. But like the rest of them, there was no way she was going to admit it. They'd all bought into the idea of emancipation and so far, none of them had breached the unspoken rule to never say a word against it.

"How's the computer stuff going?" Grace asked.

Maya leaned lazily on the edge of the balcony and stared up at the canopies of the palm trees, black fronds of silhouette against the teal-green-colored sky. "It's going really well, thanks."

Candace interrupted, "So hey, guess what? I was just telling Grace that I found out that Lucy used to be on TV."

Maya glanced at Grace. She didn't seem all that impressed, either. "Really? What show?"

"We don't know," Grace said cautiously. "Did you ever see a TV show with Lucy on it?"

"I hardly ever watch TV," Maya said, in a wary tone, which struck Grace as slightly jarring.

"We could search for her online." Candace pulled up a chair and sat in front of the laptop. "Why didn't I think of this before?"

Grace froze. This wasn't taking the direction she'd expected. She wasn't sure how she felt about the housemates knowing more about Lucy. It might not be safe.

"Because you're not an actual stalker?" Grace answered, trying to sound casual.

"It's TV. Hardly a state secret," Candace said. "Presumably she wanted to have an audience."

"Is that why people act?" Grace said with an edge of challenge to her tone. "For the audience?"

Candace shrugged. "It's a big part of it."

"But in TV you usually don't see the audience."

"You still know they're there. I mean, you gotta kind of imagine them. Anyhow, Lucy actually told me she loved the buzz she got from playing on stage with Green Day."

Maya flinched. "Lucy played with Green Day?"

Candace nodded. "They got her up on stage when she was, like, fourteen."

"I didn't know that."

Grace looked at Maya with sudden curiosity. "Why would you?"

"Just seems like she'd tell us a thing like that."

"I wonder how many other secrets she's got up her sleeve," Candace mused.

Grace and Maya said nothing, exchanging uncomfortable looks.

"Okay. I can't find anything on IMDb for Lucy Long," Candace said. "Not for Lucille, either. What else is Lucy short for? Lucinda?"

Maya interrupted. "Candace, no offense but this *is* getting kinda stalkerish. If she didn't tell you the name of the show, maybe she doesn't want to talk about it? Shouldn't we respect her privacy?"

Candace looked baffled. She closed her computer and shrugged. "Whatever. I just thought you'd think it was cool is all."

Deep in thought, Grace studied Maya. Ever since the younger girl had caught her looking through Lucy's letters, Maya had been a vault. She never revealed anything about herself. It seemed everyone's secrets were safe with Maya—Grace's own crush on Paolo as well as Lucy's past. But what did they really know about Maya?

JOHN-MICHAEL
VENICE BEACH, FRIDAY, MAY 22

John-Michael was behind the wheel of the Benz within five minutes of the end of his calculus class. The shock of being accosted outside school by Judy yesterday hadn't quite left him. Maybe he was being paranoid, but John-Michael didn't want to stick around to find out if she'd be back.

The Friday afternoon commuter beach dash had already started. A five-minute drive back to Venice turned into a twenty-minute crawl in the blazing sun. He thought of the beach, the weekend ahead. He plugged in his headphones and listened to his newest pop punk playlist. Yet even as his lips moved along to the lyrics, his mind couldn't quite let go of the image of Judy.

There'd been venom in her eyes.

His dad's executor had told him how much the estate would be worth once the house sold. It wasn't a fortune, but even half of it was a whole lot more money than Judy had ever been near. He didn't regret calling her a skank. As far as he was concerned, she was a gold-digging harpy, a former stripper with zero education who'd lived off the vices of idiot hetero men for most of her life.

Now that the police had decided that his father's suicide was suspicious, however, Chuck Weller's place might forever be whispered of as "that murder house." It might affect the sale. That was all the money John-Michael would ever be able to count on. It included his mother's inheritance, which they'd used to make a sizeable down payment on the house. It made him sick to think that he might not be able to sell the place. Even as a rental, it might be hard to find a tenant. These weren't the kinds of problems he'd ever envisaged having during high school.

He parked the car in the garage spot he'd managed to secure at huge expense. During the short walk to the beach house, he gazed out at the wide stretch of sand. The ocean looked startlingly blue today. The sun was hot enough that he could feel his face smarting from the slight burn he'd gotten during the drive home. Maybe a sunbathing session was called for. He was never going to have a physique remotely like Paolo's. But he didn't have to have skin the color of milk, either.

He'd been lying on his beach towel in swimming shorts for over thirty minutes when he heard Candace's voice.

"Here you are. God, finally, a chance to get horizontal. I'm totally exhausted."

John-Michael raised his sunglasses. "The TV show?"

She nodded a confirmation and sat down, sighing with relief.

"You came to LA to work, and you're working."

Candace shook her head slowly. "Hardly."

John-Michael said, "What? I thought you loved it."

"You didn't come to the studio that time with the others. You'd understand if you had. I'm just eye candy."

"So? At least you're on TV."

Candace tugged at his towel. It was a broad bath towel, sea green with a navy blue border. Easily wide enough for two to share. "I thought so at first. But now I want more. Hey, c'mon, let me lie down."

"Ah, the human condition to always want more."

She flashed a grin. "Ain't that the truth? Anyway, I'm hanging in there for more auditions."

"You'll see, Candace, someday you'll be up for something amazing."

She flicked his shoulder playfully. "When that happens, if it happens . . ."

"You'll what?"

She rolled onto her back. "Oh! I can die happy, I guess."

"I think you'd be better to stay living and enjoy the experience, but, whatever."

Candace shoved him this time, hard enough that he rolled onto the sand. As John-Michael stood, brushing himself off in indignation, she leaned back. "Hey, did you hear about Lucy? That she used to be on TV?"

"Yeah. I know. So?"

"You knew?!" This possibility clearly hadn't crossed Candace's mind. "You knew and you didn't tell?"

John-Michael lay down once again. "Lucy doesn't like to talk about it. It's ancient history."

Candace rested her chin in her hands and peeked up at him from under a sun visor. "Do you know what show she was on?"

"Jelly and Pie."

"That?! Huh! I never saw it."

"It wasn't great. Show got canceled after three seasons."

"What was Lucy?"

"Oh, you know. The archetypal, cute, dimply, sassy black kid. Now shut up talking about it, Lucy really doesn't want it dragged up. Lay down, it's sunblock time."

Candace rolled onto her stomach and gave way to his hands as he applied lotion to her shoulders and back. She sighed and he could hear a lazy smile in her voice. "Oh, JM, if only you liked girls."

"Stop it," he said firmly, but with a grin.

"So how's it all going, on that front? You seen anyone you like?"

"No," he said, even more firmly. "You've had all the juicy gossip you're going to get here. Why don't we talk about you, not me? You seen anyone that *you* like?"

"Oh, me. Who wants to talk about that?"

"I never met a girl who didn't want to talk about herself."

Candace propped herself onto one elbow and stuck out her right hand. "Well, hello, I'm Candace Deering. There. Now you've met *one.*"

"Seriously? But you're in showbiz!"

"I play many parts." She smiled with fake modesty.

He laughed. "Yeah. I believe it. Now you're playing the introverted artiste."

"Ha. Well, maybe. I'll tell you who doesn't like to talk about herself–my stepsister."

"Yeah. She's pretty quiet. And actually, Maya."

"That's different," Candace said. "She's a geek. Not that there's anything wrong with that," she added hastily. "I love geeks. They invent all the pretty toys. But it's a lot of work–all that coding."

"She does put in a lot of late nights. I hope something comes of it."

"What do you mean?"

"Well . . . seems like a lot of time to put in for no reward."

"I think a lot of it may be her issues with dyslexia."

"She's dyslexic?"

"Yeah. Once I found her downstairs at, like, two a.m., crying 'cause she was so tired from fixing bugs in her code. She told me then. She makes a lot of mistakes because of the dyslexia. And it takes hours to debug or whatever."

John-Michael was astonished. "Whoosh. That's my respect for her shooting through the roof."

"I know."

"And all for a game-cheating app?"

"Far as I know."

"Too bad she doesn't come up with something more

unique. I had a look once—there are, like, a *million* game-cheat apps."

"Unique—yes! Then she could be the next Zuckerberg."

John-Michael lay back on his towel, staring up. He pulled his shades over his eyes. "That would be cool, to be friends with Zuck."

"Maya would be cooler."

"She'd be *so much* cooler." They were both silent for a few minutes until John-Michael said, "Way to distract me, by the way." Candace made a puzzled sound, and he smiled. "From talking about if there's a guy you like, I mean. Is there?"

"Can I tell you something?"

"Sure."

Candace grimaced. "I'm not attracted to any of the boys at school."

"None of them?"

"No. Now that I'm working with actual men on the TV show, the guys at school seem, I don't know, like kids."

"Oh—uh-huh."

"What's that mean?"

"Older dudes," he said. "I get it."

"I didn't say that."

"But you meant it. And I understand. I've met boys who've gotten into serious things with older guys. They can be very appealing. Their own place, a job, nice clothes."

She said, "I've always kinda liked guys a few years older."

"I'd settle for cute, honest, and kind."

Candace ruffled John-Michael's hair. "Aww, such a sweetie pie. And you know how to make a pie, too. Some hunk of cheesecake is sure to snap you up."

John-Michael allowed himself a quiet grin. Women could be *nice*. And he lived with four fantastic ones—more than enough to erase the memory of spiteful Judy Aherne.

LUCY
FIRST FLOOR, FRIDAY, MAY 22

Lucy and Paolo were waiting for John-Michael in the living room. Lucy tried John-Michael's cell phone but when it rang she could feel it rattle from across the kitchen table.

"He's out. And he left his cell."

But the cops just smiled humorlessly and sat down. "We'll wait."

Paolo took one look at the cops and he was out the door. Late for a lesson, apparently. But Lucy knew for a fact he'd stopped giving lessons on Friday evenings. If she didn't know how straitlaced Paolo was, she might have suspected him of wanting to avoid the police. It didn't do any good anyway, because when Paolo returned after an hour, they were still there. This time, Lucy grabbed his arm and drew him into the kitchen. "Don't you leave me alone with these Nazi pigs."

Paolo stayed after that, talking quietly or hardly at all. Grace arrived a little later, and Maya. No one left the kitchen. Grace suggested that they busy themselves with cleaning out the fridge and kitchen cabinets. It was either that or eat.

All the while, the cops waited, watching TV. One guy was Asian American, good-looking, and with a good physique, around thirty-five years old. The second was a woman, about the same age as her partner, short brunette haircut, navy pantsuit. They were playing it pretty cool, all understated. Yet something felt terribly wrong. Lucy had been on the wrong side of cops often enough to recognize a certain vibe.

They were high on anticipation. Something was going down tonight—maybe even a new break in the mysterious case of Chuck Weller's death.

John-Michael got back around six thirty. Candace was close behind. They'd been to the beach; John-Michael still wore the towel across his shoulders. When he saw the two detectives on their sofa, he barely reacted. Just gave them a passing nod and made as if to head upstairs. But those cops couldn't have been more obviously there for him; they stood up the second he walked through the door.

The woman spoke first. "John-Michael. I'm Detective Winter—we met two months ago. I'm going to have to ask you to get dressed and come down to the station with us."

John-Michael stopped in his tracks, turned, almost painfully slowly, to face Winter. "What did you say?"

"Get some pants on, son."

"Am I under arrest?"

Lucy caught his eye for the briefest instant before he

disappeared, returning three minutes later dressed in black skinny jeans and Vans, a plain white T-shirt and a black-and-purple plaid shirt.

The male officer stood very straight. He said, "John-Michael Weller, you are under arrest for the murder of Charles Durham Weller."

The female cop proceeded to read John-Michael his Miranda rights. The sound of those words was utterly chilling to Lucy. In the kitchen, amongst the housemates, there was a deathly silence. Lucy felt a tremble run through her. She stared at John-Michael, trying again to catch his eye. But he seemed unreachable. Like a lone sailboat, becalmed at sea.

Detective Winter continued. "Do you understand each of these rights I have explained to you?"

John-Michael nodded, expressionless.

"Having these rights in mind, do you wish to talk to us now?"

He shook his head.

"We're not planning to cuff you, John-Michael, but we can."

Lucy stepped forward. "I'm coming with."

The male cop set his face against hers. "I'm sorry, miss, but this is a very serious matter. It's best you don't get involved."

Lucy pushed out her lower jaw. "He's a minor. Right? And he has a right to have counsel present during the interrogation."

"We just told him he could call an attorney."

"Right. So until an attorney gets down to the station, I'm his counsel. Got that?"

John-Michael placed a hand on her arm. "You don't have to do this."

She turned to him. "Who's your lawyer, John-Michael, you know anyone?"

"I need to make my calls. I'm allowed three, right?" he asked with a glance at Detective Winter, who nodded.

Lucy continued. "I'm still coming. No way I'm gonna leave you alone with them."

"We're going to Carlsbad, miss," said the male cop. "There won't be a ride back."

She glared. "Does this face look like I care?"

Paolo was at her side a second later. In her ear he whispered, "Lucy, you sure about this?"

She glanced at Paolo in surprise, more than a little confused that he wasn't jumping in to back up their friend, too. "He's our friend. Of course I'm sure."

"Okay then, I'll drive down, too. That way you have a ride home."

Lucy nodded. Almost as an afterthought she squeezed Paolo's forearm. She couldn't tear her eyes from John-Michael. And nothing. Whatever he was feeling, if he was feeling anything, was buried down deep. She wanted to grab him by the shoulders and shake some life into him. Get him to show some goddamn emotion.

He didn't know the cops the way she did. They acted

smooth, friendly, and professional, obviously pleased that he was playing nice with them. But they were already sizing him up. Did he look like a killer, act like a killer, sound like a killer? Like a guy who would shoot his own dad full of heroin and watch him die? All he was showing was this cool, unflappable face. Easy to see it as the demeanor of a cold-blooded murderer.

Detective Winter sat next to John-Michael in the rear of the car. They put Lucy in the front passenger seat and made a big deal about the fact that they were bending the rules even letting her ride in the same car as her friend. No one spoke, all the way down to Carlsbad. The male cop—he told her his name was Shawn Leung—put the radio on to some country music station. Lucy wanted to make some crack about the weirdness of an Asian American cop listening to redneck music, but she didn't. Truth was, she kind of enjoyed it, too.

John-Michael had asked Lucy to make a call to his father's attorney, before they left the house. It was an hour before his cell rang again. Lucy turned to watch the female cop take the call. She spoke in monosyllables. When she hung up, the cop told John-Michael, "Your father's attorney is coming down."

He simply nodded once. Then back to the inscrutable, blank face. The two cops exchanged a brief, bewildered glance. Then Winter gazed with open curiosity at John-Michael.

"Quit staring at him," Lucy said.

"Miss Long, stay out of this."

"Don't let her psych you out, JM."

"Now why," puzzled Winter, "would your father's own attorney agree to act as your counsel?"

There was a brief silence. "Because he's the executor of my father's will."

The cop didn't say anything else. Lucy turned back to face forward, pondering. It was a good question, and a better move. If Chuck Weller's own lawyer was willing to back John-Michael, that certainly put a big dent in the case for any prosecution.

But John-Michael hadn't been charged yet, she reminded herself, only arrested. Pretty much everyone Lucy had seriously hung out with back in Claremont had been arrested at least once. On the other hand, being hauled in for holding, being drunk in public, or underage driving kind of paled into insignificance next to murder one. She tried not to think about it. Yeah. Maybe John-Michael's iceman routine was the way to go.

When they arrived at the station in Carlsbad, John-Michael's dad's attorney was already waiting. He was a picture of sober sincerity: smart suit, hands crossed over each other at his waist.

Lucy watched John-Michael get fingerprinted and escorted down a corridor where they took the mug shots. Paolo joined her a few minutes later in the reception area and pressed a cold can of Diet Coke into her hands. She accepted it gratefully but with a pang of guilt that she could take some comfort in the refreshment, while John-Michael remained dry-throated and scared.

In the stark, slightly shopworn surroundings of the station, a horrible sense of reality began to take form around them. A grimly familiar sensation of utter helplessness took hold of Lucy. She began to feel nauseous. The urge to get out of there was powerful. She kept thinking of JM. The apocalypse that was headed his way. Jail. Court. Prison.

John-Michael asked for a couple of minutes alone with his friends. The cops left him, but the attorney didn't. Lucy couldn't hold back any longer.

"John-Michael, what the hell?" Lucy felt the sudden gentle touch of Paolo's fingers on her arm. His eyes caught hers in silent warning.

John-Michael looked for a long moment at the attorney before answering Lucy. "I think . . . my dad's ex-girlfriend may have something to do with me being here."

The attorney seemed reluctant to speak in front of Lucy and Paolo. Paolo took the hint and slunk back toward the vending machines.

"It's okay. Lucy's my best friend," said John-Michael. "I trust her one hundred percent."

His frank sincerity clutched at her heart. In that moment, she wanted to remain at his side for as long as this took.

"This isn't going to go away easily," the attorney began. "I think you're looking at a night here, maybe two. They're trying to put a case together to charge you."

John-Michael didn't answer.

Lucy said, "Is that gonna be possible?"

"They have some pages of a draft of a will. It does look more recent than the one we've executed. They have evidence that your father created the file on his computer."

John-Michael closed his eyes and sighed. It was the first time Lucy had seen him register any emotion. And after all this, it wasn't terror, but frustration.

"Even with all that," the attorney continued, "they don't have a signed, witnessed final copy. Your dad could have toyed with the idea of leaving the whole thing to frickin' SeaWorld for all it matters. What counts is what the official will says."

"So he's clear?" Lucy said, uncertain. She still didn't really understand why a second will would be such a big deal.

"They're saying you destroyed the latest will, which I told them we know nothing about, but they're saying Chuck used a different lawyer."

"Some buddy of Judy's, no doubt," John-Michael said bitterly.

"That's a possibility," the attorney admitted cautiously. "Their theory is that we executed an earlier version of the will. That John-Michael came to the house—you were seen by the cop, John-Michael—and removed evidence."

"How'd you find all this out?" Lucy asked.

The attorney gave a pale smile. "Judy Aherne doesn't give a damn who she tells this story to. Far as she's concerned, John-Michael's already convicted."

Convicted. The word slunk behind Lucy's ears and glowed hot.

The attorney continued. "John-Michael, this entire affair is built on some fairly tenuous accusations that I think we can work on, given time. My bet is that the only way they're going to be able to charge you is if you give them something. So you give them nothing. Not a whisper. Are we clear? You tell them *diddly-squat*."

CANDACE

"Someone crack open this bottle for me, my hand's shaking so much. . . ."

Candace thrust a half-filled liter bottle of supermarket-brand Russian vodka into Grace's hands. She unscrewed the cap, then took three glass tumblers from a cabinet and made three vodka sodas on the rocks with some bottled lime juice left over from the party. She handed the drinks to Candace and Maya. Candace immediately swallowed two big gulps from hers.

The other two girls took their drinks over to the gray three-seater sofa.

"I can't believe they actually arrested him. That's pretty much the scariest thing I've ever seen," Maya said.

Grace took a sip. "It could be about to get a lot worse."

Maya stared at her. "You . . . you think John-Michael did it?!"

"I don't think he has an alibi," Candace said. "He looked terrified last time that detective was here. I saw his mood switch"—she clicked her fingers—"just like that. One minute he's making chocolate buns, next minute he's this scared little kid."

Grace said, "You were with John-Michael earlier on, Candace. Did he seem worried?"

"Not particularly. Although we weren't talking about him."

"What did you talk about?"

Candace thought for a few seconds. "We sat in the sun, we talked, we went into the ocean. We had fun. He seemed fine."

"Huh."

"Lucy might know more," Candace said. "They're obviously close. And a little while back, she was talking to me about how John-Michael got his all clear at the health clinic."

"Sure, he told us, the HIV test." Grace looked at Maya for confirmation, but the younger girl was staying quiet, listening attentively.

Candace said, "Yeah, only Lucy wasn't convinced he was getting tested for HIV. She seemed to think he had something else going on. Something connected to his father."

"Like what—a genetic disease?"

"Yes! Maybe that's what Lucy was getting at. Is it possible that John-Michael was getting tested for a genetic disease? And maybe his dad died of that?"

Grace looked doubtful. "I thought his dad died of choking. Or an overdose."

Maya finally spoke. "I thought it was choking *because* of an overdose."

They were all silent for a few moments, sipping their drinks. The alcohol had already soothed Candace. She turned on the TV, but Maya immediately grabbed the remote from her and turned it off. "Please. Can we just have some calm for a little while?" She hurled the remote back across the sofa.

Candace and Grace exchanged a single look in ominous silence. This was pretty strange behavior from Maya, at least on a day when she wasn't obviously glued to her coding.

Candace explained, "We need to watch *The Simpsons* or something. 'Cause this is a major downer."

Grace grabbed the remote. "If Maya isn't happy," she said, "I think we should leave it."

"Thank you, Grace," Maya said. She glared at Candace, who lapsed into stony silence.

But Candace didn't feel like letting it go. After a while she said thoughtfully, "You think maybe his dad killed himself because of the illness? Maybe it was incurable?"

"Some of those genetic diseases are pretty horrible. What if JM's dad knew he was going to die from something real nasty, and decided to kill himself first? What if he asked John-Michael to get him some H?"

"John-Michael said he never used H."

"No, but, come on, Grace. He lived on the streets for, like, a year. He's gotta know people who deal it."

"You think maybe he was with his dad when he died?"

Maya said, "If he bought him H and gave it to his dad, knowing that he was gonna kill himself, that's a crime. I don't know what level of crime it is, but I'm pretty sure that's illegal."

Grace could barely conceal her scorn. "Of course that's illegal! It's assisted suicide. Second-degree murder. You do prison time for that."

"That's insane," Candace said. "No way should you do time for assisted suicide."

"Are you kidding?" Grace countered angrily. "What if I come around and 'assist' you to death, huh? Or your little ol' grammy? That okay by you?"

Maya said, "Okay, okay, let's not get into this. Maybe we agree, maybe we don't. But if it's illegal, it's illegal. And John-Michael could be in big trouble if he actually did it."

"Let's hope Lucy can keep him quiet," Grace said.

Candace's cell buzzed with a call from Lucy. Candace signaled urgently for silence and then answered. She barely said anything, listening to Lucy, exhausted, tell her they'd be home in a couple of hours—*without* John-Michael.

When Candace informed the other girls, they paled.

"No me digas," Maya pronounced slowly. "Is it possible . . . that he did it?"

"It would explain a lot," Candace mused. "John-Michael's dad finds out he's sick. Maybe he's known a while. Maybe he only decides to tell JM at the end. When he's already decided to end it."

Grace glanced at the other two girls. They'd grown somber, nodding in quiet agreement. Incredulous, she said, "So we've already decided, have we? He's guilty? He helped his father to die?"

"It fits the facts," Candace admitted.

"Would it really be so bad?" Maya said. "If his dad was scared, maybe already suffering? It could be a kindness."

"You gotta be kidding me," Grace said. "I sure hope I'm not around any of you when I start getting old."

Candace shrugged. "I'd switch you off if you asked me, sis—if you were suffering. But what I don't get is why a sweet guy like John-Michael, who was thrown out on the streets by his jerk of a dad, would want to do him any favors?"

"He gets to keep all the money," Maya said quietly. "Whichever way you look at it, things got better for John-Michael after his old man died."

"That'll work against him," Candace said.

"I don't think we should talk about it any more," Maya said, reddening.

Candace groaned. "Now can we please watch TV?"

Grace handed her the remote. "I'm not in the mood." She rose to her feet. There was only ice in her glass now. "I'm going to my room."

Neither Candace nor Maya followed her. They wanted to be there when Lucy and Paolo got back. Maya glanced at Grace before she left. Candace couldn't tell whether it was sympathetic or judgmental.

After two hours watching a TV show called *Deadbeat*,

which starred a very cute actor that Maya clearly liked, they heard the front door open.

It was Lucy and Paolo, back from Carlsbad.

Maya and Candace rushed over to the kitchen, where a very subdued Paolo made cup of hot tea. Grace joined them, murmuring some vague platitudes. But they were all tense with anticipation. There was only one thing they wanted to know.

Lucy cradled the mug. She took tiny sips like a little kid. Finally, she faced them, shyly.

"It's not looking good."

They waited, too appalled to speak.

Lucy shook her head. Candace couldn't help noticing how Paolo hovered close at hand, his face written with concern. He turned toward the girls, his eyes glistening. "It's a difficult set of circumstances. John-Michael's going to be in jail for at least a night. They're trying to collect enough evidence to charge him."

Lucy drew breath, spoke in an unbroken monotone. "They've got a witness who says they can prove John-Michael had a motive. He's got no alibi. Someone who fits his height was caught on a security video leaving the murder scene around the time of death. He was seen at the scene some weeks later. They suspect he was removing evidence."

Candace blinked, trying to absorb the vacant horror of it. "And what does John-Michael say?"

With blunt finality Lucy said, "Nothing."

GRACE
KITCHEN, SATURDAY, MAY 23

"Can I make you something to eat?" Grace stepped up to the kitchen counter and started pulling out plates and napkins. "You guys must be exhausted."

"Thanks," Lucy said. She leaned against the kitchen table, eyes glazed.

"Are we allowed to talk to John-Michael? I mean, can he contact us?" Grace asked. She arranged ham and turkey slices on four pieces of Wonder Bread, then squirted each with mustard and mayo and pressed them into sandwiches.

Lucy reached for hers. "That's enough for me, thanks, Grace. I'm not hungry, I just don't want to go to bed on an empty stomach." Within a couple of minutes she'd finished the snack. Paolo ate his in four ravenous bites.

"I don't know what John-Michael can and can't do," Lucy said in a weary voice. "I just know he's in a whole lot of bad trouble."

They couldn't persuade Lucy to tell them more. She looked emotionally drained and went directly to her room.

After five hours of driving, Paolo was also exhausted. The moment Lucy headed for the stairs he prepared to follow her, pausing only to drink a glass of water.

Grace listened to their footsteps from the bottom of the stairs. It sounded to her as though Paolo had accompanied Lucy to the double room at the top of the house. Maybe this was the night he finally made a move. A cunning, maybe even callous strategy, no doubt, but then Grace wasn't surprised. Lucy was rarely as subdued and vulnerable as she was now. And Paolo, she suspected with aching realization, was not the type to give up. The fact that one of their friends was facing a mind-warpingly serious criminal investigation would probably only heighten the mood.

She forced her mind away from the idea of them together. Instead, she thought of John-Michael alone in his jail cell. This, too, was troubling.

Maya's cell phone rang, startling all three girls. She answered in Spanish, *"Bueno."* She nodded a couple of times and then put the cell back into her jeans pocket.

"My . . . aunt . . . Marilu is here. She wants me to go spend the night at her place."

"She's here?" Grace asked. "At the house?"

"Outside."

Grace frowned. "Kinda late, isn't it?"

"I . . . eh . . . forgot. She did mention that she might stop by. I called earlier and told her about John-Michael. I was pretty upset at the time."

The girls watched Maya go upstairs to grab some

overnight things. Candace turned to Grace. "Huh! Lying much?"

"You think?"

"Gracie, it's after midnight."

"She's Mexican," Grace replied. "They're a very family-oriented people."

Candace raised a skeptical eyebrow. She ambled over to the kitchen and peered out through the front window. "Look at her aunt's car. Tell me that isn't a fifty-thousand-dollar car."

Grace joined her at the front window. "The Cadillac? I suppose. Never really thought about it."

"If Auntie Marilu is so rich, why does Maya have to live with us?"

Grace was on the point of replying, and then stopped because Maya was back downstairs now, looking for her keys on the hooks near the front door.

"Okay, later."

"So your aunt has a pretty fancy ride," Candace said lightly.

"Oh, that's not hers," Maya replied, distracted. "Did anyone see my keys?"

"You left them on the kitchen table," Grace said, pointing. "Whose car is it?"

"It comes with the job," Maya said. "She's a driver." She plucked the keys off the table.

They watched her leave.

Grace turned to Candace. "Did you know her aunt is a driver?"

"Me? How would I know?"

"She's never mentioned that. A driver," mused Grace. "How do you like that? I wonder who she works for."

Candace shrugged. "We don't really know too much about Maya, do we?"

"We know as much about Maya as we know about anyone in this house," Grace said with care.

Candace not only agreed, but proceeded to relate the theories she and Lucy had exchanged the night after John-Michael's impromptu dinner party. "In the end," she concluded, "Lucy wondered if John-Michael had ever actually been worried about HIV. That's how messed up things are around here. Anything could be going on, underneath it all. Literally, anything."

Eventually she grimaced and said, "I don't know how any of us will sleep tonight. Poor John-Michael."

Grace had the impression that the wider implications of Maya having extra knowledge about the housemates hadn't impinged remotely on her stepsister's brain. It struck her as odd, but she guessed that Candace must already be overloaded with concern for John-Michael.

"No way I'm going to bed feeling like this," groaned Candace. "Seriously. I need to watch TV, or I'm gonna snap like a twig. And it won't be pretty."

LUCY
THIRD FLOOR, SATURDAY, MAY 23

Without a word, Paolo followed Lucy to her room. At the threshold, she took his hand and led him inside. He was silent as she walked him to her bed. Only when she sat down did an awkward tension develop. Lucy looked into his eyes. He was staring at her with unguarded longing.

"Okay," she said quietly.

It took him a minute to react. "Okay what?"

"Okay, Paolo, the answer is yes. But just tonight."

To her surprise he mumbled, "Why?"

She looked away slightly. "Why? Because I don't want to be alone. Here. In this room. Thinking about John-Michael in jail."

With a finger, he gently guided her chin back so that she was facing him again. "I meant, why just tonight?"

Lucy laid one hand on his upper arm. "Don't spoil the mood, Lawyer Boy. This isn't a negotiation."

Again, to her surprise, he became quiet, obviously thinking. Whatever private dialogue he was conducting with himself, it didn't seem to change his mind.

"All right. But can we go to my room? Candace could walk in, here."

Lucy followed him one floor down to his room. She could still hear Maya, Grace, and Candace talking in the kitchen. He closed the door behind them and turned the lock. Then, almost nervously, he took off his shirt. It wasn't the first time she'd seen Paolo shirtless. His smooth, undecorated skin struck Lucy as surprisingly vulnerable, not buff or macho.

"Why are you doing this?" he asked.

"I already told you. Do I have to spell it out?"

Lucy reached out with the tips of her fingers, ran them over his shoulders and down across his solid pecs. His eyes closed a little in response.

"Lucy, if we start, I'm not going to want to stop. I mean it." He gulped a little. This was obviously not easy for him to say. "So please don't tease me. I'm not that nice a guy."

"Who says we'd have to stop," Lucy whispered as she gently kissed the side of his neck.

She felt his skin turn to gooseflesh at her touch. When he spoke again, his voice was tight, husky. "You're really . . . I mean, would this really be your first time?"

"What?"

Paolo clasped her left hand. "Do you really want your first time to be like this?"

"Sure."

"Why?"

"Because right now, I want to," she said. "I never wanted to before. At least not when the right guy was available." She looked up into his eyes.

"That's hard to believe."

She tugged her hand away from his and wound her arms around his neck. "Is there always so much talking?"

"I just want to understand."

"What's to understand?" She tried to kiss his lips, but he didn't respond.

"I guess . . ." He seemed uncomfortable talking about this. As though he were trying to push something out of his mind. "But why? It's not like you love me. I know you don't."

"No . . ." She stared into his eyes. "But maybe you love me."

He swallowed again. And he didn't deny it.

Resolve seemed to take ahold of him. He pushed her gently backward onto the bed. He moved a hand down to her jeans and undid the clasp of her belt, the fastening on her jeans, loosened them until he could slide his hand between the fabric and her skin. He moved his hand over her hip and around back until he was clasping her flesh. Then he sighed, an exaggerated, dramatic sigh.

"I have wanted to touch you since the day I met you."

To Lucy's dismay, the sudden intimacy of his hand in her jeans did not have the effect she'd hoped for. If anything, the opposite. She could feel all her muscles stiffen. She closed her eyes for a second or two, tried to make herself relax. When he tried to move his hand back around to the front, she found her own hand stalling his.

Paolo paused, a quizzical expression on his face. He left his hand where it was, but didn't move it. Instead he kissed her. After a second she could feel his tongue trying to slide between her lips. Again she was stunned at how not into it she suddenly felt. The guy was beautiful. And he was crazy about her. What the heck was wrong?

She tolerated it for a whole minute before she made a strategic withdrawal.

It took Paolo a little while longer to catch on to what was happening. After a couple of seconds of gentle struggle beneath the waist of her jeans, his fingers wrestling hers, Paolo stopped moving. Slowly, his eyes rose to meet hers. There was puzzlement there, as well as an undercurrent of hurt.

"Too fast?" Tentatively, he withdrew his hand.

Lucy could feel a sensation of pure, hideous embarrassment sweeping through her. It was almost enough to make her pull his hand back against her.

Almost. But not quite.

For a moment they remained in the same position on the bed, neither knowing what to do next. In the end, Lucy said the only words she could think of. "I'm sorry."

He managed a wan smile. "I guess I did catch a vibe that you weren't totally into it."

She risked a grin. "Jeez. Now I've done it, right? And after you warned me you're not that nice a guy."

Paolo didn't answer. For all his calm demeanor, he seemed totally thrown.

"None of your ladies ever did this to you, I bet?"

"They didn't, no." His reply seemed wrought with concealed regret.

Lucy pulled away, sat up on the edge of his bed. She ran a hand through her hair and sighed. "I'm embarrassed."

"You're not into it," he replied softly. "It's okay, I get it."

"Don't say that. It's more complicated."

Paolo stood up and held out a hand to her. "Don't sweat it. Life is long, Lucy Long. Let's call this *deuce*."

She tried to return his smile but it probably looked just as awkward as his.

After a few minutes, they got dressed and went back down to the living room together. The moment they stepped through the door, Grace's eyes were on them. She seemed faintly relieved, if anything. Candace turned away from the TV and threw a balled-up napkin in Paolo's direction.

"Check it: Mr. Bedroom Eyes."

Paolo picked up the mustard-stained napkin from where it had fallen at his feet and tossed it into the wastepaper basket behind the lime-green futon.

"You're such a slob, Deering. And you're cranky as hell when you're tired. Good luck persuading any guy to live with you."

"Drop dead," she returned lazily, not even bothering to look up.

But Paolo wouldn't let it go. "How come when it's my

turn to cook and yours to clean, you never really clean up the kitchen? Maya, Lucy, and I are the only ones who use the bleach spray. And John-Michael and I are the only ones who ever clean out the fridge."

"Are you seriously going to whine about this right now?" Candace said. "My mom owns this house, okay? Why wouldn't I do my fair share? It's me she'll come after if we don't keep it clean."

"You don't need to keep it clean," he fired back. "Not when the rest of us are doing it for you."

"Could we please just chill?" Lucy said. Maybe she should take Paolo aside and confront him directly. What had happened in the bedroom had been a blow to their relationship for sure. But she couldn't let it ruin the atmosphere in the whole house.

"Why don't you just go call Mommy, then?" Paolo spat at Candace. His eyes were damp now. Lucy wished he'd just leave the room.

"*Me* call Mommy? What about you? You're never off the phone to her. Are you sure you like being emancipated? Maybe you should head over to Mexico, too."

He shouted back, "Never off the phone? I called her once: one time you just happened to hear it. My mom is lonely, okay? You have any idea how boring her life is now, stuck in some lousy mining town in Sonora?"

Lucy shook her head helplessly. She crossed the room to sit next to Grace on the large gray sofa that faced the wall-mounted TV. "What a crock," she said. "I feel like I've aged a bunch of years just in the few months we've been living here."

Grace nodded in agreement. "I know. *This* is not what I signed up for. Sometimes I feel more like twenty-six than sixteen."

Lucy stretched her legs out until her knees bent over the cushions at the far end of the sofa and leaned back against the pillows. "Maybe so. But it still beats the pants off living with my folks."

Grace shrugged, ambivalent, and turned back to the TV. Lucy couldn't help but notice that she seemed much happier than when Lucy had first walked in with Paolo.

Some kinds of disharmony, it seemed, weren't all bad.

MAYA

Maya had tried really, really hard to keep things together. But the day after John-Michael's arrest, it all began to unravel.

She'd begun the day doing errands with Marilu and making plans to hang out at the Amnesty International benefit at Hearst Academy, the school attended by Grace and Candace. It was late morning and Maya was on her way back to the house, riding in the white Cadillac with Marilu.

"Don't eat that burrito in the car, *mija*. The *inglesa* will smell the salsa. She'll freak."

Maya rolled her eyes. Carefully, she wrapped her breakfast back into its napkin. "How is Lady Macbeth anyhow?" she growled.

"Still the boss of me," was the terse reply. "And show some respect to Dana Alexander!"

"I am showing respect," Maya said innocently. "Isn't Lady Macbeth her most famous role?"

Marilu Soto tapped smooth pink fingernails against

the steering wheel to the beat of Selena Quintanilla singing "Baila esta cumbia." "I don't want you to miss anything today, baby. Lady Macbeth, as you call her, is going to want the full report. Things are going to happen—you'll see. John-Michael getting arrested is quite a thing. When emotions are running high, people can get to unburdening themselves. *Cuídate bien, mija.* Take care you don't get bitten by the truth bug. Might feel good at the time, like pulling a scab. But bad things can happen when you tell some truths."

"'Truth bug'?" Maya replied miserably. She shifted in her seat. "Mamá, how's that gonna happen? "I'm lying to everyone, every minute. Telling them that you're my aunt. Pretending my mother is in Mexico. I even made up a story that you were coming over, that we were going to Disneyland."

Despite herself, Marilu smiled. "*Ay*, baby. You wanna go to Disneyland? I'll take you. But take care with calling me 'Mamá.' Stick to 'Ma'—it's safer that way. They'll assume you're using a nickname."

"Will we ever be able to tell the truth?"

Her mother sighed. "The minute you decide you want to go back to Mexico, you can say whatever you like. But while the *inglesa* is my boss, we gotta do what she says."

"But . . ." Maya held back for a second, then said, "Don't you ever wonder why Dana's watching the house? I mean—have you figured out her deal?" It almost felt like an accusation to ask.

Her mother seemed to take it that way, too. "Not in a million years," she replied testily. "Who knows what her deal is? Like I always say, Hollywood people are crazy. I'm just focusing on keeping us both in this country, *mija*."

Back at the house, everyone had drifted down to the ground floor. The housemates greeted Maya with a measure of relief. It seemed there'd been some tension the night before. "Shenanigans," Lucy called it. Maya guessed that Grace was anxious about all the preparations for the Amnesty International benefit at their school that afternoon. Everyone in the house had promised to help.

Candace was preparing to go out for a shoot, only to get a call at the last minute saying that they'd rescheduled her scenes for the following week. As a consequence, she was still complaining about having dragged herself out of bed for nothing, after a night of hardly any sleep. Lucy had paused for a second, as if checking herself, and then went on to say, "That's one of the things I hated about doing TV. Weekend-morning shoots. Didn't take long for the novelty to wear off."

It was the first time Lucy had volunteered any information about her former life as a TV actor. Maya wondered how many times Lucy had been forced to bite her tongue.

Maya realized she should probably make more of an effort to act as though Lucy being a former TV star was news. Had any housemate gone to bed that night wondering why Maya hadn't seemed surprised? Had one of them somehow discovered evidence of Maya's spying? The paranoia was like a cold steel claw raking at the base of her spine.

No. Maya cradled her hot chamomile tea, thinking. If any housemate were clued in on the secret reports, it would have erupted in an almighty argument. She was being cautious, password-protecting her reports and her computer. It wasn't like her housemates were FBI agents or anything.

No one knew about Maya's situation—she felt pretty certain of that. At least she did when she forced herself to be rational.

Maybe it wasn't too late to make a big deal of Lucy's TV role? Maya remembered that down on Venice Beach every Saturday a street vendor sold secondhand CDs and DVDs. Perhaps she could find an old DVD of *Jelly and Pie?*

"Hey, anyone wanna go get a latte down on the board-walk?"

Candace glanced over from where she was perched at the kitchen table, apparently deep in thought, eating a piece of toast. Her eyes strayed to Lucy and Paolo, who were sitting on the sofa. They were watching a cartoon show together, making cute little comments to each other. Maya noticed that they were trying not to sit too close. Not quite the picture of coupledom, but barely one degree removed.

"Yeah, let's go," Candace said. There was a definite edge to her voice. She didn't even bother to dress. Plaid pajama bottoms, strappy tops, and flip-flops were ideal wear for

Saturday morning on the Venice boardwalk.

They weren't out of the house for more than five seconds before Candace turned to Maya and asked, "You think those two hooked up last night?"

From her tone, it was pretty clear that Candace thought they had. Maya lowered her sunglasses and stared out at the thick line of gunmetal gray where the ocean met the horizon. It was going to be another blazing day. Eventually she replied, "Why, did they say something?"

"They were in his room for a while last night," Candace said. "Afterward, there was a vibe."

Maya shrugged. "What if they did?"

"I'm just concerned."

"You're worried about the country club Casanova? Good luck with that."

"I'm concerned about *Grace*," Candace said.

"Oh," Maya said. "Yeah. Good point. I mean, you can see why it happened. But still."

Candace frowned. "Why it happened? Because he's into Lucy."

"I can see why it happened *last night*," Maya corrected herself. "It's obvious that Lucy is pretty shaken about John-Michael."

"We're *all* upset."

Maya pursed her lips briefly. "Really?"

Candace eyed her sharply. "You think we're not?"

"It's just . . . I'm not sure that *Grace* is upset about John-Michael." Maya chose her words carefully. "She seemed to think that assisted suicide was something he *should* do time for."

"What?! She was arguing that we shouldn't *assume* he did it!"

Maya was silent for a few seconds. "But maybe he did, Candace. And if he did, I think we should show some understanding."

"You know Grace. She thinks all killing is bad."

Maya raised an eyebrow but said nothing.

Candace came to a halt. "Hey, we passed the coffee shop already."

Maya pointed to a wide spread of tables where the street vendor's display began. "I actually wanted to stop there. Help me find a DVD of *Jelly and Pie*."

They spent about ten minutes perusing the solid collection of DVDs, VHS tapes, CDs, and audio cassettes until finally Candace unearthed one at the bottom of a box labeled *TV*. She showed it to Maya. The cover photograph was a group shot of the cast, goofing around just as they had in the few episodes of *Jelly and Pie* that Maya had seen. Lucy was almost unrecognizable. A pint-sized little nine-year-old, slightly chubby, cinnamon-colored skin, and a wide, toothy grin.

"Lucasta Jordan-Long," Maya said. "*Lucasta*. That's why you couldn't find her online."

"Jeez. Lucasta! Yeah, that sounds like a stage-brat name. Dear God," Candace continued, "check out these cast photos. It's a cheese factory. Now this we *have* to watch."

They hurried to the house, brandishing the DVD and some cans of Diet Sprite and Mountain Dew.

"You think that's appropriate?" Lucy fumed. "John-Michael spent last night in jail. Now we're supposed to reminisce about our childhoods?"

But Paolo seemed genuinely taken by the DVD cover photo. Despite Maya and Paolo cooing about how cute she'd been, Lucy stormed upstairs in a black mood. Paolo seemed torn as to whether he should follow, but the show's theme song was already running.

"I'll just take a look at the first five minutes," he conceded.

Maya watched Grace enter the living room just as Lucy was leaving. Grace stared at the TV for a second, confused and not a little annoyed.

"Guys—the benefit begins in almost four hours," she said. "Seriously. I need you to start helping me fix things up down at school. You promised."

Candace yawned. "Will you chill? It's not even noon. There's plenty of time. Didn't you already fill the freezer with all the turnovers?"

Grace visibly recoiled. She seemed on the verge of another outburst but apparently thought better of it.

Candace continued. "You're not going to believe what Maya and I found for sale on the street today. At the secondhand stall. Maya, tell her."

Maya opened three sodas and handed them out. "So guess what—Charlie from *Jelly and Pie* has been living right under our roof."

There was the briefest of hesitations. "You found a DVD of her show?"

"Yeah, that's why she left just now," Maya said.

"She doesn't want us to watch," Candace explained. "But c'mon, it's a hoot."

"Little Lucy," Maya said. "She was such a doll!"

A little suspiciously Grace said, "I thought you never saw the show before."

"I didn't say that," Maya replied a little too fast. She'd completely tripped up—again. "What I said was that I don't watch much TV. How did I know what show you were talking about? I saw *Jelly and Pie* once or twice. I just didn't pay that much attention. Hey, you've got to admit it, Lucy doesn't look anything like Charlie now."

Candace lifted the Mountain Dew to her lips. She glanced at the TV screen. The show had begun. "Sweet fancy Moses! Is *that* the legendary *Jelly and Pie*?"

LUCY

"My lawyer got me out of jail."

Lucy's relief was instant. She stood in the kitchen, one hand clutching the phone to her ear. She waved frantically with the other, trying to get her housemates' attention without interrupting John-Michael. They were still in the living room, gripped by the image of Lucy's younger self on the TV.

"The cops don't have enough to charge me," John-Michael was saying. "And it's not like they didn't try. They kept me up half the night."

"John-Michael—that's awesome!"

"That detective woman, Ellen Winter, finally signed off on my release. But I kinda got a sense that she's expecting to see me again."

"You're being too negative."

"You didn't see the look she gave me."

Moments later, Lucy planted herself on the checkered rug in front of the three-seater gray sofa. Sometimes the only way to get her friends' attention was to block the TV.

"I just spoke to John-Michael. He's doing some paper-work, then he'll start back from Carlsbad, but it's going to be a few hours. He's taking the bus. Bad news is, he's not sure he'll make it in time for the start of the benefit. And he was supposed to be arranging the ride for his buddy who was gonna play drums. With all the drama, I forgot to find someone else. Looks like it'll just be me playing guitar."

The sympathy was universal.

Lucy nodded, hiding her disappointment. She'd have to play alone until John-Michael turned up. She wanted to blame Paolo, but he'd only promised to arrange the band's transportation and electricity supply. They hadn't planned for the possibility of the rest of the band ditching Lucy at the last minute.

She could tell Paolo didn't like disappointing her. He clearly still wanted to impress her with a sweet setup at the benefit: a drummer, a bass player, a great sound system. Now they had the setup and no other musicians.

"You're pretty calm about this," Paolo observed.

Lucy paced over to the sound system, which stood beneath the wall-mounted HDTV screen. Her acoustic guitar was on a stand next to the wall, inside a hard case. She popped the case open and removed the instrument. "Learned a long time ago, a good entertainer plans for every contingency. I could walk into a kid's birthday party right now if I had to."

"Really?" Maya perked up from her spot on the sofa.

She sounded impressed. "What would you sing?"

Everyone in the living room stared at Lucy, waiting. It was a good feeling, all that hopeful expectation. Especially when she knew she could deliver. Lucy strummed a couple of chords and sang:

> *With a few good friends and a stick or two,*
> *A house is built at a corner called Pooh.*

The housemates burst into laughter.

"Carly Simon," Lucy said with a grin. "I got it covered."

Paolo said, "You should sing that today."

"JM and I were thinking more along the lines of Green Day, Rancid, Operation Ivy."

"Even better," Candace noted. "All the songs from our childhood. Plus Winnie-the-Pooh."

Paolo continued to stare at her, smiling. He looked as though he was about to say something else, but whatever it was, he kept it buried. Lucy liked the way he looked at her. It was impossible not to think back to how surprisingly sweet he'd been with her in his room. She'd told herself that the experience wouldn't be repeated, that it wasn't fair to let him think that they had a chance of a relationship together.

But maybe all the changes that were needed to make him more irresistible were superficial. She imagined his chest and arms covered in tattoos, maybe a piercing in his ear. Clothes that were a little less J. Crew. Yeah. She could see that working.

They left for the benefit an hour later, Paolo as Lucy's roadie. Candace, Grace, and Maya followed with a trunk loaded with food.

Candace and Grace's school, Hearst Academy in Malibu, was based around a sunny campus of green lawns and mission revival-style buildings of white stucco and terra-cotta-tiled roofs. The flower beds were tight with brightly colored hibiscus; the walls crawled with violet and pink bougainvillea.

Grace had managed to persuade the school's administration to let them use the central quad for the Amnesty International benefit. Lucy reflected that it didn't hurt that Candace's quasi-stepfather, the Dope Fiend, was a generous benefactor of the school. They'd probably have let the Deering girls organize an acid-fueled rave on the school grounds, so long as their coffers kept bulging. Lucy would certainly have enjoyed a rave a lot more.

A huge red Amnesty banner hung between the windows of two classrooms and across half of the quad. Beneath it, tables were arranged. They were filling fast with aluminum trays of cakes, pizza slices, quiche, fried chicken, paper bags and napkins, and cans of soda in deep plastic trays of ice. On the opposite side of the quad, two boys from Paolo and John-Michael's school were unloading amplifiers and microphones. Lucy almost laughed when she imagined herself alone in that setup. Never mind. She'd rock it out.

"Hey—is this the place for the impromptu Lucy Long gig?" The question came from behind her, a deadpan voice.

Lucy peered between the faces that were crowding around the food tables, looking for the source. When she found it, she couldn't help grinning widely.

"Ruben!"

"Hey, girlfriend," Ruben said with an ironic grin. "Am I too late to help out?" He stood clutching a conga drum to his chest, a cigarette dangling from his lips.

"Congas . . . ?"

"Only just got your text. I was on the way back from a lesson. It's all I had time to bring."

Lucy waited for Ruben to put the conga down. She hugged him tight. "Thank you, babe. I owe you."

"You don't owe me, dude. If anything, I owe you for letting Bailey be such a nimrod."

"I knew Bailey was gonna have a problem with me. I totally got that from him the first time we met at the audition. I just gave him the excuse he needed to ditch me."

"Look, I've known him for years. He's a good musician and we mesh okay together but . . . way I see it, Bailey's jerkitude is all his own."

Lucy smiled, staring down at the conga drum. "You really know how to play that?"

"Like I was Ray Barretto. This is the *conga*; I got a *quinto* in the car."

"You think you can play along with my kinda set?"

"Babe, it's cool, we'll improvise."

The audience was beginning to assemble. Ruben must have called some friends because several people called out to him as he began to set up his drums alongside Lucy's guitar and mike stand.

A few minutes later they were ready for a sound check. Ruben was already entertaining the gathered crowd with some conga riffs.

At the edge of her vision, Lucy could see Paolo watching them. He was pretending to help with the audio setup, but she could tell that he was mainly keeping an eye on her interaction with Ruben. It was impossible not to compare the two guys. Paolo was younger by at least two years, fresh-faced and athletic. Ruben, on the other hand, a Puerto Rican high school dropout, had ink-black spiky hair to match his dark eyes, piercings in his ear, cheekbones you could whet a knife on, and a *Sex Pistols—Never Mind the Bollocks* tattoo across his upper right arm, always on display under the rolled-up sleeve of his T-shirt. Ruben, who as far as Lucy had seen, lived for rhythm and punk.

If Ruben ever made a move, he'd be difficult to resist.

PAOLO

"Quit staring. You look like a stalker."

Lucy and Ruben were playing a song that Paolo didn't recognize when Paolo flipped around to see Candace eyeing him with a wily grin.

"Saw you look."

Paolo adopted a nonchalant stance. "I'm just keeping an eye on the sound equipment. It's all rented."

"Oh, stop it. We all know you slept with her."

For a moment, Paolo froze. He tried to brush it off with a bashful smile. The memory of that encounter was only becoming more miserable as the hours passed.

"Small house and loose tongues, Paolo."

"There I was thinking we were a pretty closemouthed bunch. Lucy being a child star, for example."

Candace looked puzzled. "So?"

"You don't think it's weird that Lucy didn't tell you of all people that she used to have the same job as you? I mean—a TV show. It's kind of a big deal."

"I guess. I assumed it was because she was embarrassed about being in rehab afterward," Candace said.

Stunned, Paolo said, "She was in rehab?"

Candace flinched, as if annoyed at herself and Paolo, too. "See, I'll bet that's exactly the kind of reaction she's trying to avoid. It was years ago and it's not like she's the only child star to go that way. Get over it."

"*You* get over it." Paolo could feel himself reddening in anger.

They were silent for a moment.

Paolo regarded Candace with a circumspect, almost suspicious air. There were his own secret misdemeanors, too, of course. He was fairly certain that no one in the house had a clue about those. He knew how to keep a secret. He wondered, then, was Candace concealing something, too?

"And what about you, Candace?"

Coquettishly, she tipped her head. "Me? I'm just the girl next door."

The sound of Lucy's acoustic guitar strumming chords hit the air, then her voice.

"Hey, if you've just arrived, we're Lucy and Ruben," Lucy said into the microphone.

"And now, we're gonna play you some of our favorite songs," Ruben added.

Cheers went up from the assembled crowd of high schoolers.

After a minute Ruben settled into a steady rhythm as Lucy began, very laid-back, to sing the lyrics of

"Knowledge" by Operation Ivy. Paolo listened for a minute. It was clear from the delight on their faces and from the occasional small mistakes they'd never played this together. Yet there was a chaotic synergy between them. And the audience responded with ever-building delight.

Paolo leaned over. "You think she likes him?"

Candace smiled. "Already? Man. You got it bad." She might have been about to say more, but at that moment Maya joined them, beaming. She was carrying a paper napkin wrapped around some toasted golden pastries.

"Did you try Grace's turnovers yet? Melt-in-the-mouth good."

They each took one. On the stage, Lucy stepped up the tempo. Another cheer rose up.

Maya said, openmouthed, "That is one talented *morena*."

"She's *his* talented *morena*," Candace said with a nudge of Paolo. She turned to him. "So you two finally—?"

Paolo found himself unable to reply. He didn't want to tell the truth. It was just too awkward. But on the other hand, he didn't want to lie. Lucy would find out and that would be another nail in his coffin.

"She's not 'mine,'" he ventured. "Don't be going around saying that, okay?"

Candace lifted her bottle to toast him. "Cheers, brat."

Maya continued. "Lucy's gonna be so goddamn famous one day."

"Don't be so sure," Candace muttered.

"Sure she is. Look at her," Paolo said. "She's sexy, she

sounds amazing, she's got crazy talent on the guitar."

"You should get a load of the girls that show up at my auditions," Candace added. "They have talent in spades."

"Yeah, and you beat them to the part," Maya reminded her.

Candace gave a sharp laugh. "I beat them to a basically nonspeaking part. I'm there because I've got the right look, mainly."

"Just the same, Candace. You got your foot in the door," Maya said. "And it's gonna lead to incredible things for you. It's in the air. I feel it."

"What, you got some Mexican *Santería* going on?"

"My family's from Mexico City, you redneck. We don't go in for any of that Caribbean nonsense."

Paolo leaned back, enjoying the spectacle of the two girls arguing.

Candace gave Maya's arm an affectionate squeeze. "Hey, you know I'm only joking, right? Thank you for saying you believe in me."

Maya grinned back. "You wait. You're gonna be huge. And Lucy, too."

Candace said with an air of finality, "Wake me up when it happens, okay? I wouldn't want to miss it."

Paolo listened with a sense of unease. He wanted Maya to be right about Lucy. Watching her on stage, he was in awe. It only made him want her more. Right now, she didn't want him at all and that situation would only get worse if she became famous.

As the song finished, Paolo noticed a third dark head bobbing up between Lucy and Ruben, attaching a lead to the amplifier. When the guy straightened up, Paolo realized it was John-Michael.

"Let me introduce our newest band member," Ruben rumbled throatily into the microphone. "On rhythm guitar, all the way from the Carlsbad police department, where he's just been acquitted of murder, John-Michael Weller!"

The inappropriateness of the comment drew a gasp from Paolo, Candace, and Maya. Paolo tried to catch a glimpse of John-Michael's reaction but his back was turned to the crowd. Lucy grimaced for a second, but then gave John-Michael a heartfelt smile of encouragement.

"We're gonna punk it up for you good people now," Ruben said. There was raw energy and joy in his voice. "Please give it up for Lucy Long on lead guitar and vocals and a little number by Rancid!"

Paolo stood back a little, found a vantage point from which he had a direct line of sight to Lucy singing.

Good morning heartache, you're like an old friend.

Every lyric struck straight to his core. Paolo couldn't take his eyes off her lips, the flutter of eyelashes when she closed her eyes. Both triggered sensory memories, the few moments in which they'd been close. He could feel unhappiness stirring inside him, a dull ache. The thought of never having her made him almost physically weak.

What was happening to him?

He shouldn't have tried to sleep with Lucy so soon. Or maybe he should have made a move earlier? He had no idea where he'd gone wrong. This felt bad, really bad. He could scarcely comprehend how miserable he was beginning to feel.

GRACE
HEARST ACADEMY, SATURDAY, MAY 23

From the cypress trees about twenty yards away, Grace watched Lucy back away from John-Michael. He didn't make any move to follow her, although their body language suggested that they'd had some kind of disagreement. Grace waited a minute, until Lucy was back with her other friends. Then she waved John-Michael over. As he sauntered toward her, she wondered about the twist of fate that had brought her under the same roof as Lucasta Jordan-Long.

When Grace had first heard the name of the fifth person that John-Michael had found for the house, she had assumed she'd heard it wrong.

Lucy Long, from Claremont.

She wasn't mistaken. Grace could still remember the creep in her skin as she'd let those words settle inside her.

Lucasta Jordan-Long.

A buried name with a hollow legacy.

Hearing that her soon-to-be-housemate "Lucy" was

■341

the daughter of assistant secretary Robert Long and Anne-Marie Jordan had confirmed it. The former child star's name was one of the "secrets" lovingly exchanged on the small-but-devoted online forum dedicated to *Jelly and Pie*. Grace had trawled the forum for the latest news. It was true. Their beloved Lucy was getting emancipated—thrilling news for hopeful fans who could now fantasize that they'd be able to befriend the parent-free teenager.

At first, it didn't seem possible. How could Grace share living space with the one person whose silence had condemned her father? It was then she'd realized that all those years of reasoning with her father hadn't calmed her down.

I think someone might have seen.

Grace's father couldn't remember. He'd been too wasted. His pathetic, drink-and-drug addled statement had pretty much shackled him to the gurney in the execution chamber. Vague entreaties that someone, maybe a kid, had been wandering around the house that night as well as him did not cut it.

Not without anyone else to corroborate. And no one would.

Lucasta Jordan-Long.

Marc Honeydew.

Alexis Silber-McCarthy.

Tyger Watanabe.

The only four children in the house the night of the party at which Tyson Drew had been killed. Grace had known the names for as long as she could remember. She'd followed their careers. Three had burned out early. Rehab for Tyger and Lucasta. College and an academic career for Marc. Only Alexis was still going strong.

Grace had assumed the witness was Alexis. She was the oldest, the most visibly precocious. Grace could just imagine her management talking a kid like that out of giving testimony. Untold potential damage to her career. For years, Grace had fantasized about what she'd do if she ever found herself in an elevator with Alexis Silber-McCarthy.

Until she read an interview with Lucy Long.

Lucy, in many ways, had suffered through the worst "post-child star" trauma. She'd been nine years old when it happened, and hadn't even lasted the rest of the season of *Jelly and Pie*. She'd disappeared off the radar for a few years. And then at age fourteen, she'd reemerged in a scandalous story about former child stars who went off the rails. You'd think five years would be enough time to get over the loss of fame or the pressure to get back, or whatever it was that kicked off the rush to alcohol. But apparently not.

Lucy had agreed to an interview about her trauma. She must have been fifteen at the time. In the interview, she'd said something. The moment she'd read it, Grace had known.

Lucy was the one who'd seen the murder.

Acting is lying. It's pretending to be someone you aren't. I had enough of that. Just suddenly, it came to me, like a revelation. I wanted to be authentic. That's why I went toward music.

Grace was going to be sharing a house with Lucasta Jordan-Long.

And thus her plan had been born.

Grace wasn't surprised that Lucy made darn sure that no one ever called her Lucasta, or ever wrote to her with her stage surname of Jordan-Long. Her name had been printed in many of the articles written about the Tyson Drew case.

There'd been open speculation that one of the children might have been seen wandering around the house in the middle of the night. Grace's father was one of those who'd insisted that she might be a witness. But little Lucasta herself had denied it. Her parents had threatened lawsuits to anyone who repeated the allegations. If she'd seen anything, if she'd lied to the police, only Lucasta herself could admit it.

Unless Grace found some way to persuade Lucy/Lucasta to talk about it, her own dad was going to die.

So far, things weren't going well. Something or someone always seemed to conspire to stop her finding anything concrete about Lucy's past, or at least anything that Grace didn't already know. She wasn't succeeding in getting closer to Lucy, either. In fact, Grace had to admit: although she'd never sensed any direct animosity, she was probably Lucy's least-best friend in the house.

And now the situation between Lucy and Paolo. A shiver of self-loathing ran through Grace for the briefest moment. Of all the idiotic emotions to feel—why did it have to be jealousy?

Lucy's audience began to applaud as she once again

donned the guitar. The crowd swelled rapidly. From their attitude toward the band, Grace guessed they were friends or even fans of Ruben. Soon enough she couldn't see Lucy or Ruben between the bodies. She heard Lucy mutter into the microphone, "John-Michael, get your ass over here."

The crowd began to cheer and call out song requests. Grace watched Lucy and Ruben nodding enthusiastically as they recognized certain songs. When John-Michael joined them on the shallow, makeshift stage, their three heads met briefly.

When they separated, Lucy and Ruben were grinning widely. John-Michael, however, looked nervous. Within seconds, Ruben was riffing a conga rhythm. Lucy and John-Michael joined in on electric guitars, pounding out steady chords. After a few seconds, John-Michael began to sing, taking over lead vocals. He seemed unsure of himself, half mumbling at first. Grace didn't recognize the song until the chorus. Plenty of the audience did, however. They began to leap and bounce, joining in.

I fought the law and the law won.

Grace started walking. She bumped into Candace at the food and drinks tables. Candace was close enough that Grace caught the scent of vodka on her breath as the two girls collided.

"Candace, tell me you didn't bring booze to a benefit!"

"Do I *look* like an idiot? We made Sea Breezes at home

while we were getting everything ready. Don't whine—you basically took off while all the work happened. You don't get to lay down the law, little sis."

"Are you drunk?"

"Give me a break. We just needed something to lift the mood."

"The occasion wasn't enough?"

"Fine, be a pain. I won't tell you my big, secret news."

"Like you ever would."

"Jeez, don't be all like a kid whose lunch got stolen. All right, I'll tell you."

Grace turned back to face the stage. "Yeah, yeah, let's talk about you. As usual."

"Okay, well, listen. My agent called. That guy from *Deadbeat*—the one everyone thinks is so cute—got the lead in a new TV show for a major cable channel. Science fiction adventure crapola, you know the type of thing. But done properly, big budget. The sci-fi *Game of Thrones* is what my agent said."

"And . . . ?"

"That Ricardo Adams dude from *Deadbeat*, he saw the pilot of *Downtowners*. And he told the director I'd be perfect for this part in the new show."

"You? But aren't you locked in as Gina?"

"Apparently, it's negotiable. My agent told them to up my part, like, a lot. Or to release me from the contract."

"Kill Gina off?"

"Let's face it, it's amazing that she's survived this far.

She's just so darn scrappy. Someone's bound to ice her."

Grace marveled. "So this is how it works, huh?"

"Looks like it."

"I'm impressed."

Candace smiled. "Finally."

"Is it a lot more work?"

"I think it may be. And you can't say anything. This is strictly for the vault. It's not a done deal yet. I still gotta audition, screen-test with Ricardo Adams. Plus, my agent has some dancing to do."

"Jeez. Candace. You're snowballing."

Candace winked. "Baby, I'm only just getting started." She turned on her heels and walked off, grinning.

Grace watched her go, then almost by reflex sought Paolo's face in the audience. Just as she'd expected, he was watching the band from close by. Eyes fixed on Lucy. Probably wondering was she his girl now, or just another name to be added to a list he'd recite again one day, perhaps to another group around a table?

Candace had Paolo all wrong, Grace was certain. There was more to Paolo than he was letting them see. Grace couldn't help but pity him, even while enduring the gnawing ache of frustration—at herself for not *being* herself in his presence and at him for taking her studied indifference at face value.

Maybe he didn't understand yet that simply by existing you could cause someone to suffer. Maybe Lucy would be the one to teach him.

JOHN-MICHAEL

VENICE BEACH, SUNDAY, MAY 24

"Hey, Grace. It's John-Michael." He had to tell someone. Something made him choose Grace. A finger stalled over her name as it appeared in the list on his phone. When he chose to touch the screen, John-Michael didn't know why. Later on, he understood.

It was 7:40 in the morning. A nightmare had woken him an hour before. It had taken him a couple of moments to remember that it was still only Sunday. Tomorrow was Memorial Day: no school. At first, relief had washed over him. Then came the familiar weight that seemed to get denser with the passing of time instead of lighter. No school meant no distraction. Right now, he needed as much distraction as he could get.

He'd gone to the bathroom and the sight of the early-morning sunshine had instantly cheered him. He'd dressed quickly hurried outside and spun down the spiral staircase and onto the path toward the boardwalk. Here and there the soft, sandy banks near the path were still dotted with sleeping bags, their vagrant contents snuggled tight against the cool of the night. The air came straight in off the ocean, fresh and sweet. John-Michael breathed it deeply. Moments later he worked up the courage to dial.

"John-Michael?" Grace's response was predictably dozy, confused. "Where the heck are you? It's so early."

He cradled the phone now, held it close to his mouth, spoke quietly. "I'm out on the boardwalk. I couldn't sleep, didn't want to wake you and Maya."

He took a deep breath and plunged in. "I want to take you back to San Quentin."

San Quentin. Even the thought of seeing that place again was like an icicle in his chest. Yet he couldn't help it. The dread of a long night in a cell was at his back, but it cast a shadow he could only think of one way to erase.

"You should visit your guy on death row," John-Michael said. "I've been thinking a lot about him."

"You've been thinking about . . . *Alan?*" Grace whispered in sheer disbelief.

"A night in jail isn't like any other, Gracie. You say he's innocent. I believe you. I got some new perspective on this, okay? A tiny idea of what he might be going through. And . . . I really think you should go see him. You're all he has, right? We'll drive up there together, visit him, then chill for the rest of the day, stay over. I'll pay for the motel. Tomorrow's Memorial Day—so we don't even need to hurry back."

Grace sounded tired. "I'd have to call ahead to get

permission—you need an appointment to visit a death row prisoner. Plus I'd have to get my cousin Angela on board again."

But with only a little more muted protest, Grace eventually agreed to make the necessary calls and to meet John-Michael on the side road where he'd parked the Benz.

When she first saw him, Grace didn't move right away to hug him. John-Michael walked over to her slowly, held out his arms at the last minute to receive her. A lot was transmitted between them in the hug that followed.

All he said was, "You hungry?"

"Starved."

"Let's go to breakfast first. IHOP or whatever. Then we'll get started on the road north."

She just nodded uh-huh, sticking her hands in the back pockets of her jeans.

"If it's okay with you I thought we'd go up on the 5. It's not as pretty as the Pacific Coast Highway. But it's a lot faster. We can come back down on the 1, so it's not just a long boring drive."

Grace agreed. Still sleepy, she slid into the passenger seat and buckled up.

Over strawberry-banana pancakes at an International House of Pancakes, he told her what he'd been thinking. Before he spoke, he glanced around. Not the easiest place to unburden himself. The place was half full. It smelled of coffee, bacon, and Sunday-morning virtue.

But he couldn't bear to wait a minute longer.

"You think I killed my dad," he began. "Don't you?"

She let out a little gasp, just enough for him to realize he was right. She stared at him with transparent anxiety.

"It's okay. You don't need to say anything. I heard it in your voice the minute I got back from Carlsbad."

"I . . . John-Michael, why would you say that?"

But she wasn't a good enough actress.

"Maybe it's because I agree with you."

She gasped again. "You did it?!"

He replied with another question. "I need to know: Do the others think I killed him, too?"

She stared. "Do they think . . . ? No."

"So it *is* just you?" He gave a sad smile. "How did you know? The cops can't pin anything on me, but somehow they know. They just need me to say it. To say anything. A little thing would tip this thing over right now."

"The cops don't have any evidence?"

He shook his head. Softly he said, "There's nothing to prove beyond reasonable doubt that I left LA on December first. No solid reason to doubt my dad's suicide note. No motive. Turns out the ex-girlfriend's electronic draft of the will doesn't count for much. It was created when they were dating. She could easily have used his computer to write it herself. And even if she didn't . . ."

Grace picked up her fork, thoughtful. "What counts is the will he signed?"

He was relieved to see her exuding empathy. She was the first person he'd told. The conversation could easily have gone horribly wrong. "Only what he signed," John-Michael agreed.

They were quiet for several moments, eating their pancakes, fruit, and whipped cream, sipping their drinks; herb tea for Grace and coffee for him.

Then, "You wanna know how I did it?"

Grace turned to him with eyes that were grave but unafraid. "Did you get him the heroin?"

"When he called, I'd just finished the morning shift at this conference center where I was working. I was with Felipe. We were at the beach. We were so happy. Watching the surfers, drinking a couple of beers. Did you ever get a call that, like, from the minute you picked up the phone, you knew that everything was gonna change, like, irrevocably? Like you reached a point in the road and someone put a giant goddamn fork in the middle of it and made you choose?"

With unwavering resolve she replied, "I've never had any doubts about where I wanted to go. There's only ever been one path."

"Then you're lucky," he said, his eyes heavy with regret. "The road I chose, I didn't want. You understand? I knew from the outset that it would be dark. That I'd have to meet a version of myself that I didn't want to believe existed."

Grace had no answer for this but the touch of her hand on his.

Later, after they'd returned to Venice Beach in a blaze of infamy, he would remember this moment. He'd remember his lack of a physical response when she'd tried to comfort him. He'd remember the way he felt at that moment, as though a curtain had descended. It separated the past from his future, and he needed to do the same.

Most of all, he couldn't forget what he'd told her then.

"I chose an old road, Grace. A bad, old road that lies in wait. Better hope you never find it."

The words had stayed in his mind on their return journey all the way down the Pacific Coast Highway. Until he couldn't bear to hear them anymore.

GRACE

HIGHWAY 5, SUNDAY, MAY 24

"Why didn't you just tell him no?"

John-Michael turned down the volume on the car stereo. It had taken her until they were halfway to San Francisco before she'd dared to broach the subject once again. Grace waited, anxious. Somehow, John-Michael had guessed that she suspected he'd helped his father die. He was probably expecting sympathy. People who confessed usually did. They didn't want to hear their worst fears confirmed—that they were guilty and deserved punishment.

It wouldn't be easy to say to his face.

"My dad hardly ever asked me for anything. Prided himself on it. He had to be the big man, the provider. It almost killed him to acknowledge that when my mom died he turned to Jell-O for about a month. Maybe if I'd turned out to be more what he'd hoped? Who knows? But things being what they were—what they *are*—he wasn't about to let me help. It's why he didn't tell me until he'd already made up his mind. And then, he didn't ask, he ordered. He said—and let me try to give you his precise words—*Get your fucking queer, lazy ass down here with some heroin. Enough to kill a man.*"

John-Michael spoke very calmly, in an even, almost conversational tone. His eyes rarely strayed from the road ahead. Only occasionally, in the tension of his hands and arms, did Grace detect any sign of stress.

He continued. "And why didn't I say no? To start off, I did. Ended up hanging up on him. Ten minutes later, he calls me back. This time, whole different story. He's crying. My dad, Chuck Weller. Never saw him cry since Mom died. *Please, John-Michael. You're the only one I can ask. I can't do it alone. What if I do it wrong? I might wind up in the nuthouse. I need you, John-Michael, I've never given up hope that you'd come home. Some things are just for family.*"

"Did he tell you why?"

Grimly, John-Michael nodded. "Oh yeah. The sicko despised me too much to pass up that particular little gem. *It's gonna kill me, kid. And guess what? Chances are, it's gonna kill you too.*"

"He had a genetic disease?"

He turned to Grace, realization lighting up his eyes. "My blood test. That's how you guessed I was involved in his death?"

"Lucy and Candace talked about it after the dinner party—Candace told me all about it. She said Lucy assumed you got tested for HIV. But later, they realized you weren't really at risk, given what you told us all about your history.

Then Lucy remembered that you never mentioned HIV."

"I wasn't sure what to tell Lucy when I went for the test," John-Michael admitted. "I was so scared. I mean, you can hardly imagine. So when she went straight to HIV, I didn't correct her."

"But you don't have that. Thank God. What was the test for?"

"You ever hear of Huntington's disease?"

"No."

"My dad had known there was something off for years. Little things were going wrong. Neurological glitches, problems with swallowing. He thought he was just tired. And then there were the mood swings. He was always an angry, boneheaded type. But this was way worse. He'd fly into these insane rages. Like the day he threw me out. His girlfriend dumped him—later on I wondered if it was because of what the disease was doing to him. Eventually he couldn't ignore that there was something wrong. Not that he told me about any of this. No. If he was angry it was because I'm the loser, the lousy homo who didn't even want to be a 'real man.'"

"You think all that was the disease?"

"His rampant homophobia? If only. It would make it easier. But he'd been that way about gay people since I was a little kid. I mean, I knew when I was like eight, nine. Didn't dare tell him, though. Did my best to hide it. The indie-kid thing was useful. It gave me an excuse to dress different. He called all goths and emos 'gay.' He knew they weren't, not really."

"This Huntington's disease—is it fatal?"

"Incurable, mostly untreatable, and fatal. And fifty-fifty that it gets passed on to your kids. As sickness goes it's pretty much up there as your worst nightmare. People who die from it wind up totally helpless, seriously depressed. There was no way Chuck Weller was going to end up like that—dependent on me to feed him and wipe his ass? No way. From the moment he knew he had it, he was planning the end."

"Did you stay with him while he did it?"

"Did I stay with him . . . ?" John-Michael gazed at her, bewildered. "Of course I stayed with him. That's how he wanted it. He made me promise to stay to the end. To see it through."

Grace stared into the barren scrub of their surroundings. Hills dotted with occasional pines whizzed past, wisps of grass burned yellow. Hardy desert shrubs stubbornly clustered across the terrain. The smooth gray tarmac slicing its inexorable path through California. In truth, she'd already heard enough. But she forced herself to keep listening. Now that she'd heard the awful story, she had to know how it finished.

"What was it like at the end?"

"We did the legal stuff first. There was his new will—he'd been meaning to destroy it ever since Judy left him. We burned that, rinsed the ashes down the sink, deleted all the copies on his computer. Then he hid all his medical notes.

He didn't want anyone to know the real reason. His note just said: *I've had enough of this. That is all. Good luck to John-Michael, may his fate be better than mine.*

"I didn't understand that," John-Michael said, "because he was saying it was all depression, right? And surely that's just as 'weak' as killing yourself because you don't want to go through some horrible sickness. But I guess in the end, it's because of how my mom died. She died pretty slowly. Suffered a lot. He was there for her the whole time. I guess he thought that if she could take a death like that, he should be able to as well. And he didn't want people to know that when it came down to it, he couldn't."

"God, John-Michael, that's just awful. I'm *so* sorry."

John-Michael just shook his head. Grace checked quickly, but there was no hint of tears in his eyes. He was very calm, one hand on the wheel, his left palm laid flat and easy on a knee.

"So anyway, I got there, showed him how to do the injection. He hated needles, said he wouldn't be able to find a vein. Okay, I didn't know how, either. But I'd seen it done plenty of times. The begging really scared me. He was never like that with me. I could see he was fighting his own impulse to scream at me and order me to do it. Like, he could barely manage to control himself. He must have known that soon he wouldn't be able to do even that."

A silence followed. John-Michael looked at Grace briefly. "This is where you say—'You had to do it, he made you.' Something on those lines."

She returned his gaze, blinking back tears.

"But you're not going to, Grace, are you?" His eyes were back on the road. "Have you guessed what I did next?"

"You told us he choked to death."

"He must have been drinking. I mean, before. Maybe to get the courage or dull the pain. Deep inside his heroin coma, he started to vomit, to choke. Really fighting for air. I couldn't help it—instinctively, I turned him over, started clearing his mouth and throat. He regained consciousness. Then I realized what I was doing. He wasn't going to die. He opened an eye and kinda roared at me. A horrible sound; wrong. Like a gurgle. A sound that just didn't belong to him. Didn't belong to a human. *Finish me!*

"I took a pillow. He saw what I was doing. Just gave a nod. I put it over his face. He was too weak to resist. It was over a couple of minutes later. I changed the pillowcase so it didn't have any puke on it. I put the pillow back on the other side of the bed. I checked to make sure there were no signs I'd been there. Then I left. Ditched the dirty pillowcase in a garbage can back in LA."

Grace breathed out slowly, then asked the question she'd been waiting to ask.

"Why are you telling me?"

He gave her a sad smile. "The cops have already guessed this much. You telling them wouldn't be enough to convict me. There's no corroborating evidence. And of course I'd deny it in court. I don't want to go to prison, Grace."

"John-Michael—you didn't answer my question."

"I thought you more than anyone would understand why I don't want to go to prison."

"Because I visit a man on death row?"

"When it came down to it, Grace, he was my dad. And he was *pleading* for my help. I couldn't say no to him, I couldn't. He never asked me for anything before, except not to be gay. I couldn't do that for him. You understand? I couldn't do anything to make him happy. But I could do this."

"Well," Grace admitted, "I'd do anything for my dad, too."

John-Michael nodded in sympathy. "Where is your dad anyhow? You never talk about him."

"I talk about him all the time," she said with a glance at John-Michael. "We're on our way to see him right now."

He'd gone quiet then, but there had been a wild light in his eyes—fearful and unpredictable, like a trapped animal scouting for a way to escape.

Later she'd wonder if that was the moment when he'd first had the idea.

JOHN-MICHAEL
BALCONY, MEMORIAL DAY, EVENING

John-Michael and Grace arrived back late on Memorial Day. They'd had to call Paolo to come to pick them up along the Pacific Coast Highway. Everyone in the house was shaken by what John-Michael had done on the drive back.

They didn't understand. How could they? They just thought it was a horrible loss. Wasteful and pointless.

Beyond stupid.

"You'll have to come up with some kind of excuse for what happened on the road," Grace warned John-Michael as they stood together on the balcony, exhausted after the long day. "Maybe even say you were stoned or something. Whatever you do, don't tell them what you told me about your father." There was an uncomfortable pause. "Maybe you shouldn't even have told me."

John-Michael knew Grace was right. The confession had been cathartic. And as he'd pointed out to her, without evidence or a written confession, what he'd told her couldn't convict him. But it still wouldn't be good if the information got out. Who knew where it could lead?

He'd bound himself to Grace forever, had to trust that she could keep a secret. Otherwise he would drive himself crazy, worrying about it. It made him feel more secure to know she'd kept one of her own. But maybe he'd just lost all good sense a while back and now he was running on the heady vapor of hope.

Without knowing what had really happened with his father, however, the other housemates couldn't possibly begin to understand what he'd done on their way home.

Even Grace was taken aback at first, but once she'd recovered from the shock of it, Grace had understood. He knew she would. She had a darker heart than any of the others might suspect.

Prison had a way of contaminating everyone it touched. Now Grace was urging him to rein in the secrets he'd unleashed.

"I'm done talking about what happened with my dad," John-Michael said. "I mean it. But seriously, you don't think Lucy has already guessed?"

"Perhaps. But if Lucy did hook up with Paolo—I'm not so sure she's a safe bet. Pillow talk—it's notorious."

"So I'll deny it."

"I mean it," Grace insisted. "Don't even get into a conversation about fathers. You never know where talk like that might lead."

"Oh, I get it. You're worried that if I talk about fathers

then people might start asking about *your* dad."

For a moment a look of sharp anxiety had appeared on her face. "John-Michael, this isn't about me. Sure, I prefer it if people don't start up about my dad. Candace doesn't know about him—my mom wanted it that way. If she finds out I've been hiding it all these years, I don't know if she'll ever trust me again. But mainly, it's about you. You committed a serious crime. That's a secret you'll have to keep—maybe for the rest of your life."

"Hey, hey, I know. You can trust me. On the subject of fathers, I'm all, like, zip-lipped. I'm an Easter Island statue." His face wore an immobile frown until Grace reluctantly smiled.

"Okay," Grace said. But then, "Oh, I don't know. Maybe you should talk to Lucy about what happened. Why we went to San Quentin, I mean."

"I should tell Lucy about *your* dad?"

Grace nodded. "Lucy. But *only* her. And only about my dad. Not the stuff about *your* dad."

John-Michael still couldn't figure why Grace thought Lucy was a safe bet with Grace's secret about her father and not with John-Michael's secret about his. Yet she insisted.

"Lucy's your best friend in the house. She's going to expect some explanation for why you upped and decided to spend your holiday weekend taking me to visit some con. Being a total statue about it will only rouse her suspicions. Tell her about my dad. And *nothing* else."

His first chance to speak alone to Lucy came later that night.

"Come up for a smoke."

"On the balcony—are you insane? The SoCal offenserati will be walking their dogs right about now. They'll sue you for giving them cancer."

John-Michael tipped his head toward the rear of the house. "In the backyard then?"

"Fine." Lucy followed him outside.

He reached into his jeans for a packet of cigarettes, snapped a lighter, and fired up. Wordlessly, Lucy plucked the cigarette from his fingers. She took two drags and handed it back.

"I'm quitting," she told him with an easy confidence. "First, I only bum smokes from other people. Next month I go cold turkey."

With an almost seductive swing of her hips, Lucy settled into one of the leather-backed easy chairs on the tiny lawn. She folded her arms. The skin of her shoulders, neck, and arms was glossy with a sheen of perspiration. John-Michael admired her poised sexuality.

"What is it, JM? What really happened on the road today? I mean, dude, why'd you do it? C'mon now and talk to Lucy."

He ignored her question and went straight to what he'd agreed on with Grace. "Grace needed to see her father."

The mental processes were almost evident on Lucy's face. After a moment she said, "What are you saying—you didn't go to San Quentin after all?"

He kept his eyes on hers. "Oh, we went to San Quentin all right."

Grace had instructed him very firmly against actually making the final connection for Lucy. With nothing but silence and his firm gaze between them, Lucy finally caved in and said it. Just as Grace had predicted she would.

"Grace's *dad* is Dead Man Walking . . . ?"

Slowly, he nodded. "Grace's mom made all the kids from her first marriage take her second husband's name—Deering. But her real name is Grace Vesper. And her father is Alex Vesper. 'Alan Vernon' is just a name she made up. Vesper is who she's been writing to, been seeing."

Lucy didn't visibly react. "Is that supposed to mean something?"

"It didn't to me, either. But just take a look on the internet. He's all over it. Around eight years ago." He waited for Lucy to say something. She didn't. "That Hollywood murder in the swimming pool? Tyson Drew, the movie star?"

Finally, Lucy responded. "Grace's dad killed Tyson Drew?"

"No. He didn't. Cops pinned it on him anyhow. Grace's mom's managed to get her family away from the stigma. They were separated at the time it happened anyway, so no love lost. Poor guy doesn't have too many folks believing in him."

"But Gracie believes."

He knocked cigarette ash onto the nearby strip of

lumpy, reddish-brown dirt. "Yeah."

"I see." Lucy's expression was grave, calm. Yet there was calculation behind those eyes. Her profound silence told him that.

John-Michael continued. "Can you imagine the pain of something like that? I spent one night in jail, Lucy, and I'm not ashamed to admit it, I was fuckin' terrified. The moment they lock that door. And you know for the next however many hours, that's your world. The stink of piss, stale tobacco breath, sweat. I was lucky—I'm a minor, they couldn't lock me up with any of the lousy scumbags they were bringing in. But I saw them when I was waiting. Drunks, junkies, guys from rough neighborhoods looking at me like I was something to slice up and lay on a sandwich. And I'm not a wuss, I've spent nights under freeways. That was sweet blessed freedom and perfumed sheets by comparison."

She said nothing. Lucy stared back at him with eyes that were only now beginning to register anguish.

"Imagine all the soul and life sucked out of a building and replaced with fear and despair and rage that's barely suppressed. That's San Quentin. Last time, when I went with Paolo and Gracie, I stayed in the car and Grace went in with her cousin Angela. I didn't go in. I couldn't. This time, she made me go in with them. Said she wanted me to meet her old man. So I'd understand. And I did. I thought that night in jail had toughened me up. But no. The minute that security gate closed behind us, I felt the walls closing in. Throat all tight. Like all the air was used up. Like any minute someone would tap me on the shoulder and say, 'Hey, pal, there's been a mistake, it's your time.'"

Barely audible she whispered, "But they didn't."

"How I didn't just turn around and run screaming out of the place, I don't know. Maybe I was afraid I'd look guilty. Anyway, I sat down with Gracie in front of some glass. Alex Vesper on the other side. Eight years on death row, you gotta figure that's going to waste a man, right? Well, I never saw the dude before, so maybe he was a fat slob once, but I doubt it."

Her voice quavered. "How'd he look?"

"A real tough guy. Not an ounce of fat on him. Face hard, like granite. But in his eyes, he's all Grace. Glacier-blue. When he smiled at her, it was like a sledgehammer cracked open that ice. Smiled at me, too. Grateful to me for driving her up there. Two visits in a month. That's better than the last six. Gracie told him what was going on with me. And he told me: *Don't expect the truth to protect you. That's a crock.*"

He paused then, waiting for Lucy to respond. But all she did was to take his cigarette, and return his gaze with a level stare. After a minute, she stood, paced over to the French doors, slid the door open, and stepped into the living room. She closed the door, didn't look back even once.

For a moment John-Michael just stood there, stunned. He'd poured his heart out to her, but nothing. Lucy was as inscrutable as she was evidently irresistible.

He pitied any guy who got too close.

GRACE
PACIFIC COAST HIGHWAY,
MEMORIAL DAY, AFTERNOON

The ocean shimmered. It had a particular deep blue brilliance in the midafternoon that drew the eye, so long as you could bear its dazzle.

From behind dark brown sunglasses, Grace watched John-Michael. He was driving with one arm resting lazily on the open window of the Benz. The car sped around the cliffs of the coastal road, its tires clinging to the tarmac as they took each bend.

Grace marveled at the aerodynamic design of the convertible, so perfectly engineered that even with the top down, her hair barely moved. The car stereo was playing the Shins track "New Slang" from John-Michael's indie music playlist. Not the kind of music that she would have picked for a road trip. Yet for a long, long time after that day, the tune would instantly evoke in Grace an exquisite ache of nostalgia; the memory of their drive back from San Quentin along the Pacific Coast Highway.

And all that had begun and ended on that day.

John-Michael had barely spoken a word in the last fifty minutes. It was the longest stretch they'd gone without conversation. Initially, she'd thought he was just enjoying the music. But when she'd asked him the name of the track that had been playing at the time, it was obvious that he wasn't tuned in to the music. His eyes were on the road; his mind was somewhere else entirely.

She watched him awhile. As she did, Grace became aware of John-Michael's male physicality. His forearms weren't as developed as Paolo's, but they were covered with fine light hair, and the muscles beneath were strong, lithe. She'd always thought of John-Michael as skinny, but firm thighs filled his pale blue jeans. In fact, she realized, it was only his torso and hips that were slender. In the shoulders and arms were hints of a powerful, if underexercised body.

Weirdly, she'd never really looked at him that way before. His face was angular and sallow, but without the usual touch of eyeliner and with a few days of dark stubble on his face and throat, his look was much tougher than she was used to. Normally, John-Michael had such a calm, gentle expression.

Today, something deep was troubling him. He looked older. For a moment she thought she was catching a glimpse of how he'd look as a middle-aged man: saturnine and wary.

Yet surprisingly attractive.

She looked away, a little disturbed by the sudden stirrings he was causing within her. Falling for a gay friend?

She imagined Candace's response.

Yeah, go there. Way to make Paolo look like a realistic prospect.

What was wrong with Grace?

Kind of obvious, sis, you need to get laid.

Maybe that was it? Or was it because now Grace knew that John-Michael wasn't just the sweet, amiable housemate she believed him to be? He had a darker edge. Was it possible she was only attracted to boys with a dark side?

But she had to admit still another explanation. It ran like a current through her. Maybe it was because of the new, secret bond between her and John-Michael.

Grace felt dizzy when she really thought about how much he'd trusted her. The power it gave her over him. She wondered if he had any idea how fiercely protective she felt toward him now.

Her eyes strayed back to the road, carefully avoiding any part of John-Michael. On the stretch of road ahead, the green tent of a roadside booth billowed in the offshore breeze. She could just make out the writing on the sign: CARAMEL APPLES—FRESH.

"Omigod, caramel apples," Grace said. "We gotta get some. Pull over."

John-Michael eyed her, slow and curious. Silently, he did as she'd asked. The Benz rolled to a soft halt, crunching in the fine gravel of the hard shoulder. They were at the edge of the coastal road. Seven feet to the right, a scrub-covered rocky hillside rolled steeply down. At the bottom, rocks crumbled into the ocean. Waves crashed against a thin strip of pale golden beach.

John-Michael didn't make any move to get out of the car. He took a cigarette from the pocket of his checked shirt, lit it with a flick of his Zippo lighter.

Grace undid her seat belt, opened the passenger door. She stretched her legs for a second before getting out.

"You want one?"

"I'll take one to go."

"I'll call Maya to see if the others want some. We'll be home in two hours. They'd still be pretty fresh."

Plucking her cell phone from her back pocket, Grace strolled over to the stall, which was about fifty feet away. A single car was parked between the Benz and the caramel apple stall. Inside, a family of three was watching a Disney movie on the DVD screens, each eating a big, juicy apple coated in soft caramel. She could smell the buttery warm candy as she passed. Close to the stall it was almost overpowering. Under a clear plastic box, rows of identically sized, glossy caramel apples stood on their heads, wooden sticks in the air. Behind the counter, the vendor grinned.

"I'll take one," she told him. The call connected. Maya picked up. "Hey, Maya," Grace began. "What do you say to some caramel apples?" She tucked the phone between her chin and shoulder as the vendor handed her one apple.

"I say 'hey there, little fella,'" she heard Maya say warmly. "I say, 'Now, you are one fine-lookin' piece of fruit.'"

Grace smiled. "That's what I thought." With the phone

still under her chin, she nodded at the vendor. "And five more to go." The vendor wrapped the take-out apples smartly in clear, red-tinted cellophane and put them in a candy-striped paper bag. Grace got her wallet, began to count out some dollars.

Without warning, the vendor's expression shifted, frozen in stark fear. She spun around, following his stare.

John-Michael's Mercedes-Benz convertible was rolling over the crest of the hill. A second later, it pitched toward the steep section. The car picked up speed.

The vendor managed to gasp, "Is that your car . . . ?"

And then there was nothing but the shattering sound of a car crunching into the rocky beach below. Three seconds later, an explosion. A fireball engulfed the entire Benz. The roar and boom pulsed through her body, a shock wave of raw energy.

For a second, Grace was paralyzed. On autopilot, she slid her phone from between her chin and shoulder and back into her jeans pocket.

She could tell the vendor was trying to say something else to her. But she didn't hear it. She didn't notice her caramel apple flying through the air, flung aside as she turned, racing toward the spot from where John-Michael's car had plunged toward the ocean. Her voice was caught up in her throat, tight and stifled. She could feel her breath coming in gulps. Panic engulfed her.

Then she saw him. Climbing slowly over the rise of the hill, framed with the ultramarine blue of the sea.

John-Michael.

As he came closer, she thought she could almost detect a lightness to his step. When he reached her, to her amazement, he smiled.

"Hello, Grace." He leaned in, planted a soft kiss on her cheek. "Thank you for being here."

She was too stunned to move. In the distance behind John-Michael, she watched the car with the family of three pull sharply into the road and speed away. Over in his stall, the caramel apple vendor simply stared in horror.

"What . . . did you do?"

John-Michael looked straight into her eyes. "The only thing I could."

"You . . . were you trying to kill yourself?"

"I jumped out, Gracie. It's a convertible."

"Why?"

"Why did I jump out?" He glanced over his shoulder to the blazing heap of crushed metal below. "I'd have thought that was kind of obvious."

"*Why* did you total your *beautiful* car?"

Slowly, he shook his head. "Not my car. Chuck's car. Chuck's car where he shagged Judy. Chuck's car that he loved more than he ever loved me. I thought it could be mine but how, Grace, how could it? Think about what I did to make it mine."

On the last sentence, his voice broke. A hand went up to his eyes. "You think I can ever forget what I did to get it?"

She put both arms around him, pulled him against her

shoulder. Behind his back, she watched thick black smoke twist into the air. The breeze changed for a second and she caught a scent of gasoline and burning rubber.

John-Michael pushed back, wiped his eyes. He turned to face the ocean.

"Good-bye, Dad," he breathed softly.

She sighed deeply; relief mixed with resignation. "I hope you have a plan for how you're going to explain this."

"I'll think of something."

"How about a plan for getting us back to LA?"

He took out his cell phone. "Let's call the house, ask someone to come get us."

"Candace won't. She's gonna think you've lost your mind."

"Paolo, then. He's a good guy."

"Yeah, Paolo. Good ol' reliable Paolo and his Chevy Malibu."

John-Michael slid an arm around her waist. He drew her gently against him. She responded by putting her own arm around him. They began to walk. In front of them, a narrow ribbon of smoke rose from the side of the road. It began to thread through the air toward them, smoldering tar and burned aluminum on the wind. Until they walked right through.

For a second, Grace felt John-Michael's grip tighten. But he didn't look back.

MAYA
BALCONY, MEMORIAL DAY, AFTERNOON

Candace looked up wearily from her homework. "Hey, is someone gonna get the phone?"

It was lunchtime on the Monday after the benefit at Hearst Academy. Everyone was relaxing at the house except John-Michael and Grace, who'd taken off to San Francisco in John-Michael's Benz.

Utterly distracted by what she'd just heard on her cell, Maya ignored Candace as well as the house phone.

Candace was stretched on the gray sofa, flipping through the pages of *Variety* with one eye on the TV, totally uninterested in picking up the call. Dozing on the futon sofa, Paolo stirred. He looked around hopefully for Maya. Before he could object, Maya withdrew hurriedly. She stepped outside the front door and climbed the stairs to the balcony. Then she took out her own cell phone and continued to listen.

Maya's cell was still connected to Grace's phone. She could hear, very clearly, John-Michael's end of the conversation with Paolo, who had just picked up the call on the house phone. John-Michael was laughing about driving his car off a cliff on the Pacific Coast Highway, but Paolo didn't seem to find it funny. Not at all. From what Maya could tell from John-Michael's end of the conversation, Paolo was appalled.

It wasn't in the same category of shock as Maya's own reaction when she'd heard Grace gasping aloud, the explosion, and then the terrified yelling—presumably Grace and whoever else saw it happen. It had seemed like an age before she'd heard Grace's voice again. Maya had waited, scarcely daring to breathe as all hell broke loose on the other end of the call.

For at least two minutes, Maya had assumed that John-Michael was dead.

Grace hadn't heard Maya's desperate pleading into the phone. She'd forgotten that the call was still in progress. She must have pocketed the phone, still connected to Maya's.

And now Maya could do nothing but listen in silence to Grace and John-Michael, presumably until the battery of Grace's cell phone ran out.

"Is Paolo coming to get us?" Grace asked.

John-Michael gave an audible chuckle. "Yeah. He was all, like, 'Man, have you gone nuts?'"

"What'd I tell you?"

"He'd understand. They all would. If they knew what happened with my dad."

Maya was seized with curiosity. There was an actual

reason for John-Michael trashing that beautiful Mercedes-Benz? She moved from the edge of the balcony where she'd been staring into the flat line of the ocean, and settled into one of the rattan easy chairs.

This conversation sounded way too good to miss. And since it hadn't even happened in the house, technically, Maya felt under zero obligation to report it to Dana Alexander. She was already fencing off as much as she dared. So long as the woman got some kind of information about the housemates, and some of it at least was verifiable, their agreement was valid—in Maya's eyes.

Anyway—how exactly was Dana Alexander going to know what might be going on in the house, apart from what Maya was telling her? Unless one of the other housemates was also a spy . . . ?

It was a chilling idea. For a few seconds it broke right across Maya's thoughts. After a moment or two she dismissed it as crazy paranoia. Surely Alexander wouldn't go that far? Whatever problem the woman had with Lucy and Grace, it couldn't be so serious that she needed a backup spy.

When Maya finally tuned back into the phone conversation, it seemed that John-Michael and Grace had moved on from talking about John-Michael's car.

"Oh," Grace was saying, "I know why Lucy didn't want us to know about *Jelly and Pie*. And it wasn't just because the show blew chunks."

John-Michael replied, "Really? Huh, I kinda liked it,

but then I have a high tolerance for cheesy TV. I thought the aunt character was pretty cool. And Lucy was way cute."

"You actually watched it?"

"I wasn't a fanboy, if that's what you mean. But yeah, I used to leave the channel if it was on. And when I met Lucy at rock camp and realized that she was Charlie, yeah, I admit it, I was kind of psyched."

"Uh-huh." Then Grace became strangely silent.

"So," John-Michael said, "you think it was because of the rehab?"

"Do I think *what* was because of the rehab?"

"Lucy. The reason she doesn't talk about being on TV. After the show. She was in rehab. Maybe you didn't know?"

Maya became alert, waiting to hear Grace confirm. But she sidestepped his question with a totally left-field question of her own: "How much do you remember about the Tyson Drew case?"

John-Michael didn't reply. When Grace began to talk again, Maya guessed that he must have simply shaken his head, because he didn't seem to know anything at all. Grace began to explain what sounded like the whole story. Tyson Drew, a party in Hollywood, a murder. Reports in the news about some child TV stars being in the house—maybe they'd witnessed something? Lucy–Lucasta, as she was known in those days; the phone was cutting in and out but Maya managed to pick out the most important details: Charlie from *Jelly and Pie* had been one of the children in the house. Some kind of confusion over the witness reports. A man being found guilty of drowning Tyson Drew. Somebody named Alec Vespa maybe? . . . Alex Vesper!

The name practically stopped Maya's heart.

Vesper. It couldn't be a coincidence. The same last name as Grace before her mother remarried Candace's father.

Alex Vesper.

And that's when Maya realized. It was like something was hollowing out her insides. She felt as though she might actually be sick. She leaned forward on the chair and stared at the brilliant white shine of the ocean. She simply tried to breathe.

Alex Vesper was Grace's father. Grace's father was on death row.

"So that's why Lucy didn't want us talking about *Jelly and Pie!*" she heard John-Michael say. "She didn't want us wondering about why she changed her name, maybe looking it up on the internet. I have to say, never in a million years would I have guessed that Lucy was at the Tyson Drew murder party."

"Me neither," said Grace. "It's as if Lucy's gotten used to hiding it. Like she's used to living with suspicion. Makes you wonder why."

Maya felt as though tumblers were falling inside her mind, cogs locking into place. Slowly a key turned, and on the other side was nothing but fear. Betrayal.

Danger.

She was afraid to search for the news story. But Maya knew that she must. Her fingers trembled as she tapped the screen of her smartphone, brought up a web browser, and searched.

"Dana Alexander" "Tyson Drew"

Something cold stirred deep within as the results came up.

The name didn't appear in the headline. Only one newspaper had even reported it. A casual reader might assume it was a mistake. But there it was on a list of famous people who'd been at the Hollywood party at which Tyson Drew had been found dead.

Dana Alexander.

The bigger newspapers didn't mention her. She'd been a huge star back then. In her youthful prime; two years before she played Lady Macbeth in Hollywood's biggest adaptation of the Shakespearean tragedy.

Was it possible that Dana Alexander had the kind of power that could keep her name out of a story like that?

Maya shivered, thinking of the latest report she'd typed up for the woman.

All these years later and Dana Alexander was still keeping tabs on Lucy and Grace. The only thing that Maya could see that connected the two girls was the man on death row.

A cool breeze blew in from the water. Maya began steadily to shake.

It finally made sense, the reason why Alexander was watching the house. Lucy or Grace: one of them knew something. Lucy was at the Tyson Drew murder party. Grace was Alex Vesper's daughter.

What if Vesper wasn't guilty?

What would Dana Alexander be prepared to do if Lucy remembered something about that Hollywood party, something that might save Grace's dad from death row?

What would Dana Alexander do if everyone *told the truth*?

ARIANA CALLS THE WEST COAST
MEMORIAL DAY, EVENING

"This isn't working out quite as I'd hoped." Dana Alexander's voice was silky smooth, clinically cool in its expression of disdain.

Ariana pursed her lips. Sometimes it was downright irritating talking to the British woman, with her supercilious airs and her stuck-up accent. It wasn't like Ariana to experience xenophobia—she had nothing against folks seeking a new life in the United States. But *sweet Lord of mercy*, some Europeans were just so damn precious.

"Only so far I can push things with the girl. It gets to looking like harassment."

"No doubt," came the dry response. "That's why I made provision for an alternative source of information. But things have dried up on that front, too."

"You absolutely certain? Maybe the kids just got settled into a routine?"

"Always a possibility," said Alexander. "And yet, I think

not. Their lives were just getting so interesting. Lucy almost expelled, John-Michael being investigated by the police, Paolo hiding something—I still don't know what. And now? All I'm hearing is 'sweet little Grace, the devoted daughter.' Such an angel, what a saint! So dedicated to her cause, to her pen pals, the poor lonely prisoners."

"Maya doesn't know that the guy on death row is Grace's father. Gotta expect the girl to have a little bit of fellow feeling for her."

Alexander's response was fiercely snapped out. "Of course Maya doesn't know! The fact that Vesper is that girl's father just makes her all the more sympathetic. If Maya were ever to discover that particular gem, I doubt I'll ever hear anything else from that little brat house again."

"Sounds like Maya is already choosing her words more carefully."

"Indeed. That's why it may be time to proceed to Plan B."

"There's a Plan B?"

"There's always a Plan B. Pack your bags. You'd better pop along to LA. Surely you're overdue an unfortunate fall from the wagon? Booze or pills—I don't care which you tell her you've gone for. Poor you, you've no one to turn to except dear little Lucasta from rehab. In the words of Lady Macbeth, darling, *'Screw your courage to the sticking-place, and we'll not fail.'*"

Ariana could almost hear the smug smile on the other end of the phone. But then there was a marked shift in

Dana Alexander's tone. This time it was pure ice.

"There's nothing I despise so much as a spoiled child, Ariana. It's time I took a more active role in their lives. Time to bring the heat to Venice Beach."

ACKNOWLEDGMENTS

It's always tricky for an author to break out of a pattern and innovate into a very different style of writing, but thanks to some brilliant, talented friends and editors, writing *Emancipated* has been a joy.

To Michael Grant, whose wealth of experience as a children's and young adult author I have been able to rely on in so many ways—as a mentor and manuscript critiquer, as a story adviser and a guide to Venice Beach and Santa Monica. The reason there is a Mercedes-Benz in this story is down to a car rental snafu and Michael's glee at driving around all day in a high-end convertible during my visit to LA.

To Hoku Janbazian and my aunt, Tere Reyes, for taking care of me and showing me around LA during my trip to research the locations for *Emancipated*.

A fantastic editorial team is the best gift an author can have: Elizabeth Law's single-minded dedication to helping me make this series as great as possible. It's not every editor who can analyze character development in reference to nuance in *Mad Men* and *Breaking Bad*, and fewer who'll do the same over Skype from Paris!

At HarperCollins, thanks to Katherine Tegen, Katie Bignell, Bethany Reis, Veronica Ambrose, and especially Maria Barbo for such careful, thoughtful consideration of the manuscript at each stage of its evolution, for such clear and confident guidance.

On this side of the Atlantic, thanks to my lovely friend and fellow YA author Susie Day for beta-reading an early draft and persuading me to write a better ending! Robert Kirby of United Agents has been a fantastic source of advice and support throughout.

And without my wonderful family, David, Josie, and Lilia, this would all be a fairly meaningless endeavor!

Turn the page for a **sneak peek**
at the **next gripping** book in
the **Emancipated** trilogy.

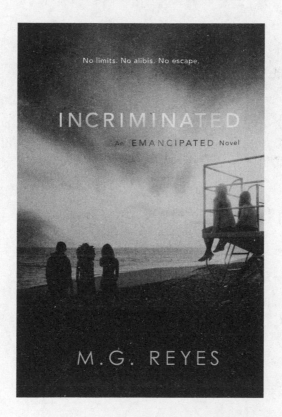

MAYA
TRIPLE BEDROOM, VENICE BEACH HOUSE,

Jack Cato was waiting with Grace at the bottom of the spiral staircase. Maya could guess why she hadn't invited him inside the house. The smell of smoke from the couch fire still hung over the ground floor. Without the replacement, which was due to be delivered the following day, the living space looked sparse. Or as Candace preferred, "minimalist."

"Morning," Jack said, beaming. "Beautiful day, isn't it?"

Maya grinned. "It is on the outside. Inside, it's kind of smoky."

He looked puzzled. "Did something happen?"

"A fire," Grace commented. "RIP sofa. So, you're taking Maya to a business brunch?"

"It's more of an entrepreneurs' breakfast," Jack said with a chuckle that brought an instant smile to Maya's lips. "But broadly speaking, yes."

"Jack was a finalist in some big-deal entrepreneur

competition for schoolkids in England," Maya told Grace. "And he got to meet lots of famous people and investors who started successful companies. He found out how all that stuff works, so he's taking me along to this thing at Caltech."

"We're just having a go at rustling up some interest," Jack said with self-effacing modesty. Maya doubted that he could be more adorable if he tried.

Three hours later, Maya was collapsing against the wall at the conference center at Caltech. On the other side of the wall was a room full of rich geeks, some barely out of college, who'd just witnessed her first-ever tech presentation. Her heart was still pounding loudly and steady in her own ears as it had throughout the longest five minutes of her life.

"That was bloody brilliant!" Jack said, breathless. She felt his hand, tentatively reaching for her shoulder and then pulling back at the last moment.

Maya couldn't stop a radiant smile.

"I can't believe it!" she said. He was gazing at her so intently that she wanted to look away but she couldn't seem to do it. "Two of them! *Two* of those guys want to invest in my app! Actual backers. This is unreal."

"You did it, champ," he said, straining to sound humorous. He gave her a playful punch on the shoulder. Their eyes caught for a second and she sensed an undercurrent of tension. This was either more adorable British reticence or he really, really wanted to touch her and didn't know how.

The whole event had been pretty casual, like an

open-mike type thing. Jack had put Maya forward to do a five-minute "bit" about her new Promisr app, and Maya had stood there pitching her social-bartering app in front of everyone, her voice shaking a little bit. It was like some terrifying kind of entrepreneur comedy club.

Halfway through, she'd decided the best thing was simply to demonstrate her app. A cluster of potential investors had gathered the instant she'd finished; all of them young men, none older than thirty.

"I've never seen investors jump like that," Jack marveled, running one hand through his unruly fair hair as he struggled to absorb what had just happened. "You don't get it! Mostly they're kind of bored, actually. You really made those nerds light up!"

"I did, didn't I?" Maya said, equally dazed. "It's incredible to think that some people can just drop that kind of money after a five-minute presentation."

"Well, they did get to grill you for a good hour or so afterward. They can drop a lot more, too. They *will* drop a lot more. You'll see. A hundred K is nothing to these guys. It's not just the tech, it's you. Maya, you wowed them."

"But why?" she asked, bemused.

"Because you're young, brilliant, gorgeous, and, as a girl, you stand out! These guys are dreaming of the day that your photo is on the cover of *Wired* magazine. Or even *Time*!"

Maya beamed, and then shoved him lightly in the chest. "Oh, please. Now you're exaggerating."

Jack caught both her hands in his. She could feel her knees buckling slightly, unable to concentrate on anything but the sensation of his fingers intertwining with hers.

"Are you okay?" he said as she closed her eyes, suddenly leaning against him for support.

Maya was experiencing an exhilarating jumble of emotions. Relief and excitement, but also fear. "Jack, what if I screw this up? I can write code, but what do I know about running a business of any kind?"

"Oh, you shouldn't worry about that. They're counting on you to write the code. You're the brains, the creativity. The business side of things, that's their end."

Her eyes fluttered open. Now she really did feel scared. "You think—you think there's any chance I could get ripped off? It happens."

He raised a finger to her cheek and stroked her skin lightly. "Hey," he said very softly. "I'm the one who got you into this. You think I'd stand by and watch you get ripped off?"

She felt an overwhelming surge of gratitude toward him. "If it wasn't for you, I'd still be fixing bugs in Cheetr, just watching downloads mount up. This is a whole other league. It's major."

"What nonsense," he murmured, his fingers still caressing her cheek. "You'd already started work on Promisr when you first talked to me."

They were standing very close now, enough that she could feel the whisper of his breath, which smelled sweet, of orange juice. She shivered in anticipation of more but instead he pulled away a little, before letting his hand fall to his side. Maya realized with a start that she'd been willing him to kiss her. She released a held breath when he turned away.

"Um, so we'd better get back in time for the next round of presentations. It'd look rude to miss them," he said with obvious effort.

Why won't he kiss me?

Maya thought Jack was cute the first time she saw him but now it was as though some kind of filter had lifted away and she could finally see him. The longer she stared, the sexier he became.

"Jack," she said quietly, not moving from where he'd left her, by the wall. Jack stalled on his way to the door and turned. Frustration clouded his expression.

In that moment, Jack stopped being her tutor, a chemistry genius, a business coach. All Maya could think about was a cute guy with the sexiest accent ever, and everything he'd done for her. At that moment, all *she* wanted to do was kiss *him*.

Maya strode across to Jack and grabbed him by the arms.

She drew him closer, until he was no more than a slight lean of her head away. She sensed that he was still waiting for her to make the first move. A feeling of euphoria went through her and her skin buzzed all over. Then Maya leaned in, no tentativeness now, pushing herself against him, challenging him to resist. The softness of his lips surprised her, something that she'd think about many hours later when the shock of the initial contact had passed.

This time, he didn't hold still. Their mouths seemed to melt together and she reached her arms around his neck, clinging on to him while they kissed.

"Good Lord," he murmured faintly, pulling away.

Maya released her fingers from his hair and stepped away. "Your first kiss?" she said, trying to sound innocent. Who was she kidding? She'd never kissed a boy like that.

"Might as well be," he said with a nervous laugh. "Look, Maya, I . . ."

"Is it because you're my tutor?"

"No! I mean, yeah, a bit, but that wouldn't stop me. I mean if that were an issue I'd ask them to find you another . . . it's just that . . ." His lips twisted in a grimace. "Clarissa," he concluded bitterly.

"Your ex-girlfriend?" Maya could barely contain her disappointment. "You told me it was over. I thought she'd gone back to England."

"And it is, but she's going to be here a bit longer, as it turns out," he said, more than a little guiltily. "She's found some wretched course she wants to do at UCLA. Now she's waiting to see if her uni will let her onto an exchange program."

"Okay but—what's that to you?"

"Maya, I'm the only person she knows in LA. I can't just abandon her. Clarissa is from a tiny village in Suffolk.

LA is bloody terrifying to a girl like her."

Maya couldn't speak. A hundred arguments and insults lined up in her mind.

"Hey," she said, drawing herself up with effort. "It was only a thank-you kiss. If you want to keep this strictly business, then just say so."

"I didn't say that, Maya," Jack said unhappily. But she'd already turned to leave.

Don't miss all the steamy drama in the Emancipated series by
M. G. REYES

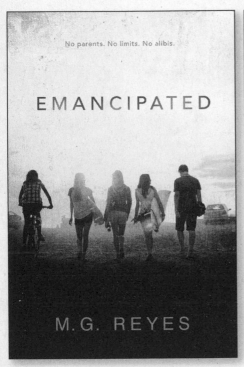

No parents. No limits. No alibis.

EMANCIPATED

M.G. REYES

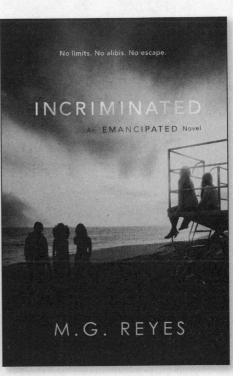

No limits. No alibis. No escape.

INCRIMINATED

An EMANCIPATED Novel

M.G. REYES

Six teens. One house on Venice Beach.
What could possibly go wrong?

JOIN THE

Epic Reads

COMMUNITY

THE ULTIMATE YA DESTINATION

◀ **DISCOVER** ▶
your next favorite read

◀ **MEET** ▶
new authors to love

◀ **WIN** ▶
free books

◀ **SHARE** ▶
infographics, playlists, quizzes, and more

◀ **WATCH** ▶
the latest videos

◀ **TUNE IN** ▶
to Tea Time with Team Epic Reads

    Find us at **www.epicreads.com** and **@epicreads**

More praise for

THE COYOTE KINGS OF THE
SPACE-AGE BACHELOR PAD

Ω

"*The Coyote Kings* is outrageously hilarious and horrifying by turns. With a sharply satiric intelligence and immense imagination, Minister Faust is an exciting new voice in the field."

> —SHEREE R. THOMAS,
> editor of the World Fantasy Award–winning
> *Dark Matter: A Century of Speculative Fiction*
> *from the African Diaspora*

Ω

"Minister Faust has a voice that has to be experienced to be believed. Once you read *Coyote Kings,* you'll never forget it."

> —STEVEN BARNES,
> author of *Lion's Blood* and *Zulu Heart*